Other Books by Donald Willerton

The Mogi Franklin Mystery Series (2012)
    The Ghosts of the San Juan
    The Lost Children
    The Secret of La Rosa
    The Hidden River
    The Lake of Fire
    The Lady in White

Smoke Dreams

By

Donald Willerton

Please visit the website of the author for more information:
www.donwillerton.com

ISBN 978-0-615-97402-6

Cover design by Lisa Kratzer
House image face by Joshua Willerton
House image is used by permission and is from
BARBER'S Turn-of-the-Century Houses
Elevations and Floor Plans
Third Edition
ISBN-13: 978-0-486-46527-2
George F. Barber & Co.
Dover Publications, Inc., Mineola, New York
Copyright 2008

Smoke Dreams

The Mulvaney Mansion

Prologue

Late September, 1870

Cyrus Mulvaney felt the sweat on his upper lip as he stepped from his single-horse carriage onto the wood plank walkway that fronted the stores around the plaza. He was a large man—a good five inches above six feet and three hundred pounds—and was not accustomed to the desperation that made his hands shake as he tied the horse to the post. It was late as he turned and walked in front of the stores, the sun hovering just above the horizon. The shopkeepers were shuttering their windows while the saloons, gambling halls and bordellos were preparing to accommodate the raucous crowds that would soon appear and remain all night.

Cyrus hesitated in front of the law office door. Throughout the long ride from the ranch, he had rehearsed what would play out once he opened the door. He now hoped he had the courage to follow through.

Mulvaney and Hetley had been the dominant law office of Las Vegas, New Mexico Territory for several years. Taking advantage of the loose laws imposed when the former northern part of Mexico was made a U. S. Territory, the two lawyers cheated, intimidated, coerced, and extorted the original land owners out of much of the property bestowed on them as part of Spanish and Mexican land grants. Under the guise of representing the holders in matters of land arbitration, the men charged a percentage of the land for their services instead of the usual monetary fees. Delaying the wheels of justice as they worked through a system that flowed in English but balked in Spanish, the native language of most of the land holders,

[1]

they bilked their clients on a consistent basis, ending up owning more than a million acres without spending a penny of their own money.

Three years ago Cyrus Mulvaney traded his scattered parcels of land to his partner to buy one monstrous tract of land northeast of the city, a hundred thousand acres of prime tall-grass prairie that he intended to turn into a cattle shipping depot. It was his expectation that, once he became a wealthy cattle baron, it wouldn't be long before he was ushered into the position of Territorial Governor.

But all his plans had gone wrong.

"Well, look what the cat dragged in," Clarence Hetley said as his former partner stepped through the door. The short rotund man leaned back in his office chair behind a huge desk, his feet propped up, a mild sneer on his face.

Cyrus moved slowly to the chair in front of the desk, lowered himself into the padded seat, and stretched as he leaned back. He couldn't remember ever being so tired. The last two months had been a blur. First Sam, then Violet, now Lucy.

"I'm sorry about your boy," Hetley said, plopping his feet down against the rug and pulling his chair up to his desk. "About Vi too. I hear she's gone addled."

Cyrus only nodded. He was sure that Hetley's commiseration was sincere, but his former partner's backroom dealing with the railroad boys was responsible for a lot of Cyrus's troubled finances.

"I'll get to the point," Cyrus began, looking across the desk. "The cattlemen changed their trails to the east, taking away their need for pasturing on my land. Your under-the-table deal with the railroad cheated me out of their business and made my planned depot business a complete failure. The Comanche wreaked havoc on my ranch, and building the house drained me of every spare nickel. Sam was taken by the Indians, Violet's gone mad, and I just sent Lucy to St. Louis to live with family until I can get Violet back there and into an asylum. Everything I planned for has failed, and everything I own has become a liability."

Cyrus leaned forward, his hand gripping the edge of the desk.

"I give up. I need to get out of here, go back to St. Louis, and start over. But I need to sell everything I own to start free and clear, to have enough money to set up an office."

He looked Hetley in the eyes. "I want you to buy me out. I've improved the land considerably—stockyards, fencing, corrals, hay barns, water tanks. The canyon has the house, barn, sheds, and bunkhouses. And the house is worth every penny that I've put into it; you've been there and you know there's nothing else like it in the Territory.

"For all the things that we did together, for helping make us both rich, I need you to do this."

Clarence Hetley listened, his face impassive. He let the silence stand for a beat or two, then started his pitch.

"Cyrus, I said I was sorry about the boy, and I'm even more sorry about Violet, she being a favorite of mine. But that railroad business was exactly that, business, and you know it. You make money when you can, and you do whatever it takes. You just misjudged the situation.

"I told you three years ago that becoming a cattleman was a bad idea. Law is always the way to make money and develop power. But you were bullheaded and wouldn't listen. You went ahead and then things didn't work out like you planned. I understand your plight. I really do. And I understand your desire to move back to St. Louis. But the railroad out here wants to move people and goods, not cattle, and you built that monster house of yours smack dab in the middle of the Comanche's backyard, not to mention that it's a half day's ride from town.

"That precious land that you wanted so bad is too dry to farm and too big to fence so the buffalo don't eat all the grass. The house is too damn big and expensive to maintain, which shows that your high falutin' tastes got the best of you. But I sympathize, and so here's what I can do."

Hetley wrote a number on a piece of paper and slid it to other side of the desk.

The knot in Cyrus's stomach flared into a burn. He expected that Hetley would make him squirm, but he thought the man had enough grit not to cheat him outright. The price was a tenth of what the land was worth and would leave him penniless.

"That's not enough," Cyrus said, bitterly. "You're leaving me nothing. I couldn't buy a drink with what's left after I pay the debts."

Hetley was unfazed. "Cyrus, you got this idea of being governor in your head, and you suddenly went moral on me, started talking about how noble this country is and how you could lead it into greatness, how bad the Indians and the Mexicans had been treated by the white man and how we needed to reform the laws. Suddenly, you were better than the rest of us and made us out to be a bunch of damn crooks. I was happy to trade you land just to get rid of you. You were beginning to make me sick." The sneer on his face turned into something more sinister.

"Now you're back with your tail between your legs whining about how bad life has treated you, and how you need to get out of this noble land and go back to the big city. Meanwhile, you got all the people riled up against me and the legislature, making it a lot harder to get my business done. Well, if you want to leave, then have at it. Don't let the door hit you on the way out. But it's going to cost you. You made me out to be a criminal, a leech on society, if I remember correctly, so don't expect that, just because you had an attack of conscience, it's earned you the right to leave without regrets."

Cyrus Mulvaney's Irish heritage had brought him his size and his flaming red hair, but he could hear every ancestor roll over in their grave when he got out of his chair, kneeled on the floor, lowered his head, and begged.

"Clarence, I'm asking you as a longtime friend. If you don't consider me a friend anymore, then at least remember the money we made for each other. Maybe I did get a little heady with my pride and all, and maybe I was already practicing politics, but I didn't do you any lasting harm. Please," Cyrus said in a low voice, "don't bottom me on this. I need to get out and I need money to do it. Please."

Cyrus could beg but he wasn't about to raise his eyes to see Hetley gloat.

Hetley stood, walked around the desk, bent down to see Cyrus's face, and smiled.

"No one will give you better, Cyrus," he said softly. "I've made sure of it. My friends and I want you to leave. You've been a burr under our saddle for a long time. But if you're going to run like a little rabbit, then I want everything you have. I want everything you've even thought of having. I'll take your land and

[4]

your house, and I don't care if you're left with anything more than the clothes on your back."

Hetley extended his hand and patted Cyrus Mulvaney on the cheek.

The ferocious fist that exploded from the man kneeling on the floor, a fist that had years of resentment behind it, caught the smaller man beneath the jaw, close to the neck. The power in the blow lifted Hetley's body several inches off the floor.

Cyrus heard a sharp sound as Hetley's head jerked back and to the side, and he knew that Hetley's neck had snapped like a chicken's.

There was silence in the office as the body slumped onto the desk, then slid to the floor. Cyrus, his chest heaving, stood tall over the body.

His fount of rage slackened but he could find no sorrow for his action. Cyrus had not planned on even touching the man, but Hetley deserved what he received. Cyrus's mind raced as he tried to figure out what to do next. He briefly thought of throwing the body in the floor of the carriage, hiding the murder, and escaping in the night. But there were too many people around the plaza to go out the front unnoticed, and the alley was always full of drunks and whores. He thought about making it look like an accident, but the chances of him being believed were slim. He thought about setting fire to the building and attempting to cover up the crime, but it was a sure thing that he would be caught before he got out of town. Even a fire wouldn't disguise a broken neck.

The only advantage he had was that the confrontation had made little sound, probably not even being heard outside the office. Even doing nothing, the body would not be discovered until Hetley's assistants came to work in the morning. That would give Cyrus time to get back to the ranch, a thought that gave him a sense of certainty that he had not had recently.

Since Sam had been kidnapped, Cyrus's life had been a rollercoaster of emotions. Violet had always been delicate, but the loneliness of the frontier had turned her fragile. When Sam suddenly vanished and the horrors of what must have happened to him settled in, she must have snapped on the inside, losing first her ability to cope, then to communicate, and then shuttering herself completely, staying in a corner of the house where she alternated weeping with staring blankly. She no longer talked nor heard anything around her.

Cyrus had almost joined her as he watched her descend into madness. It made the decision to send six year-old Lucy to Violet's sister both easy and hard—easy because Violet's condition would no longer be a daily presence to the child and hard because she was all he had left. With his daughter gone, his abandonment was total. As would be his daughter's sense of her own life as well, he was sure. Her sweet disposition and loving ways would never be the same.

Lucy had cried in the arms of the lady companion hired for the trip as they said goodbye, and her departure left Cyrus feeling utterly alone and weary, sorrowful to the bone to have seen his family disintegrate before his eyes. He pledged to himself, as he watched the dust of the stage retreat to the horizon, to close down the ranch and raise as much money as he could. Selling everything to Hetley was his last choice, but it would allow him to pay off the massive debts that were driving him toward prison. It didn't help to see Hetley's friends lurking as they watched his demise, waiting to pounce on the remains like vultures.

Now, standing over Hetley's body and running through all that he might do, Cyrus sharply regretted that his life had come undone. He knew there was only one real option now, even as he yearned to be back in the house, the home he had built, for it all to be resolved.

Cyrus closed the office like he used to, drawing the front curtains, dousing the flames of the lamps, and locking the door. He was soon back in his carriage, winding through the loud streets of the night.

Several hours later, he came out of the narrow canyon and drove through the gate of the Mulvaney ranch. Of the large staff that used to care for the house and grounds, only the two housemaids remained. Their time was now spent watching over Violet. Pulling up to the barn, Cyrus calculated when the body would probably be found, when the sheriff would get organized, and how long it would take them to ride to the ranch. All taken into account, he expected to see a posse about noon.

There would be no question that Cyrus Mulvaney killed Clarence Hetley. Cyrus had made no attempt to hide his visit the evening before. As big as he was and as well-known a figure as he

[6]

had become over the years, he would not have gone unnoticed by the people milling about the plaza. His very presence at the office would be enough for the sheriff, and Cyrus expected that justice would be served at the end of a rope. Such was the no-frills loyalty that Hetley had bought, for the sheriff had been on Hetley's payroll for years.

Cyrus was in no rush. He took the rigging off the horse, gave the beast a well-earned brush by the light of a lantern, then let it into the side corral. He added an extra scoop of oats to the feed trough. Walking to the house, he looked up at what two years of building had produced. It would have been a major house in St. Louis, but out in the barren adobe-dominated Southwest, his Victorian mansion was one of the grandest houses for five hundred miles in every direction. He had always been proud of the place, even when he was spending far more than he had estimated. Living in it, entertaining in it, receiving all the important people that he could find had been his delight. This was his magnificent dream home, and its opulence was to have been a statement of his success.

He caught a short nap until the light of dawn came into his room, then rose, showered, dressed, and went downstairs. In his office Cyrus composed such legal papers as were needed to complement his will, formally updated the situation with regard to the children, and made specific recommendations for Violet. He expected that her father would take care of the arrangements in St. Louis, and he might even come to escort her back to her childhood home. Cyrus did not have any positive expectations regarding her condition, and the thought made him feel guilty. Violet had been a good wife, and he would never have brought his family to the ranch had he known how much she would suffer from the isolation.

It was midmorning when he finished his paperwork, called in the housemaids to witness the changes, walked to the barn to get a rope, then returned to his third-floor bedroom. Forming a good noose around his neck, he tied a short length of the rope to the balcony railing, and stepped off into the thin air.

1

Present Day

I should be unfazed by heat and cold, but in fact, I hate them both. The intense cold of winter makes me feel hard and brittle, and the waves of endless radiation from the summer sun make me slump all over. Today hardly even counts as summer, but the heat has already made me listless and inattentive. It wasn't until the snake moved out of the rocks that it finally caught my attention.

A large diamondback rattler had slipped onto the grass and was on its way to the back door. It slithered up and over some miniature sand dunes next to the old gate, and then slid down onto the sidewalk. Apparently not bothered by the hot cement, I watched the snake smoothly zigzag until it reached the thick pile of rubble. Several winters ago, a massive snowfall collapsed the back porch roof, crushing the porch under hundreds of heavy slate shingles, leaving a large mound of broken wood and stone heaped against the house. One corner of the roof above the door had failed to break loose and still clung to the brickwork like a ripped curtain.

Picking its way through the mess and around the bottom of the lopsided roof, the snake levered its belly against a mound of shingles, lifted itself through the empty doorway, and glided over the worn threshold. It stopped, moved its head side to side, flitting its tongue in and out, tasting the air. Apparently satisfied, it moved further into the abandoned kitchen, sliding around the tumbleweeds piled against the cabinets, and skimmed over the dirty linoleum tiles with a perfect quiet. Coiling itself near a back corner of the room, the snake lowered its head and watched.

Not long afterward, a deer mouse peeked out of a hole in a floorboard. Cautiously, it crawled out, erratically moved its head back and forth, and twitched its nose hairs like the feelers of an ant. Feeling safe, it skittered along the base of the wall.

The snake struck in an instant, drove its fangs into the mouse's neck and held it firm until the quivering stopped. The snake then worked its lunch through its jaws and squeezed the lump downward into its body. Finally content, it stretched into the familiar zigzag pattern and returned the way it had come, slithering across the floor, out the doorway, and down onto the wreckage of the porch.

As the snake glided beside the hanging portion of the old roof, I wiggled out a couple of nails that held a shingle in place. The shingle shifted slightly, let go, and the heavy sharp-edged piece of slate slid past its neighbors, gained momentum in the six or seven feet of freefall, and struck the snake directly behind its head. The snake's body twisted rapidly into a spiral, released and reversed, then curled up and around and sideways in a frenzy of deathly confusion. I watched until it finally relaxed and lay still.

It wasn't that I disliked the snake. I had just grown fond of the mouse.

Dealing with the snake was, at best, idle play, minor entertainment to keep from being completely bored. Few things of interest ever happen here anymore, and the tedium can be wearing. So I sometimes play as if there is a point to my being the dominant presence in the canyon. Being dominant is not what I chose to be— I'm made to be protective not aggressive—but my abilities do make me overwhelming compared to the other creatures.

I am a house, and a very nice one, at that. Not that I have other houses to compare myself to, having lived a solitary life in the canyon, but I accept the accolades given me by many of my visitors through the years. They never knew that, when they were looking me over, I was looking back.

But I'm getting ahead of myself. The fact that I am a house and am alive is not easy to comprehend for most people. I understand. Living entities are usually, well, lifelike, and structures assembled from inanimate pieces don't normally display lifelike qualities. But hear my story, if you will. I will start at the very beginning, a long, long time ago.

I was already fully built and furnished when clouds of smoke slapped me awake. My windows and doors had been opened and there were bonfires roaring in the yards on each side of me. The billowing clouds of smoke from burning logs and branches flooded my rooms, my stairways, my cellar, and attic, making me woozy to begin with but then shaking me to attention. It was as if I had awakened inside a deflated bag and was slowly expanding myself against the fabric to inhabit it. I felt my individual parts: my foundation, my timbers, the supports on my porch, the wood within my walls, the glass in my windows, and the slate upon my roof. I could even feel the large decorative brass rods attached to my roof, hot and sizzling beneath the desert sun.

The wonder of waking up and feeling my housely parts was nearly dwarfed by the feel of the grass jostling in the current along the banks of the river, the swishing of the tall cottonwoods in the wind, the sand swirling on the road, and even the sun beating down on the cliffs behind me. I was feeling not only myself but the whole canyon in which I resided. It was as if I had roots fanning out below the ground and spreading their way throughout the soil and rock of the valley, roots bringing me vibrations and pressures and textures as if I had a vast multitude of fingertips. Were the roots part of my structure? If so, was I built that way or somehow acquired them after being here for some period of time? Or were the roots no part of me at all, but part of the earth and I just shared in their connection somehow? I was not sure what do with those bewildering sensations.

All I know is that the more I felt alive, the more I wanted to be alive. I swallowed. I gulped. I inhaled long deep breaths. I was enthralled with this awakening. I also found myself with abilities that surprised me. As I absorbed more of the smoke, I began to smell its pungent odors, as if I had a nose. I could taste, too, though I knew I had no tongue. I could hear, though I knew I had no ears. I could see, though I had no eyes.

Now more engaged with my surroundings, I discovered a man—tall, deeply tanned, bare-chested, muscled, and covered in colored stripes. He was dancing around the bonfires. He twirled, he leaped, and he ran from one fire to the other, singing. He came in my doors, onto my floors, into my rooms, commanding the smoke that swirled about him.

He must have been the one who called me from darkness. He must have used the smoke to bring me to life.

Whoever he was, I fell into the rhythm of his singing and felt the cadence of his dancing.

As he danced, his movements drew me in. As he sang, the sounds swept around me. I was not one place and not one thing—the wall, the chimney, the lights, or the air—I was *all* of the place. The four levels of my many rooms, the large porches around me, the vast roof, and the big yards—it was *all* me. I was flooded with sensations.

The panting, sweating, painted man finally ended his dance and came to my front door. He sprinkled powder across my threshold and threw it against my door's lintel and the frame. Taking a knife from his belt, he sliced across his palm, a cut that rapidly filled with blood. Opening and closing his hand until it was covered with red, he placed bloody handprints on my lintel, then on my uprights, and finally bled on my threshold until tiny droplets ran together on my floor. He rubbed his hands together, placed them both flat on my threshold, then chanted in a low voice.

As soon as his bloody hands touched me, a frenzy of feelings jolted me. My first emotions were of surprise and terror, but then more and more emotions assaulted me—pain, joy, anger, agony, happiness, tragedy, excitement. So many I felt caught in a swirling brew of feelings.

Memories flooded me and pulses of energy rocked me. Thoughts flashed into my senses and the man became known to me. I began to see his history, who he was and where he had been and what he had done. And I felt his loneliness; there was a great deal of loneliness.

Even as I was feeling his emotions, I began feeling my own. How confusing emotions are! Initially there were only external sensations, but now I was swelling with internal feelings that were not his but mine.

I had building within me the heart-centered qualities of a soul.

As powerful as becoming conscious was, being vested with a soul brought even more wonder. I was not the man at my threshold—I was a house, not a man—but I now had a context for my life, a framework of what had happened to me from the time I was built and the roles this man had played before my awakening. As savage as his life had been, my own life had been shocking as well. I was first built out of optimism and pride, but I was soon invaded by evil. Terrible things happened within my doors. My story spoke of pain, misery, sadness, and shame. My rooms were soaked in tragedy and tears had etched themselves into my floors.

The tall man in my doorway, his hands still on my threshold, finished his chanting. He spoke to me.

"This is what I want," he whispered. "This is why I brought you to life."

He talked to me of protection, of patience, of preservation, and of the secrets that existed within me. Then he gave me a charge, a command, for what I was to do.

"Keep all things in order. She will come. I will return."

The man declared my purpose, set my destiny. I was now complete. All that had happened that day, the fullness of being awakened and the soul that I was given, culminated in the simple task of maintaining myself to protect the secrets inside me until the woman and he returned. My secrets would then be revealed.

The man wrapped his hand, mounted his horse, and rode into the canyon of the river.

That was many, many years ago.

I have waited. Forever, it seems, I have waited.

She never came. He never returned.

I tell my tale of sadness and of pain because I am dying. My roots are over-extended and broken, my foundation trembles, my structure sags. My vision is cloudy and I do not sense all that is around me like I did years ago. The vibrations and pressures at the end of my fingertips go unanswered, and I, though still dominant in the canyon, feel aimless and distracted. Abandoned, I am ready to collapse, ready for what remains of my great heights to fall down and to slowly sink into the ground.

I deeply regret that the charge the man gave me goes unfulfilled, but there is nothing I can do. My future is now as simple as the snake's. I expect to return to darkness as suddenly as I arose out of it the day the man danced and chanted in the smoke.

But there is a vehicle coming down the canyon road. I can hear the tires on the gravel and I can feel the lugging of the engine as it goes up and down the dips. I used to be curious about who was coming and what they were coming for. I would watch them, and I would listen, thinking that they might make a difference in my existence, be part of my destiny. I have always been disappointed. In the past years, people have come only to stare and to walk around, then insult me—saying I am old and decrepit and smell stale and dirty, that my yards have returned to weeds and wildness. Of course I look old. I am old, older than anyone who looks at me.

It has been years since an experienced builder has looked me over. Any craftsman would see my fundamentals and admire them. He could see my potential, my fine lines, and my beauty. If the right people would only look and listen and touch, they could see me and I would see them.

If anyone would only give me the time, I would surprise them.

2

Tucker Whitby slid off the gray leather passenger seat to stand on the hard-packed dirt in front of the house. He could see that the house was obviously large as they drove up, but now, standing in front of it as he craned his neck upward, removing his ball cap to see the topmost gables, he realized that it was far beyond large. It was huge, easily the biggest Victorian house he had ever seen. The picture in the ad hadn't come close to revealing its true size.

"So, this is the Mulvaney Mansion," he said. "It looks pretty good for being almost a hundred and fifty years old."

"It was started in 1867 and finished in 1869," Lynn Anderson said. "That makes it a hundred and forty or so. But we've had it inspected and it's in really good shape, all things considered."

Lynn had opened the back of the SUV and gotten the Mulvaney file from a cardboard box. First snugging a broad-brimmed floppy hat on her head to shield her from the hot sun, she pushed a button and the door was closing as she walked up next to Tucker.

"You want to see the outside, or do you want to go inside first?" she asked.

"If you don't mind, I'd like to go back up the road and start at the gate."

"That's fine. Whatever you'd like to do. At some point, though, you have to walk along the riverbank. It's a wonderful feature of the ranch, and I haven't seen a property with this much river frontage in a long time. You'll love it."

Tucker took a small bag from the SUV and the two of them walked fifty or so yards back to the open metal-pipe gate that represented the start of the Mulvaney Ranch. He already knew that the house was much too big for him, but it was always fun to check out a new place. No reason to waste the trip completely.

"The property includes what?" he asked.

Lynn removed a property map from her folder, and holding it flat in her hand, oriented it to the scene before them. She pointed to where the fence ran across the river from the cliffs on the left to the cliffs on the right, stretching across the river in the middle. That was the north boundary. The cliffs along each side of the valley determined the west and east boundaries. She pointed to where the cliffs turned and came together in the distance, the river disappearing through a gap in the middle. That was the south boundary.

"An official plat survey hasn't been done in thirty years, but it's about sixteen or so acres. If you decide to buy, we'll get it updated. All the water and mineral rights come with the property, and there're only a couple of state laws about the amount of water you can pump from the river if you want to irrigate a garden or an orchard."

The river was a lazy, flat-rock laden, quiet piece of water bound on each side by yards of green grass, flat angular boulders, and cattails. There was a slow but steady flow, Tucker noted, as water rushed through the occasional rock contours, and the riverbed was sufficiently wide to make a good dip in the landscape. The view was the definition of peaceful.

Living in this valley would be a dream, Tucker thought, and he was already wishing the house was smaller. It had been almost twenty years since he had lived in a house for longer than a year or two, preferring to fix a house up, sell it, and then move on to another one. But he was going to be sixty in a couple of months and he thought it was time to look for something permanent. He had saved enough money to buy whatever he wanted, and what he wanted was an old place with land, an interesting house that was challenging enough to be a long project, and someplace remote.

And if this place was anything, he was thinking, it was remote. It had taken most of an hour to get to the ranch from town. The southernmost tip of the Rocky Mountains was directly west about forty miles, right on the other side of Las Vegas, New Mexico. Between there and where Tucker stood, the foothills of the mountain range splayed out into a vast high-altitude prairie, rich in grass and fertile topsoil.

Within a few miles of the ranch, the land fell off into a maze of canyons that started an almost thousand-foot drop in elevation, which to the east of the property resulted in the land finally becoming the real prairie, the Great Plains. Extending across to Oklahoma, the Plains went as far north as the Dakotas and as far south as halfway through Texas.

In the middle of the canyons, right under Tucker's feet, a man named Cyrus Mulvaney decided to build his house. That he began this house in 1867 was hard to grasp. The builder was digging ditches for the foundation just a couple of years after Abraham Lincoln was assassinated.

Tucker walked into the sage brush to get a better look at the course of the river. Behind him, about two hundred yards upriver from the fence where the canyons of the Mora and the Canadian rivers came together, was a grove of cottonwood trees. Closer to the house, a wide patch of purple flowers carpeted a portion of the bank, and on the other side were thickets of dark green and red oak trees bunched along the bottom of the east bluffs. The river then narrowed considerably as it disappeared between the south cliffs. Quite a picture, he thought. The ranch was a rare find.

"Okay," he said. "We can move closer to the house."

He and Lynn moved up a small rise from the gate, followed the road down to where the SUV was parked, then walked toward the river to an old cement sidewalk that circled the house. It ran from the front porch to behind the house and then over to the cliffs of the south boundary, where it turned, followed the riverbank where the stream was straight, and came back to the house. Tucker guessed the entire loop might be a quarter mile or more in length.

"Who put in the flagpole?"

Lynn looked to the side of the house at the large open yard. A pole with splotches of silver color stood in the center of the grass, a small ring of rocks around the base. No flag flew, but an old steel cable hung loose from swiveled pulleys at the top and bottom. The pole appeared to sag in the afternoon heat like everything else.

"The VA, I would guess," she answered.

Tucker had taken a pair binoculars from his bag and was peering at the outside details of the house.

"What are you looking for?" Lynn asked.

"Trying to see the 'bones,'" he said. "Most people think that the interior of a house tells you the important things about its condition. I look for those things that are mostly hidden, like the internal timber structure, the basic proportions of the floors and walls, the foundation, the shape of the roof, the straightness of the chimneys, the way the dormers and gables are attached—things like that. You can't actually see the bones so you have to imagine what they look like by judging what's on top of them.

"So I start outside. The roof is the biggest element of protection for a house in this climate. It takes the rain, the snow, the sun, the wind—all the big weather that happens hits the roof the hardest. If you've got a good roof, you've probably got a house that can be rebuilt. If you've got a bad roof, it will take a lot more money and effort and may not be worth either. But if what I'm seeing are real slate shingles, fixing anything wrong with this roof may not even be possible." He lowered the binoculars to look at the house without them, then raised them to his eyes again.

"The foundation is next and then everything in between, like where each story of the house connects to the story below it. I look for bulging walls, misaligned porch connections, crooked window frames, sway-backed eaves, and sagging timbers.

"I also check the overall straightness of the house." He reached into his bag and held up a weight on a string. "Using a plumb bob, I can get an idea of whether the corners of the house are still straight up and down. You hold this at arm's length and look at the house to see if the corners line up with the string."

Tucker showed Lynn how to site down her arm, and then how to hold the plumb bob so it lined up with the corners, trim, and posts of the house.

"Wow. You must be a pro at this stuff."

Tucker smiled, appreciating that the woman seemed genuinely interested.

"Well, hardly as a good as a professional. My dad was a carpenter, and so I worked on a lot of houses when I was a teenager. That convinced me to go to college, but my educated life didn't turn out like I expected, so I came back to construction. I took a fancy to rebuilding Victorian houses, which is what I've been doing for the last several years."

"You've remodeled a Victorian house before?"

"Seven, but none were this big."

Seven? Lynn sighed at the thought. She should have known that a house this different was going to bring in the fringe players. She expected experienced builders or remodelers but somebody who actually specialized in Victorian houses?

She had moved from Century 21 to the Coldwell Banker office a year ago. She'd been a realtor for a long time but balanced a part-time job with staying at home with her kids, who were now grown. Her husband of thirty years had finally signed the divorce papers and they were waiting for their house to sell. Being a single woman demanded more income, and so she switched to the realty office that had the most houses on the Multiple Listing Source. The choice was proving to be a good one and she was doing better than she had expected. It was a competitive office, but in spite of having a few more years, and pounds, on the flashier women with the god-awful nails, she had held her own. Five hundred thousand dollars more in sales this year and she could take home the Realtor of the Year trophy.

She hadn't hesitated when they asked her to represent the Mulvaney property, but she realized later that she hadn't understood the situation. Advertised as a historical ranch house with river frontage, it was, in fact, an ancient, broken down monstrosity of a house in the middle of nowhere.

When she went through the master file, she found years of efforts by a dozen realtors to find a way to characterize the Mulvaney house as something someone would want to buy. The current owner was an oil company in Texas, which had bought the property thirty-odd years before, expecting to convert it into an executive retreat center, a fun place for executives to bring their families on vacation and for the occasional off-site business meeting. After discovering how much it would cost just to make it usable, the company decided it was more profitable to over-state its value, write off the taxes, and take the improvement and maintenance costs as depreciations. That wasn't a bad strategy at the time, but they neither improved it nor maintained it. Less than a decade later, they were stuck with a house and property valued at far less than their original investment. So the place was given over to realtors to market as they could.

In fact, after the company was bought by a bigger corporation last year, the pressure to sell the ranch had increased. With the house a continuing liability on paper, the decision was made to sell it, burn it, or tear it down—whatever it took to get it off the books.

It was now Lynn Anderson's responsibility to sell it before any drastic measures had to be used. Tucker Whitby was the only person who responded to the ad, and she had met him for the first time that morning. She prided herself on being able to read people, and he fit right into the preferred profile buyer for such a property: a retiree with money who was looking for something to keep himself busy. She thought he was probably in his mid-fifties, possibly a little younger, and noted that he had broad shoulders and muscular forearms, that his hands were thick and calloused, and he stood straight and tall. She liked him. He talked well, if not very much, and they had a good visit during the drive to the ranch. She had already gleaned that he was an experienced builder. He didn't seem to have a family, didn't seem to be married, and didn't seem too worried about the price of the property. By the time they had made it to the ranch gate, she thought she had a buyer.

And, a little embarrassed at noticing more than once, she thought that he was reasonably handsome—his eyes were a beautiful blue and he had a ready smile. It had been a long time since she'd talked that long with an attractive single man, and by the time they'd arrived, she was hoping he'd want to see more of her. Worn out by the years of working on a divorce, suffering it, and now biding her time to get the details finished off, she had little to no social life. She could use a good friend.

But Mr. Whitby was turning out to be far more experienced with old houses than she had anticipated, which dashed her hopes for a quick sale; it didn't take an expert to see how much work this house would require. From what her officemates had told her, anyone familiar with remodeling, rebuilding, or restoring houses would not be interested in the Mulvaney Mansion because it would obviously cost far more than anyone could possibly want to spend on it.

Now the best hope for selling the place was finding a buyer who would tear the house down and salvage the materials to build a new house. That was the approach her bosses had recommended: let the guy look at it, decide not to take it, then draw him a picture of how great a nice bright new house would look in this beautiful river valley. Sell it, even if she had to give him the price of the land without the house, were her instructions.

That plan was clearly not going to work with Tucker Whitby. Anybody who had rebuilt seven Victorian houses was not going to tear one down, no matter what shape it was in. He'll just walk away.

Lynn came out of her reverie and noticed that Tucker had stopped looking through his binoculars and was walking up and down the sidewalk, peering at the house. He was chuckling.

"What?" she asked.

"Look at the front of the house. It's watching us."

She looked but didn't see anything. "What do you mean," she asked.

"It's watching us. Have you seen those pictures of people, portraits to which the artist has done something to the eyes so that, no matter where you are, the eyes seem to be looking right at you?"

"Oh, okay. It's some kind of optical illusion, right?"

"Yeah. Well, look at the front of the house. Imagine the windows are eyes. Now, walk to the side. See? It's like, wherever we are, the windows seem to be looking straight at us."

Lynn thought it was a little spooky. She didn't want a house looking at her.

Tucker laughed, then reached for his bag. He noticed the purple flowers a few feet away.

"Oh, hey, lavender."

Lynn watched her client suddenly brighten as he walked into the patch of blossoming stalks between the sidewalk and the river. Before she knew it, he was absorbed in the haze of the light purple plants bunched along the slope and had lost all focus on the house.

There were several large plants scattered along the bank, obviously planted as part of a flower garden. Uncared for, the plants were thin and haggard and crowded by an invasion of weeds, grasses, and yucca plants.

Tucker dropped to his knees, picked a couple of long stems, rolled the flowers between his hands, closed his eyes, and held them to his nose.

[21]

The aroma flooded his sinuses. It was Jennie. Most people had roses at their weddings, but Jennie would have nothing but the soft purple flowers of lavender. Every table at the reception had its own bunch, making the whole room smell of soft purple. Every time they went to arts and crafts fairs or farmer's markets, she'd buy bouquets of lavender, bars of soap made with lavender, or bottles of lavender body wash. Every bathroom in the house smelled purple for a month.

Just like her, he thought. Soft, kind, and gentle—a whiff of simple beauty in the air.

Tucker opened his eyes. It had been a long time since she had become so vivid in his thoughts. He was used to keeping the memories in the back of his mind, holding them far away so they seemed small, but the smell brought everything forward. When thoughts of her barged in, the pain and sadness came with them and he had to allow the feelings their due, then wait for the feelings to subside.

She would have loved this place, he thought, as he struggled back to reality. She would have loved having her own lavender garden. And she would have dearly loved this house.

There was a faint clanging of the cable against the flagpole as he finally stood and brushed the dirt from his knees.

"I've never seen a man who knows the name of a lavender plant much less be so taken by the sight of one," Lynn said as Tucker came back to the sidewalk. He had surprised her, bounding suddenly away from his deliberate and measured style of looking at the house only to delight in flowers. What a free response, she had thought, and he did it without a hint of embarrassment. She felt like reaching down and grabbing a few stalks herself, and she didn't even like lavender.

Tucker's face reddened with his response. "My wife loved lavender," he said. "She'd buy bouquets, soaps, scented candles, whatever she could find that had lavender in it."

"Then she'll really love this place," she said, failing to notice his use of the past tense.

"Oh, my wife died several years ago, in a car accident," he said.

"Oh, I'm sorry," Lynn said hesitantly, not wanting to say the wrong thing.

"No, no. That's fine. I had a teenage daughter, and she also died. I'm just a single wandering builder-guy now," he said with a soft smile.

"I am so sorry. I hope that... Well, I mean that it must have been terrible... I'm so sorry."

"It's okay. It was a long time ago. Let's move over into the shade. It's pretty hot out here."

He and Lynn moved across the yard. Tucker touched the flagpole as they passed, swinging the worn cable, listening to it clang as it clumsily swung back and forth against the pipe. It was a sharp sound but, at the same time, lonesome as it echoed from the surrounding rock walls. A faint memory of its sound occurred to him, but realized that there was no breeze to swing the cable; he must have imagined it.

They stood in the shadow of the south cliffs, on the sidewalk that now ran along the bottom. They were on the opposite side of the house as the gate. Tucker's bag was open again, the binoculars and plumb bob out, and he was focused on the southern side of the house. With one pass over the south view of the roof, he lowered the binoculars and was silent as he cocked his head to one side.

He had worked on houses for a long, long time, and he had built up considerable intuition about them, and his intuition was telling him that some things weren't adding up.

"What?" Lynn asked, seeing him again distracted.

Tucker wiped the sweat from around his eyes, raised the binoculars, and reexamined the various high points of the house, half talking to her and half to himself.

"The best lookout spot in this whole valley is on that roof. You can see twice as much grass at half the distance from up there as you can from anywhere along the canyon rim. But if there had been birds on the roof, there'd be big splotches of poop all over it. Pigeons, ravens, crows, hawks, eagles, owls—they all poop a lot. Against the dark of the shingles, you'd see it everywhere. But there's not a single splotch, not on the ridges, the gables, or even below the metal roof ornaments. It looks like not a single bird has spent time on the roof."

He looked at her with a puzzled expression. "Why would they not perch on the roof? And look at the window sills—nothing.

Clean as a whistle. I've never known a pigeon or a dove that could resist a window sill. Weird."

Lynn was hoping that her red face wasn't noticeable in the shade. After she had accepted the responsibility of selling the house, her boss had taken her aside and told her the stories and rumors: strange noises, music, lights that went on and off, horses refusing to come close to the house, stray cattle that wouldn't eat the grass in the yard, dogs that wouldn't venture inside the front door. "Things aren't natural with that house," her boss had said. "We're pretty sure it's haunted." She hadn't believed any of it on general principle. New Mexico had hundreds of ghost stories, and although it was sometimes fun to imagine historical spirits flying around old houses, she didn't believe any of them.

She did have a favorite ghost story that was connected with this house, however. It was from a collection of ghostly tales published years ago for a Las Vegas historical celebration. The story was called "The Dancing Lady of Mulvaney Mansion." Supposedly, right after the house had been abandoned in the 1870s, reports came from prospectors, ranch hands, Indians, and others passing by of a lady wearing a long white dress dancing on the porch of the house. Sometimes she was in the yard and sometimes down by the river, but the stories always had her swinging and swaying, led by an invisible partner as if they were dancing to an orchestra. Lynn couldn't help but prefer that image over faces in windows or howling noises on full-moon nights. That particular ghost story was romantic, she thought, with her kind of ghost.

Still shaking his head, Tucker glanced over at the dormitory building.

"That's the dormitory built by the VA? What's the history behind it?"

Lynn readjusted her floppy hat and flipped through the pages of her file. She pulled out a history crib sheet that gave a detailed description and dates of the various major owners of the house.

"Let's see," she said. "The house was finished in 1869 and abandoned within a couple of years. Around the turn of the century, the property was leased by the Sisters of the Holy Light out of Santa Fe and opened as a tuberculosis sanatorium. Lots of people were moving to New Mexico and Arizona because of the dry climate, and the Archbishop of Santa Fe felt it a good idea to develop a facility

[24]

for them. The house was updated at that time, though it didn't need much beyond paint and a good cleaning because it had been virtually untouched for years."

"TB asylums were a big deal in the early 1900s," Tucker said. "Tucson had to build tent cities to accommodate everyone who came."

"The sanatorium," Lynn continued, "did well enough, and then was swamped by troops coming back from the First World War when it was expanded to treat soldiers who had been exposed to trench gasses. The place was crowded but well-regarded for the services it performed. The dust bowl and the depression in the twenties brought the business to a standstill. The sanatorium was officially closed in 1931, though some of the Sisters of the Holy Light stayed on for a number of years, the church in Santa Fe using it as a convent and a retreat center.

"World War II created the need for rehabilitation facilities for injured troops, so the Veterans Administration bought the property in 1943 and completely redid it. That's when they put in electricity, new plumbing, new floors, laid on new paint, installed a telephone system, and changed the heating system from coal to gas. And that's when they built the dormitory."

"Let's take a look," Tucker said, slipping his binoculars back into the bag. He was still thinking about the birds, but a few steps later he was laughing again.

"See, see," he said, pointing at the windows. "Now the windows on this side look like they're watching us. This is great."

Lynn was just sorry to leave the shade of the cliffs.

They followed the sidewalk up to the austere-looking building. Built along the base of the cliffs behind the house, the dormitory was located about fifty feet from the back door of the house. Tucker smiled as he recognized the rudimentary construction as the kind of building that became the run-down flea-bag motels that he remembered seeing along the highways in New Jersey as a kid. The building had two long wings, each wing having six rooms one after another like dominos in the box. It had a flat roof pitched to the back that was supported in front and back by slanted metal pipes. The common areas of the structure centered between the two wings consisted of his and her bathrooms and shower rooms and what Lynn referred to as an entertainment room. All the walls were concrete block, the floors cement, and the ceilings nondescript fiberboard sandwiched between the steel trusses and the tarred plywood of the roof.

Lynn following close behind, Tucker made a quick inspection of the hallway rooms, which were barren and made for two beds. Each room had two built-in desks, one closet, a sink, and a steel-framed window centered on the back wall. He checked the bathrooms to find only a few toilets intact, no sinks, and a deeply engrained bad smell. The entertainment room had been used as a dump for leftover papers, books, and magazines, two ancient plastic-covered sofas, old bed springs, and a broken office chair.

Tucker assumed that the building had been ignored by any owners or renters after the VA, although some industrious family had converted the last bedroom in the north wing into a chicken coop. Having tame chickens in their own coop at least confined their mess to one place; the rest of the dorm looked like an abandoned zoo. Poop was everywhere, discarded bones, old snakeskins, feathers, nests, and large piles of whatever the raccoons, skunks, and coyotes could find to shred for beds.

Once back out the front door, Tucker and Lynn stood in the shade of the corrugated overhang of the entry patio taking deep breaths of fresh air.

"The VA made the house a hospital? And built the dorm?" he asked.

"Yes," she replied. "The house was remodeled into a hospital environment, with doctors upstairs and the first floor wings for patients and the kitchen facilities. The dorm was used to house the nurses and staff."

"This is hardly the place for emergency medicine," Tucker said. "Was it a mental institution, by chance?"

Lynn had skipped over the name—the Veterans Hospital for the Insane. She hated to use that last word; soldiers deserved better. "Well, yes. It was created for those returning from the war who had, um, mental difficulties. I think they called it 'shell shock' in those days."

"What happened after the war?" Tucker asked.

"In the mid-fifties," Lynn continued reading, "when the VA decided that the hospital wasn't needed anymore, the ranch was again abandoned. It stayed on the government surplus property list for several years and was eventually bought by the Boy Scouts. However, with the growth of the Philmont Scout Ranch, they defaulted on the loan a few years later and let the place go.

"After that, it was rented, leased, or owned by small ranchers, a civic organization, and a historical society who had more vision than money. It was finally bought by the current owner, a Texas oil company, in 1980."

"That's quite a history," Tucker said. "It's amazing that a house this old is still standing, much less a house that has had such rugged use. It's a great location, but imagine a house full of people with no air conditioning, one kitchen, and only one bathroom. And the radiators must have creaked and pinged and moaned all winter long."

When they reached the corner of the house, passing by the large pile of rubble from the collapsed back porch, Tucker looked at the abandoned power pole that stood twenty feet away. He wouldn't even guess at the number of years since the house had seen electricity.

They walked down the north sidewalk. Tucker was satisfied that he had noted all of the house's exterior features and possible problems. Reaching the SUV, he set his bag on the front steps and the two of them retreated into the shade of the house.

"What do you think?" Lynn asked.

3

Tucker's initial impression had not changed: it was way too much house for him. He intended to slow down on his next project, not die from it. The location was unique, no question, and having a house on a river was one of his dreams. But every piece of new material, hired contractor, or day-to-day supplies would, at minimum, be an hour away and two hours roundtrip. He was interested in remote, but rebuilding this house would be like working in a foreign country.

On the other hand, he'd never seen a house so well-suited to a property, nor a property that had so much self-contained beauty. The dormitory was a detractor, but it could be cleaned up and provide workshop space and tool storage, which would let the entire house be available and uncluttered until it was completely finished, a very attractive idea. And where else would he get a river all to himself?

Tucker sighed, ran his hand along some of the stones in the foundation of the porch, and thought about whether he could possibly take this house on. It would take a lot longer than any other house he'd redone. If he staged it out, though, and only did pieces at a time, well... He could use as many years as he wanted, he reasoned, and maybe that's what he needed. Maybe this was finally the house that would keep him grounded for a while.

He backed away from the house and looked up.

It was unquestionably a high-dollar Victorian, and an absolutely regal mansion when it was new. A wrap-around porch dominated the front and sides of the house, providing a sheltered entrance to the front door as well as lots of socializing room for wandering guests. To the left of the front door, a gazebo roof covered a semi-circular part of the porch that extended out into the yard. All across the bottom of the porch was stonework, giving the house a solid and even more massive appearance than its sheer size already inspired.

The second story matched the shape of the first floor, probably with bedrooms replacing the social rooms, and the third floor matched the second, with maybe even more bedrooms. If so, Tucker guessed the house had nine or ten sleeping rooms and at least three sleeping porches where beds would be moved in the summer.

An almost circular bay window swept out on the first floor, with the same shape copied on the second and third floors. This gave the house a "tower" complete with a cone-shaped rooftop, which really made the house look grand.

Brick had been used to cover every outside wall, from the foundation to below the gables, which was pretty unusual in Tucker's experience but the protection was supreme. The brick looked in good shape too. With assistance from a mason or two, the brick wouldn't be hard to restore.

But the porch's roof all around the house was sagging between the support posts, and the ornate wood corbels on top of the posts had popped out or disintegrated and most of the posts themselves were rotted. The floors of the front porch and side porch were warped, rising up and down in frozen waves. Any paint had long been sandblasted away by the canyon winds.

The windows varied from being in good shape to missing altogether. Ancient in their construction, they would all have to be replaced. Tucker had counted the windows as he walked around it, giving up at fifty. Getting the windows modernized would be an immense cost.

The foundation seemed firm. He saw no patterns in the brick that indicated foundation cracking or failure, but he would need to go into the basement for a true inspection.

The roof looked in remarkably good shape. His binocular inspection revealed that some of the flashing around the chimney had separated, and indicated that a roof valley was partially caved in. He expected to see water damage inside.

All in all, the outside was workable. It would just take time, effort, and money. The house obviously did not have electricity, and he assumed that it did not have a working water system and would probably need a new septic system as well. He suspected that any heating system was also long gone.

That brought him back to a more fundamental question: why was this house still standing at all? His intuition continued to tell him that things weren't what they appeared to be.

The absence of birds could possibly be explained by bad wind currents or smelly anti-bird mold on the ridge shingles, maybe something about the slate itself, or maybe something else he could not imagine. Possibly. But he had worked on Victorian houses half the age of this one and they hadn't been anywhere near as straight. The corners of this place were still intact and perfectly vertical. Sighting down the outside walls showed no bowing in or out, and the ridges of the roof appeared level. The valleys of the roof indicated that the dormers had all stayed true. And even the stonework around the house was still level.

This house had been abandoned for considerable periods of its lifetime—thirty, fifty, maybe even seventy years? It's one thing for an old house to survive if it's been constantly occupied, but a house abandoned and left to the elements had almost zero chance of staying together. Wood wasn't that long-lasting when unprotected.

In his estimation, this house should have collapsed a long time ago. Something very strange was going on.

"Did I see that you brought some chairs?" Tucker asked. "Maybe we could sit on the porch and take a break before we go into the house."

"Oh, that's a great idea," Lynn responded. "And I brought some drinks to help us cool off a bit."

It took a couple of minutes to gather the lawn chairs and cooler from her SUV. The air was still hot, and not a breath of wind helped cool the front of the house. The shade on the porch, however, was a comfort, and the cold drinks a relief. Sitting in the folding chairs was pleasing to them both.

"I wish the house wasn't so big," Tucker said, balancing a can of Coke on his knee. "It's a beautiful piece of property, and the valley would be a fine place to live, even being so far from town. But the house is too big for one person to rebuild, not to mention that it would be incredibly hard for one person to take care of after it's finished."

Lynn had expected to hear no less trepidation after watching Tucker go methodically through his evaluation and listening to his comments as he pointed out aspects in need of repair and the difficulties of working on a house forty feet tall. It was easy to understand why it was an impossible job. She couldn't even imagine how much work it would take. However, she could tell that he was becoming attracted to the idea.

"What can you tell me about the guy who built this monster?" Tucker asked. "It's quite a house for the 1800s frontier."

"There's a small blurb in the paperwork, but I know a little more from stories that I've heard around town. Cyrus Mulvaney was a hotshot lawyer in town for many years, and he made a lot of money working in the land grant business. He had a wife named Violet, a boy named Samuel, and a younger daughter named Lucille. Not satisfied with being a lawyer, he decided to make himself into a cattle baron, and so he bought a hundred thousand acres northeast of town to serve as grazing pastures for cattle drives on the way north. He expected the railroads to eventually build into New Mexico, and wanted to have stockyards ready like those in Kansas, using the railroad to ship the cattle back east.

"Assuming that he would become extremely rich and famous, he built this house as a monument to his success. Unfortunately, within two years of living in it, his ten year-old son was kidnapped by the Comanche Indians, on his birthday, no less. His wife went insane as a result, and he gave up his six year-old daughter to relatives. Meanwhile, all of his business ventures had failed. He ended up hanging himself from one of the balconies.

"And, if that wasn't enough, his wife disappeared after the funeral. She was being watched by the house maids because of her mental condition, and then suddenly vanished; they couldn't find her anywhere. The local judge finally declared that she must have thrown herself into the river, but they never found a body."

"That's a pretty tragic tale," Tucker said. "And pretty depressing. That means that we're sitting on the porch of a house that has been the site of a child kidnapping, a suicide, a disappearance, a sanatorium, and a convent, as well as a long-term engagement as an insane asylum. This house, throughout its history, must have witnessed almost every kind of human horror imaginable.

"And you'd like me to live here," he said, looking at her with a wry smile.

Listing all of the historical troubles all at once caught Lynn off guard. It really put a dark shade on the house. On the other hand, that darkness gave another strong reason for tearing the house down.

"I do want you to live here," she said, sitting straight in her chair and looking him in the eye. "But not in this house. You've made the perfect argument that it's time to tear this house down and build smaller, better, and smarter." She learned the last phrase at a realtor's convention.

Tucker was about to reply when the cable on the flagpole began to beat against the metal, making sharp, raspy, clanging sounds.

As Tucker and Lynn jerked around to watch the thrashing cable, the rhythm increased and the sounds became more erratic.

Behind them, a noise came from within the house, first like a creak and then more of a hollow sound, like a finger rubbed across a drum. It grew into a full-throated moan, then a wail. The front door slammed open and the sound screamed out across the deck at the two of them.

The floor under Lynn's chair swayed, jolted her sideways, cracked, then gave way, plunging the chair, and her, toward a rapidly expanding hole. Barely making it to his feet in time, Tucker grabbed her hand and pulled her out of the chair as it collapsed into the empty space beneath the floor.

Both of them stumbled down the steps as the wooden floor shook, twisted, and vibrated, as if an invisible hand had reached out and was pounding on the boards.

* * *

I do not like this woman! I may be old and rundown, a house that has outlived its time, and I may die at any moment, but I will not be murdered.

Who is this woman that she would throw me away? Does she know nothing of honor and endurance? Has she no appreciation of wood and craftsmanship? Can she not respect me for what I am? She is shallow and is interested only in the man and his money.

The man I like; he has a careful eye for my structure. I watched them both as they went around me, and I appreciate the comments he made. I liked him when he knelt among the flowers. There was sensitivity in his hands and caring in his heart. I heard the echoes of pain and anguish; there is more to hear from this man.

I am glad that he has found me well cared for, though it disturbs him that he can't find a reason. Good. He should wonder. I have done well to preserve myself. I have always followed the command given me by the shaman and will continue to do so. The man will have to work a little harder, be a little more trusting, and listen longer if he wishes to understand.

The woman can just go away.

4

Tucker held on to Lynn's arm, half-directing, half-pulling her down the front steps. Stumbling into the yard and away from the house, they were short of breath by the time they had gotten far enough away to feel safe.

The floor stopped shaking, the moaning quit, and the flagpole fell silent.

"What happened?" Lynn stammered, wide-eyed and breathing hard.

Tucker steadied his voice. "I have no idea." He calmed himself and slowly walked nearer the porch. He peered over the steps to where his chair sat upright whereas Lynn's was now caught in the splintered opening, hanging only by one leg and the material on the back. The floor could no doubt be rotten in places, but it would have to be a mighty big coincidence that the lady just happened to be sitting exactly on the bad spot, he thought.

Getting as close to the house as her SUV, Lynn called over that she was all for abandoning the chairs and cooler and getting the hell out of there.

Tucker was more contemplative, fearful of what he had seen but wildly curious. He didn't believe it was an earthquake or a sudden downdraft or vibrations from the wind, or in fact any ordinary phenomena. And chances were that even rotten boards wouldn't suddenly collapse in such a neat hole. But if those were ruled out, he was left with nothing to cause what had happened. Any natural cause, anyway, which left him thinking about the supernatural. It was his experience that old houses, especially old, elegant Victorians, were sometimes different from regular houses. His previous houses had never felt especially supernatural one way or the other, but he had always wondered what a haunted house would be like—and wondered what difference it would make if you were to try to remodel one.

He decided to keep his thoughts to himself.

Lynn had already climbed into the seat of the SUV. She was now a believer in every single thing that her boss had told her.

"Wait a minute," Tucker called out, not wanting to leave.

"Are you kidding? We were just attacked by a house! We need to get out of here."

Tucker moved around to her side of the SUV and tried to calm her down.

"I still want to see the inside. I assume that you're not going to increase the price just because it's haunted," he said with a smile.

"Haunted is right, and we should leave any ghosts to themselves. What do you want to see the inside for? Would you live in a house that had screamed at you as it was throwing you off the porch?" Tucker noticed that her hands were shaking as she held onto the steering wheel.

"I'm not saying that I'm ready to live here. I just want to see the inside of the house. Maybe it will show that the house is really sensitive to spurious air currents or has really bad rot problems. I don't know. But, hey, we're here. Why don't you stay in the car and I'll do a quick look around?"

"You mean sit in the car until nightfall when I finally go in the house and find that some ghost has ripped all of your flesh off?" she said, looking him sternly in the eyes.

"Well, okay. Don't sit in the car. You can stand on the porch, or maybe at the bottom of the steps. I guarantee that I won't let any ghost do anything to me. I promise."

Tucker looked at her and smiled. He had known there was something else going on. His intuition wasn't so far off, after all. He wasn't sure if it was a *who* or an *it*, but something had been keeping this house from crumbling into the dirt. Typically, he wasn't a believer in the supernatural, but he wasn't a nonbeliever either. And when nothing natural made sense…

"I just want to see the inside," he insisted.

It took a few concessions. Lynn would stay at the bottom of the steps and close to the SUV, and Tucker would call back to her if she called to him. Tucker grabbed his bag off the front steps and was through the front doorway before she had time to renegotiate.

Tucker stopped in the reception room and stood still, listening, looking, and surveying everything around him. The house looked old, smelled old, and had the usual creaks and groans like it was old. This was the part of seeing an old house that he liked most—examining the floors, the walls, the ceilings, the stairs, the hallways—imagining what it must have been like to live in the house. He liked seeing a house's colors, its textures, its lighting, liked to smell its smells and see its dusty spaces and guess at the ambiance that the occupants would have experienced. He liked seeing the layout of the rooms and imagining what the original designer thought when he drew the plans on a drawing board. Of course, this house wasn't furnished, which dictated a lot of the feelings, but the high ceilings, the woodwork, the size of the doors between the rooms, the width of the hallways, the ornateness of the ceiling fixtures all factored into how people felt at home.

He walked through quickly, more to force himself not to dawdle than to save the minutes of agony for Lynn. Tucker, in fact, had been in so many old Victorians that he didn't expect to find significantly different building problems, which meant that he could probably fix any problem he found. He moved through the parlor, the library, the kitchen, and the large oval dining room in a few minutes. The rooms were huge compared to a modern house.

He made his way up the back stairs to the second level. The bedrooms were similarly sized and shaped as those rooms downstairs, though another bedroom and the bathroom were now above the kitchen and pantry areas. As with the parlor and library downstairs, the two major rooms had fireplaces with wood boxes built into the walls next to them.

There was carpet in three of the rooms. Tucker laughed. The carpet was, no doubt, laid in the sixties. He pulled back a corner and confirmed that it had been laid over square motley-white hard-surfaced linoleum tiles, probably installed by the VA. The tiles would have been standard for hospital environments of the day.

Now he felt the adventure of archaeology—peeling back the layers of generations before him. He wasn't offended by the carpet, and in fact, he liked carpet. If he was offended, it was by the linoleum tile. Using his knife, he loosened several of the floor tiles and revealed the floor beneath. It was oak, or maybe mahogany, probably brought from someplace in the east. It would have been a beautiful floor when new, and it was a tragedy that the tiles covered it up.

When he returned to the stairs and walked up to the third floor, he thought the spaces seemed less busy than the other levels, which Tucker attributed to smaller hallways, smaller rooms, and lower ceilings. As he stepped into the hallway, it seemed strange that the whole space was relatively cool. Typically, the hot air coming through the windows would rise up into the higher parts of the house. He was sure that there was no insulation below the roof and so the slate shingles should have been passing on the intense heat from the desert sun.

But it wasn't hot at all. Either the roof vents were turning in a magical performance or this was another thing that went on the "weird" list Tucker was keeping in his head. It was almost like something wanted him to move through the house as comfortably as possible.

He was looking at the river through the corner "tower" room when he heard sounds echoing in the house.

Footsteps. Slow but definite.

He turned slowly and listened as the footsteps faded away, then grew louder. Something was coming up the stairway. The footpads were sometimes too soft to make out, but the creaking of the stair treads was unmistakable. He heard the final footstep at the top of the stairs and then a slow procession down the hall.

He set his bag quietly on the floor and stood ready, intensely focused on the doorway in front of him.

"Mr. Whitby?" a small voice called.

"Yeah, in here."

Lynn hurried through the door and moved quickly beside him.

"I thought you weren't coming inside," he said.

Lynn was flustered and clearly nervous, and she moved close to him, grabbing hold of his arm. "Well, I wasn't, you know," she said with a slightly quaking voice, "but the longer I was alone, the more I thought that I was safer with you. So, how's the house?"

Tucker laughed. "Pretty ordinary, so far. I was just looking at the floor. The first and second floors are covered with linoleum tiles, but this floor is the original wood. And the walls haven't been painted as much up here. In fact, I think a couple of the rooms have the original wallpaper. That's highly unusual and would be a historian's dream. Let me show you."

Entering the room next to the stairway landing with Lynn close behind, Tucker ran his hand over the faded print on the wall. It had a rough surface and was coated with dirt, dust, and soot. He licked his thumb and rubbed hard. Five or six rubs later, blue and yellow barely peaked through.

The room was big enough to have been either storage or a bedroom, maybe even a study, though the ceiling was at different angles. An old radiator stood beneath the window, ornate and solid, with a rough silver color that had blackened next to the floor. The window had a fine view of the south yard of the house. A fireplace was on the opposite wall next to the door, with another built-in wood bin next to it.

Satisfied with his inspection, Tucker and Lynn walked down the back stairs. Tucker paused along the way to show Lynn a couple of rooms where the plastered ceiling had ballooned downward into a bowl-shaped growth. This corresponded to a separated flashing of the roof he had seen outside, which allowed water to run down inside the walls and drip onto the ceilings. In several places, the walls had gotten wet and the wallpaper was hanging from the walls in large strips. They reached the bottom of the stairs and turned into the kitchen.

"I need to go into the basement," Tucker said, pointing to a narrow doorway. "Do you want to come? In the movies, bad things always happen in the basement."

Lynn blanched. "Uh, I think I'll stand right here and talk to you while you're checking it out. Would that be okay?"

"Sure."

Tucker took a large flashlight and a small lantern from his bag and started down the stairs. At the bottom, he stepped onto a dirt floor, the floor joists above him so low they were within his reach.

Tucker turned on the lantern and placed it on the bottom step of the stairs. He swept the flashlight around the room. He was seeking information that could only be found in the basement. The heat, water, and sewer certainly, and the foundation, but he was really looking for more.

Tucker was thinking about what had happened on the porch. He was conservative when it came to spirits and ghosts and hauntings and such, but, sometimes, supernatural manifestations were the only reasonable explanations for strange occurrences. He was glad that Lynn had not followed him. He had made a joke about the house being haunted, but in truth, if any supernatural forces were at work in the house, he believed they'd show up in the basement. And, if they did, Lynn would be even more adamant about tearing the house down. Basements were like the bowels of a body—low, central, and full of stuff trying to get out. He trusted the bowels of a house to reveal more of its spiritual condition than the upstairs.

Moving through a wandering path, he thought the basement felt ordinary. It was cramped, confining and uncomfortable, and filled with disorderly piles of boxes, wood scraps, old metal headboards and springs, busted filing cabinets, tables with missing legs, papers, and trash.

He was able to get a clear view of the foundation, which was made out of a layer of large, flat stones on the very bottom, a layer of small boulders and rocks embedded in cement on top of that, and brick layered on top of the rocks. Large timbers sat on top of the brick. It was on the timbers that the floors and walls of the house were constructed. It all looked in surprisingly good shape. The floor joists appeared straight and strong, as did the monster wooden girders, held up by brick pillars that ran down the middle of the house.

The small basement windows around the perimeter were all broken. Cast iron sewer pipes coming from above were concentrated in the back of the house, with a large pipe piercing the foundation wall on the south. That would lead to the cesspool or septic tank, Tucker surmised. There were no broken joints or pipes that he could see. Three electrical panels hung along one wall, sprouting a tangled mess of old wires leading to the walls above.

An empty cement pad sat next to the chimney. The central boiler had been removed, probably stolen, and most of the hot water pipes going up to the radiators were gone. The pipes were probably copper, Tucker thought, which made them valuable in the recycling market.

The house's central chimney was a massive square of brickwork, at least eight feet along each side. Being thirty, maybe forty feet tall, the chimney must have been a major undertaking of its own as the house was being built around it. Built into its side, like next to the fireplaces upstairs, was a storage bin for logs. Tucker guessed that they kept wood to start the fire in the furnace, after which they would pile on coal. The massive chimney was the most unusual find the basement had to offer.

That and the lack of animal tracks. There was no evidence of animals in the soft dirt at all—no paw prints, no snake trails, no scratch marks by any claws. There were no bird droppings, no nests in the corner, no bats hanging in the upper reaches of the ceilings, and no scat on the floor. Considering the dormitory zoo only a short walk away and the open basement windows that served as "rooms available" signs, Tucker found the cleanliness of the basement to be significant.

That evidence, or lack thereof in this case, confirmed that the house was cared for, which was consistent with what he had decided outside. If it was taken care of by a spirit or something, it was a whole other kind of spirit than what he normally thought of as haunting a house. Was it a general force that preserved the house or a more specific entity, like a ghostly maintenance man or caretaker?

Coming back around to the stairway, he thought about what he had learned. The bowels of the house hadn't disgorged any of the terrors in the horror movies, but neither had he felt alone. There was a benign sense of curiosity in the air, as if he was being watched.

Still, everything about the house reflected the unavoidable signs of aging, any spirit caretaker not withstanding: drooping supports, falling plaster, shrinking wood, broken windows, wavy floors, threadbare carpet, spider webs floating in the windowsills. Dirt, tumbleweeds, and mounds of sand littered every room. The smells were few, however, other than those of dust and baked dirt. The air was too dry to be musty.

Those signs of age Tucker could accept because the house was old, had been vacant, and had missing doors and windows. But beyond its appearance, something had preserved the strength of the house, had kept its structure straight and kept creatures out. That showed a high level of respect and desire for preservation. Animals had not come into the house because they had not been allowed into the house. He suspected that was true of the roof, as well, birds not landing for the same reason critters did not come downstairs.

There was one more thing Tucker wanted to look for. It was not unusual for builders of that era to sign their work. In particular, on the beams in the basement, directly beneath the front door or close to it, there would sometimes be initials, a full name, or sometimes a pithy saying carved into the timbers. Any carving would have actually been done before the beam was set in place.

Tucker trained his light above him, following the different timbers on the east end of the basement and peering closely for any marks.

"There," he said to himself, finally finding letters carved in a beam. "Arthur Crumbling. Huh, what a name for a house builder. And there's Cyrus Mulvaney's name, as well."

There was a third name but it was harder to make it out. Tucker needed to get closer. Around him was a general disarray of things, but he found a round metal trashcan that would get him close enough to the beam. He turned it upside down and scooted it beneath the carvings.

The letters were more scratched than carved, barely showing up in the rough surface. He moved his light so that it shown across the letters instead of down on them. He could make out three letters: S A M. He at first assumed that they were initials but then slowly made the connection.

It was a name: Sam. Samuel. That was Cyrus Mulvaney's son, the one kidnapped by Indians. Mulvaney's son had crawled up there and scratched his own name into the beam. Tucker reached up and touched the letters.

"Mr. Whitby? MR. WHITBY?"

Tucker felt the dirt beneath him as he lay flat on the floor, an old chair to his side and some of the dust-covered boxes across his legs. The trashcan was crumpled and lying on its side.

It was mostly dark. His flashlight and the lantern he had left on the stair step were out, leaving only the ambient light from the windows to keep total darkness from around him.

"MR. WHITBY!" Lynn screamed even louder.

[42]

Tucker sat up, shook his head, ran his hand through his hair to shake the dirt out, then grabbed his flashlight. It worked when he flipped the switch. As he struggled to his feet brushing dirt from his clothes, he sniffed a strong odor: pancakes. Pancakes? He was sure. The aroma was unmistakable. Fresh pancakes, like right off the griddle, and the rich, full smell of butter.

He was mystified. What had happened to him? The last he remembered, he was touching the scratched initials of the little boy. Then he was on the ground.

Lynn was relieved when Tucker returned to the bottom of the stairs, retrieved his lantern, and came up the steps to join her.

"WHAT HAPPENED?" she cried in a frantic voice. "I heard a crash, the light went out, and I couldn't hear you anymore. I didn't know what to do…"

"It's all fine," Tucker responded. "I was just using a trashcan to stand on and it slipped out from under me. We're good. No problem."

He noted that she looked like she believed him.

"I've got a couple more things that I'd like to do," he said. "Then we'll be out of here."

5

Tucker led Lynn to the parlor, reached into his bag, removed a long measuring tape, and handed her one end. "I'd like to get a rough idea of the dimensions of the house. If you'll hold the end of the tape just inside the window on the other side of the stairway…" He pointed. "I'll go across to the far wall."

She did as he asked, and he held his end of the tape along the outside of the parlor window frame. He noted the number, then watched as the tape was pulled to a larger number, then released inward to a smaller number.

"You need to hold it steadier, okay?" he called to Lynn.

She replied that she had hooked the tape on the window frame and wasn't holding it at all.

That was a puzzle, and so Tucker held the tape tighter against the frame and read it again. As before, it read one number and then the tape slowly creeped inward to show a bigger number, then slowly outward to a smaller number. As he continued to hold it, the movement was repeated.

It took a moment for Tucker to readjust his thinking. It wasn't the tape that was moving. It was the wall.

His intuition went off like an alarm bell—what was happening just wasn't right. Walls don't move. When walls move, buildings typically fall down. Movement means instability, and instability is, well, unstable. Tucker was confused. Whether it was the fact that it was happening or that he had no explanation for it whatsoever, he swallowed to relieve the dryness in his mouth and noticed that his heart rate had increased. He called Lynn over and showed her the movement of the tape, but he gave her no explanation.

"Okay, well, let's do the other direction," he said.

With Lynn satisfied to stay close to the front door, they repeated the procedure for the length of the house, from front door to back door. This time, the tape read a constant length.

He walked back to Lynn as he reeled the tape back into its holder.

"One last thing, I promise. I'm going to check for whether the floors are level." He removed a full roll of duct tape from the bag, walked to one side of the parlor, set the tape on its edge on the floor, aimed it for the center of the room, and gave it a little push.

"This is an old trick for testing the level of the floor from the middle of the house to the outside. If the tape accelerates, which it looks like it is, then the floor dips, which means there's probably a problem with the floor joists. Some joist has failed..."

The roll of tape had accelerated, then slowed down, and then stopped halfway across.

It slowly rolled in reverse, accelerated, then came to a stop where Tucker had first placed it. It began to roll again, back across the room, stopped, and then returned to its starting point. The roll of tape continued to repeat the process.

Tucker's face whitened and he grabbed his hands together in front of him to keep them from shaking.

"That's not good, is it?" Lynn asked him from behind.

Tucker did not reply. He picked up the roll of tape, returned it to his bag, then led Lynn out the door. She locked it behind them and grabbed the chairs as he picked up the cooler. They stored the chairs and cooler in the back of the SUV, and she had the engine running before he was completely seated.

He motioned her hand back when she reached for the gear shift. He needed a little time.

She sat looking at him sideways, the engine running and the air conditioner blowing furiously.

Tucker was at a loss. It was one thing for a house to be inhabited by a disembodied spirit that hung about in the shadows and made dramatic entrances and exits. But this house was, today, right now, empowered by something active—active to the point that it had made several weird things happen all within a single visit. It

[46]

was as if those weird things were always happening, but they had just now gotten noticed. If that was true, he was thinking, then the spirit within was an ongoing thing. Not a spirit that was *in* the house but a spirit that *was* the house.

He tried to put it all together.

Two or three minutes later, Tucker switched the fan to its lowest speed and spoke. "The house is breathing," he said.

Lynn was vastly relieved. "They talk about that in the office. The builders are always talking about houses breathing and..." Tucker stopped her.

"They're talking about air exchanges in houses, through walls and windows and cracks and such. What I mean is a literal fact, not a metaphor: this house is breathing," he said slowly, using his hands to show the expansion and contraction of a body during a breath.

She still didn't understand what he was saying. "You mean like..."

"Yeah. The house is breathing like you and I are breathing. When it inhales, the walls move out like a ribcage and the floor moves down like a diaphragm. When it exhales, the walls move in and the floor moves up."

Lynn yanked the shifter into reverse and spun the wheels as she whipped the SUV around.

"Wait, wait," Tucker said. "Please. Wait. Let me keep thinking for a moment."

She wasn't much interested in thinking, but being inside the car and having it pointed in the right direction made her more agreeable. She sat still, looking at him expectantly.

"Okay," Tucker said after a minute. "I want to try one more thing. It won't take long, but I want you to come with me."

"I'm not going into a house that's breathing!" she said, copying his hand motions to mimic the house's respiration.

"I can do this alone, and that would be fine," Tucker said, "but I feel like we're in this together. Not having you next to me makes me feel incomplete. I want to try something on the stairway. If nothing else, you'll have one more really good story to tell at the office."

Lynn had stopped listening at "not having you next to me makes me feel incomplete." She was disoriented and frightened and absolutely out of her comfort zone, but she couldn't miss feeling a deep-down thrill at his words. She couldn't remember her ex-husband ever having expressed a sentiment like that.

But this guy wanted her to go back into a haunted house. He was either monumentally stupid or the bravest man she had ever met.

And, oh, Lord, there are those blue eyes, she thought.

She took a deep breath. "Okay."

Tucker opened his bag in the backseat and removed a couple of cloths and a squeeze ketchup bottle.

Lynn cinched up her courage as much as she could and led the way, cautiously creeping up the steps, walking across the porch's floor, unlocking the door, and then meekly peeking into the reception hall. Tucker passed her and walked to the front stairway.

The stairway was good quality for 1867, with solid oak treads and risers, and it had nicely carved railings and newel posts. The arid heat of New Mexico had not been kind to it, drying the wood to a dull sand color and covering it with a thick layer of dust. A continuous line of dark stains up and down the railing witnessed to the many years of use.

Tucker took Lynn by the hand and led her up to the midway landing. He folded one of the cloths, stepped down, and wiped the round wooden knob on top of the bottom newel post, then wiped the railing, which skirted the edge of the landing, and then the dust from the second and third newel posts.

"Now we'll see what happens. Stand next to me," he said quietly, "and put your hand on my shoulder. Put your other hand on the wallpaper." He pointed to the outside wall.

Tucker took the plastic ketchup bottle, removed the top, and squirted a heavy line of liquid on the round knobs of the second and third newel posts of the landing and on the railing between. Using the second cloth, he smeared the liquid across the surfaces. It quickly disappeared into the dry wood but had filled the air with a strong odor. He squeezed more liquid from the bottle and rubbed again. The oak began to hold a wet shine.

Lynn felt and then saw the wall of the house move slightly. It continued to inch its way out, then back in, in large enough changes that it pushed against her fingers.

A quiet sound came up the stairway, much like a stifled breath.

Tucker squirted more liquid on the railing and rubbed with long, even strokes.

There was a sound like an exhale, and then another of air being drawn in, but longer this time.

"I think it likes the smell," Tucker said quietly.

He gave the round knobs another squirt.

"What is that stuff?" Lynn asked in a whisper.

"Furniture polish," he whispered back. "I always carry a little to see if old wood can still be brightened up."

The house's breaths were definitely deeper and longer now. In and out. In and out.

Suddenly, a breeze whisked up the stairway and swirled up into the stairwell, high into the ceiling above them. Tucker quickly capped the bottle, dropped it, and held on to Lynn. She circled her arms around him, holding tight.

The swirling breeze changed into a stout wind and the two were rocked back and forth as the wind curled around them. Inside the swirl, Tucker detected a murmur. It was indistinct and muffled by the wind around him, but whether it was an actual voice or not, he could not tell. It was only towards the end that he realized the wind curling around them had the deep aroma of lavender.

The wind gradually subsided and the house was again calm and quiet. Tucker gradually released his hold on Lynn's arms, though she took longer to release him. Breathing hard and unsure of his steps, Tucker retrieved his bottle and cloths from the floor and led Lynn through the front door. Lynn made sure that she securely locked it. Tucker was going to point out that the back door was missing entirely but decided not to mention it.

They were on the steps to the ground when Tucker slowed, looked back, and then returned to the door. He raised an open hand and held his palm and fingers flat against it as he closed his eyes. He held his hand there for a few seconds, then withdrew it and returned to the SUV.

"I'll make a deal with you," Tucker said after a few minutes as the SUV barreled up the canyon road. "I'll buy the house if you won't say a word about what happened today."

The tires squealed as Lynn jumped on the brakes and yanked the wheel to the right, pulling onto the side of the road.

[49]

She stared at him. "You want to buy that house? You actually want to live in that house?"

Her voice was quivering. "I'm going to tell my bosses to bring in bulldozers next week and plow the place under! Live in that house? Are you kidding me?"

Tucker's hands were amazingly quick. He shoved the shifter into park, turned off the engine, and removed the keys before she realized what he was doing.

Then he sat, silently looking out the passenger window.

Lynn was yelling at him, asking him what the hell right he had to take her keys and throwing in more of her assessment of haunted houses, stupid ghosts, and especially how she did not like being thrown off porches.

After a few moments, she had run out of anger. She took several deep breaths, wiped her eyes and sat back in her seat, her arm propped against the window sill and her hand to her mouth. She did not look at him.

"I will buy that house," Tucker said evenly, "if you won't tell anyone what happened today."

"Why shouldn't I tell what happened," she asked, still peeved at him for taking her keys, for the whole strange experience, even if it was not his fault.

"Because the place would be invaded by thousands of curious people wanting to see ghosts. There would be a never-ending line of cars at the gate and hundreds of people scaling the cliffs to look at the house. I would have a MTV film crew camping out on the rim of the canyon and watching the house twenty-four hours a day, hoping that some apparition looks out a window. I would not be left alone, ever. And by the way, neither would you. You'd have CNN asking you to show exactly how the house collapsed a chair beneath you, and requesting you estimate how strong the wind was that assaulted you on the staircase, and asking if you plan on suing the oil company for endangerment. Our lives would be forever changed."

Lynn had to smile a little at the idea of a CNN interview.

"Okay," she finally said. "But let's talk about it. I'd feel bad if I sold you a haunted house and your corpse was later found in a pool of blood."

She turned toward him and touched his hand with her fingers.

"Mr. Whitby, do you know what you're doing?"

"Absolutely not," Tucker replied. "Although I probably am not as scared as you are, I'm apprehensive to say the least. I have no explanation whatsoever for what happened today. I have never witnessed anything like it. I don't even have beliefs that support it. But I am as curious about this as I've ever been about anything in my life, and if I don't learn what's going on, if I turn away from a chance to investigate this obviously remarkable house, I'll regret it for what years I have left. Who else has this happened to? How many other people have ever experienced this? None, I'll bet. It seems like I have an opportunity here, and so I want this house to be mine."

He managed to smile at her. "Believe me, I may own this place for a couple of days and then turn around and hire you to sell it again. I don't know. But I have to take the chance."

Lynn pulled her hand back and looked down in front of her. "So, what do you want me to do?"

"You have found a buyer for the property. And the guy was stupid enough to not even haggle over the price. Let's do the paperwork, and then you move on and sell more houses. That's it."

Lynn took a deep breath. Even with the definite fear that she felt, she also hated to think that this man would be finding answers to the mysterious activities without her. Not being part of it would become her own missed opportunity.

"Is that all you want me to do?"

"No, ma'am," Tucker said. "I also think that you ought to come visit me on a regular basis. I don't know one woman in a million who would have experienced what we've been through this afternoon, and still have the courtesy to call me Mr. Whitby. That makes you pretty special."

He gave her the keys.

* * *

If I had a voice, I would sing, and the sounds would echo up and down this canyon like thunder on a rainy day.

When his hands touched me, I shivered with surprise. His hands touched my doorframe as he entered. He touched the railings of my stairs and the mantles of my fireplaces, and he ran his hand

[51]

over my wallpaper. He touched my floors and felt the smoothness of my trim. He was careful and deliberate, experienced but gentle. I know this man; his hands are the hands of a master. I have waited years for such a man.

After I was brought to life and the shaman had left, I reveled in my newfound awareness. I examined myself day after day, looking at my parts and pieces. I felt the rough saw blade marks etched in my timbers, the handprints left in the cement of my foundations, the hammer indentations in my walls, and the trowel marks in my plaster. Everywhere I looked and felt, I had the evidence of the workers who constructed me. But I did not know the builder, my designer and creator, the man whose name is carved into my beam in the basement.

I wish I had been alive when his hands were building me.

Today, I felt what my builder's hands must have felt like: a master's hands, full of strength and experience but made gentle with confidence. This man could see the essential in me, the essence of the grandeur that was displayed in the past. He has an eye for design and for craftsmanship. He loves wood. I liked it when he looked close.

Who knew that he would look for the markings on my timbers? Only a man of great experience would know to look for, let alone care to find, the signatures. And I have always loved the name of the little boy, the innocent who was taken. The scratchings feel so comfortable yet so resolute. He must have been proud to write his letters in my beam so close to his father's.

When this man touched the letters, I wanted him to understand that there is power in the boy's name. They are the stamp of his being.

What now? The man has discovered me and I have discovered him. When he spread his liquid on my railings, I couldn't contain myself. I needed to hold him, to swirl around him, and embrace him with the delight of my attention. It has been a long time since I have felt passion like this. I did not realize the depths of my loneliness until, after years in a drought of emotion, I was able to display the tenderness that I so desire.

He'll be back. I wasn't sure until he placed his hand on my door. Now I know.

He'll be back.

6

Why had he bought a haunted house? After four months of living with it, Tucker was only beginning to understand the answer. His initial wild curiosity reason hadn't proven to be sufficient. Any ghostly encounters had been fewer and far more subdued that he had expected, and provided none of the answers that his curiosity needed to be satisfied. In retrospect, he imagined he could have investigated the house with the blessing of the realty company and not even bought the place.

It had taken these four months of working with the house to finally come to an honest assessment of the "why" of the situation. He'd bought the house because he was dying. Not literally. He was more fit and healthy than any other similarly-aged person he knew. But the last few years had brought him more and more dissatisfaction. He was convinced that his life was wasting away. Moving around the country, seeing all the different houses, the different architectures, and living in the different situations had been interesting, and he liked it. But once into the projects, even doing as good a job as he did, he didn't feel the sense of wholeness that he longed for. He was always happy to sell each house when it was finished and move on, hoping that maybe the next one would bring something different, something unusual, something new. It never happened. Every house became like the one before it.

Tucker had bought the Mulvaney Mansion because it was immediately unlike the others. When he touched Sam's initials on the beam, it excited him. And lying in the dirt and darkness after his fall, he knew that something unique had happened to him. Swept up in the swirling wind on the stairway, he wished for more.

That's what he wanted. He wanted things to happen to him that he had never experienced, that he had never even thought of. As the house rocked him back and forth on the stairs, he was scared but enthralled. The house gave him a shock of emotion he hadn't felt in a long time. Maybe the house could be an adventure. Maybe it could be a thrill. He couldn't remember the last time he felt thrilled. Could he handle a house that had a ghostly presence? He hadn't been sure, but he decided that wrestling with a ghost would be worth finding out.

Tucker sat on the porch with a blanket around his shoulders, quietly sipping his tea and listening to sounds of the river. It wasn't like him to be so contemplative. But a brisk October had brought the colors of fall to the cottonwood trees at the confluence of the two rivers north of the property, and the oak leaves of the thickets across the river added deep reds to the hues of gold and yellow. The river idled by, marking time until the shallows froze and the snow along the bank dipped the tall grasses into the water to make icicles. The tall cliffs across the river from the house were the same as usual—immutable and silent—but the lower sun in the sky produced more purples and reds that coated their faces in the evening.

That made sitting on the porch in the evening an almost spiritual activity, and synchronizing his inner being with the outer world had prompted Tucker's sudden flood of reflections.

Had his expectations been fulfilled? Had his life taken on a whole new level of excitement and adventure? Maybe, he thought. Depends on how you look at it.

A house this large was certainly a bigger challenge to rebuild than his other houses. Beginning as usual, though, he had identified, estimated, prioritized, and scheduled everything in it, on it, around it, or needed for it. He might be anal, but he did know how to manage projects. That level of control didn't make it unexciting, necessarily, but it certainly set the expectation of few surprises or misadventures.

The big ticket items had been left to contractors: getting the electricity to a temporary pole by his trailer and to the old power box of the dormitory; completely redoing the sewer system, including new pipes from the house to a new septic tank; relining the well; installing a new water pump and running new pipes into the basement; and, his current pride and joy, having a company from town pour a cement floor in the basement. Finished, the place looked like a skating rink, making him wish he still had his childhood skates.

Tucker relaxed his shoulders, slumped into a comfortable position, took another sip from his mug, and considered that he had done quite a bit of work on his own as well. The collapsed porch and all its rubble was the first to go since it represented a danger, and then all of the broken gingerbread wood decoration around the porch had been torn out. He replaced the swayback crosspieces that supported the porch's roof, then repaired the decorative siding under the dormers. Just cleaning all the yards and the riverbanks had taken a full week.

He demolished and cleaned the inside of the dormitory, ripping out all the toilets, sinks, urinals, dividers, and mirrors, and tossing everything else not bolted down into the large construction trash bin leased from a waste management company in town. He also rented a high-powered washer and sprayed every surface inside the dorm until he had flooded the building. It took a week to dry but it smelled better.

Cleaning inside the house was more complicated. The Rural Electrification Act of the 1930s launched programs to bring electric power to farms and ranches. The Mulvaney house probably wasn't done until 1943, when the VA bought the property. Needing to add electricity throughout the house but faced with an acre of thick plaster, the electrical wires were run inside primitive conduit attached to the surfaces of the walls and ceilings, making the electrical service inside the house look like plant roots gone wild. It took a dedicated week to pull everything out. The nest of twisted wires around the electrical panels in the basement was removed along with the panels, and the whole mess thrown away.

Tucker swept out the tumbleweeds and dirt and sand, pulled off sagging wallpaper, hauled out the carpet, and removed the old radiators. Having done everything that was easy, he declared that he had done enough on the house's interior. His priority needed to be the exterior, getting the house enclosed for the winter. Doing some of the preliminary work, he only had the two biggest ticket items left—repairing the roof and replacing all the windows.

The canyon-echoed sounds of a vehicle on the road interrupted his thoughts, and Tucker was happy to see the black Yukon pull into the front yard.

"Hey," Lynn Anderson called as she slid out of the front seat.

"Hey," Tucker said. She had kept her promise, not uttering a word of the strange happenings at the house. And she had kept up a regular visiting schedule, which they both had grown to like. She always seemed to enjoy him, but it had taken her a while to be comfortable with the house, even though he could tell she was also curious. Tucker never avoided telling her of any interesting behaviors of the house, but he tried to sound as casual as possible, as if the unusual was utterly usual.

From his point of view, the house had been cordial and friendly, if those were good words to describe it. There had not been another explosive episode on the porch, no more swirling windstorms and no murmurs in the air.

Grabbing a large sack from the backseat of the Yukon, Lynn walked to the passenger side, took out a tall, narrow box from the front seat, and came up the steps while Tucker went inside the house and returned with his other lawn chair and another blanket.

He gave her a hug.

"Fried chicken!" he said. "Oh, I do love fried chicken. You are such a sweetheart."

She glowed with a wide smile. "It's a lot better than the microwave stuff you usually have, so enjoy it while you can. And I've got a special surprise for you. Well, actually, for both of us." She handed him the box, brightly covered in shiny paper and decorated with a large red bow.

"Go ahead. Open it."

Tucker took out his ever-present utility knife, opened the blade, and cleanly cut the ribbon and the tape holding the paper in place. Undoing the top of the box exposed a bottle of Champagne.

"Is this a special occasion?" he asked.

"You bet your ass, you old goat. I got Realtor of the Year!"

He congratulated her with a kiss on the cheek and a hug, then retrieved two plastic cups and a small folding table from the kitchen while she worked on the bottle's cork. Returning, she poured them each a good dose of cheer.

"Here's to continued success at selling houses to people who deserve them," Tucker said.

"Here's to you," Lynn replied, "who made it possible for me to have a city-wide moment of fame for being able to sell a famous haunted house. You can't believe the difference this sale made. I did make the numbers, I'll admit, and was already being courted for the prize. And, by the way, the oil company gave me a special plaque for what they considered a great achievement."

"Did you tell them how hard it was to convince the guy to buy the house?"

"I told them that you were a pushover for antiques and didn't have a clue how much work you were signing up for."

"Well, now, the second part was certainly true."

Tucker laid the box of chicken, the mashed potatoes and gravy, and the coleslaw on the table. He finished three big pieces of chicken before he took his first drink of the bubbly. After fifteen or twenty minutes, they wiped their hands, put the sack on the floor, and refilled the small cups until the bottle was half empty.

"It's beautiful out here," Lynn said, casually swinging a leg that crossed her knee.

"This is a good time to be here. In about thirty minutes, you'll see the swallows come down to the river to feed on the insects."

She looked over to him, then used her swinging foot to nudge his knee.

"How are you doing, friend?"

Tucker was slow to answer. "You always ask me that. One of these days I'm going to watch TV and find out the latest fad that people are dying of and tell you that I've just been diagnosed with it."

"And I'd know you were lying, you dog, so tell me the truth."

"Okay," he said, and took a deep breath. "Overall, I wouldn't want to be anywhere else. Building with a spirit-partner is something new, but it's added a flavor to building that I've never had. And I'm very happy to get some of the foundational elements improved, like the water, sewer, and the new floor in the basement. There have been, however, a lot of lonely hours. I've been alone for most of my life, and so I know how to be alone, but the isolation of this place is far more than what I've experienced. Even a ghost hanging around hasn't made up for it."

He moved his head from side to side. "I think that I'm feeling lonely every now and then."

"I would think," Lynn blurted out. "I don't know how you do it! This is as isolated a place as anywhere in the country. You ought to come to town more often, take a vacation, go on a cruise, or something." She nudged him again. "Come see me—I'll show you a good time."

Tucker smiled quietly but kept his head lowered. "Oh, I can take it. I've got my internet, and my dish gets me all the TV I want."

"Which is ZERO," Lynn interrupted. "You need to find something fun to do, honey."

"I have fun," he protested. "I have fun every day."

"You're nuts. Having fun is something you do with somebody else. How come you don't have anybody else?"

Tucker was silent and looked away, knowing that his face was turning red. Lynn knew that his wife and daughter were dead. What she didn't know was that he was responsible for their deaths.

"Here," she said as she refilled his cup, knowing that she had embarrassed him. "If we're not going to do anything, we can always drink."

Their conversation on the topic always went this far and no farther. She knew that it wasn't something he was able to talk about, but she really wished he would. His reticence seemed sentimental a few months ago, but now it just seemed like avoidance and was mildly irritating. She didn't know if it was a tragic memory, a general phobia, or an inherited trait to not talk about his past. But you can't help someone who doesn't want help, she told herself, and so she always backed off. One of these days, she was going to pin him down. She wanted to know.

Lynn noticed the first time she came back to visit that he had built a rock border around the lavender patch. It had been weeded and a curving rock path to the house had been started. She asked about it, but he dodged giving her anything besides liking the color. He had admitted that his wife liked lavender that first day, but there was more to it than that. There was something about lavender that was key to a mystery lurking inside him. A few weeks later, he had added a birdbath and a stone bench. She could also tell that he had been watering the plot: the plants had doubled in size and the blossoms were far healthier.

She kept coming back to the house because she had grown fond of him. The age difference was, what, fifteen years, maybe only ten? That kept their relationship from progressing beyond the friendly kiss, but she could tell that he was a much younger person inside. For some reason, he did not allow that person to come out, and for that she was truly sorry. She always left the ranch wanting more.

Tucker accepted the refilled cup with a thank you, and then listened as she told him of the office, the recent houses that she had or had not sold, and the funniness of the people she dealt with. She railed against the town council and the corrupt building inspector and finally wound down with a report on her kids. They were all doing fine.

Tucker enjoyed listening. It felt good to hear something other than news reports and commercials, and God knows he spent too much time on the computer. It was good to hear the voice of a friend. It was true that he felt lonely. In fact, he ached for company. But there was always work to do, and if he was good at anything, it was getting work done. If he could reach a certain point, a point where the major things were done, and he had a good start on the other stuff and wasn't always up against the calendar, then maybe…

He always stopped his thoughts there. His past was his barrier, and he never allowed himself any more than a brief peek at it, let alone crossed it.

Following her tales of the week, Tucker told Lynn what he had done, and that he had two more major contractors coming, the two most expensive yet to work on the house. He hoped to get the house closed in before mid-December, the first of January at the latest. He was looking forward to seeing the house under the first blanket of snow.

"You may have a visitor one of these days," Lynn said. "I'm working with a client to find a rental for the year. His name is Larry Jackson, and he and his wife seem really nice. He's the new Building Trades teacher at the high school. I told him he needed to

[59]

come and see the house, since you guys are kind of in the same business."

"He has my sympathies if he's teaching high school kids," Tucker said. "I'd never have the courage. Have him come out and I'll give him the grand tour."

"He also may have some workers for you," Lynn continued. "The school has already contacted him about several of the students wanting jobs who aren't old enough to work for contractors around town. Are you interested in having any help during the summer?"

"Maybe. I've scheduled the overhaul of the porches for June and July, with painting in August. I want to redo the floors, ceilings, and railings, so it's a lot of work without requiring much in the way of skill. When he comes to visit, I'll see who he has to offer."

In fact, Tucker thought, hiring temporary help might be a real time saver. He'd planned on using the whole summer to fix the porches, then start on taking down the plaster next fall. If he could finish the porches early, maybe the hired hands could help inside the house.

"How's Casper?" Lynn asked with a smile.

Tucker grinned. "Go ahead and make fun, but we're in serious territory here. I've been rebuilding houses a large part of my life, first with my dad and then on my own. It's my experience that old houses are especially hard to work on. Nonstandard wood sizes, nonstandard plumbing, nonstandard electrical, decades-old glue, caulking, and patches—all drive me crazy. You always have to fix something before you can fix something else. It's a constant struggle to get old floors pulled up, window frames removed, piping yanked out, foundations leveled, concrete demolished, or woodwork re-stained. Rebuilding an old house, especially an old Victorian, has sometimes taken three times more money than I've planned on and four times as long."

He leaned back into his chair and crossed his arms. "But this house is different. The broken wood on the front steps came out as if it wasn't nailed in, and worn out door thresholds pulled up without destroying the door frames. Sagging wallpaper came right off, and not once did I cut myself while removing the broken panes from the windows in the basement. After the glass was removed, I'd take the old window frame out, add a few boards here and there, and the new window would go in like it was being sucked into place.

"It's like the house wants to be fixed, like it's partnering with me to get the work done. And, by the way, if I finish something important that it approves of, I smell a distinct aroma of lavender. How's that for an approving partner?"

He looked at Lynn and smiled. "We're getting along fine, actually, if that's what you're really asking. It knows that I'm here to stay and to only do good things. There was only one incident when the house got nervous with all the people and big machines, but after I talked to it and calmed it down, everything worked out okay."

Lynn tilted her head and looked at him skeptically. "You're not going crazy on me, are you?"

Tucker laughed. "Okay. I can see your level of skepticism has not improved, and so you will get what you asked for. Come with me."

He held her hand as they walked into the reception hall and climbed the stairs to the second floor.

"Okay. Do what I do." Tucker stood close to the inside hallway wall, gently leaned in, and placed his ear against the plaster while putting his hands flat against the wall on either side of his head.

He watched as Lynn did the same. "Now, close your eyes and listen."

Lynn was used to the breathing of the house, and so she wasn't surprised to hear a quiet whooshing sound. But that was with the ear away from the wall. She tried to ignore the breathing sound and gently pressed her ear against the plaster.

"I'm not going to hear a toilet flush, am I?"

"Hush. Relax and listen."

After perhaps a minute in this position with her eyes closed, she heard a faint thump, a rhythmic repeating thump of the quietest sort. Slowly beating, one thump after another.

"Ahhh!" she cried as she jumped back from the wall.

Tucker smiled. "You were the one making fun of Casper."

"Oh, my God! That's not what I think it is, is it? A heartbeat?"

He laughed a little laugh. "I believe so. I was walking through the house one night running my hands over the walls, and for some reason, I had my ear up against the plaster. There it was, quiet but constant. I don't have any idea of how it does it. I've looked all over the house, and I've listened to it in different places but still don't have a clue where it's coming from."

They walked down the stairway and back outside.

"Houses don't have hearts, do they?" she asked, pretty sure of herself but never doubting that Tucker might reveal some deep, dark secret hidden from the uninitiated.

"Nope. Houses don't have beating hearts, and they don't have breathing lungs. I've worked on a lot of houses and have never fixed any hearts, lungs, eyes, brains, or ears."

They sat down.

"Then help me understand," she said. They had talked about it before, but neither of them had developed what the other considered a reasonable explanation for how a house could possibly be a living entity.

"Well, like usual," Tucker said, "I cannot tell you why this house is alive or how it got that way. I have, however, considered some of the things that it does. Let's take for granted that it is alive and that it knows that it's alive. It hasn't traveled, hasn't had any schooling, and hasn't had a house next door to know what a typical house acts like. The only experiences it has had are what's taken place inside of it.

"It, therefore, has seen beings with eyes, ears, noses, arms, legs, lungs, hearts, and minds; and it knows how those beings go about living every day. And I'm sure that there have been dead people in the house, which would show a body that doesn't have all those sounds and movements. So it knows what the absence of life looks like. I think that this house is like a child who imitates what it sees. Therefore, it figures out how to act like it's breathing; and, therefore, it figures out some way to act like it has a heartbeat. The house is mimicking what it has experienced within its walls."

Lynn felt way out of her league in any such discussion, but she had been around the house enough to appreciate that some *thing*, or some *one*, lived in or through the house. Tucker wouldn't lie about these things, and he was certainly not one to ignore reality. And he had, indeed, turned out to be bravest man she had ever met.

Her real problem was that the house dominated his thinking. Builders were like that, she understood; she had witnessed "builder widows" several times. But this house wasn't a static object that Tucker was working on, and certainly not an ordinary remodel. The house was like a person he was having a relationship with, one that expected, even demanded, his attentions. It wasn't absorbing only his time but his emotions, which even fried chicken every night wasn't going to cure.

She hated herself when she thought that way. When she was direct and honest, she knew how to describe what she was feeling and she did not like the sound of it one bit: she was jealous of the house. And that made her think that she was becoming as crazy as he was.

It was late and Lynn needed to get back to town. They finished a final drink, rose from their chairs, embraced, kissed, and then she was gone.

Watching the taillights fade into the darkness of late dusk, Tucker returned to his question before Lynn arrived: had the house brought the energized life that he wished for? Had it rejuvenated his spirit?

His answer was still a definite "it depends how you look at it." This house was significantly different than any other house he had worked on, and the reward was commensurate with the situation. It had definitely moved his life up a big notch. He was pleased to own something different, to experience something so off the charts that he didn't dare speak of it to anyone except Lynn. And that's where he had to qualify his answer. The house had pulled him out of his depression and given him energy for a different life. In that regard, buying this house and working on it these last many months was an unqualified success. But that same success revealed that some of the withering of his life was never going to be solved by a house; it was tied to his lack of someone to share it with.

He was not surprised by this realization and it was sobering to see that it was plainly visible. He had known for years that his isolation from other people was haunting him as much as this house was haunted. He was alone, and it wasn't due to his constant change of address. Unfortunately, he just had to live with it. His isolation was his destiny, his sentence for the deeds of his past, and not even a haunted house could provide a remedy for a broken life.

* * *

He is a fine man, but sometimes he confuses me. He does what he chooses to do, and yet his joys are short-lived. He desires wholeness but accepts an image of himself as a broken man whose desires will never be attained. I cannot read the whole story that he has to tell.

But I have delighted in the things that have been done to me. I do miss my dirt in the basement; the hard surface seems so impersonal. But the rest of my fixes have filled me with renewed attentiveness. I am beginning to feel my roots again, and once again I look forward to the vibrations of the day.

The man has more than knowledge—he is indeed the craftsman that I always wished for—and I will serve him as I can. But I want more for the man, more that will help him find his way.

7

Instead of December as he'd hoped, it was February before Tucker could stand in the parlor and not feel a breeze. Repairing the roof had been a complex affair. He contracted with a firm out of Pueblo, Colorado that specialized in tile roofing, and even they were intimidated by the size and height of the house. It took them three weeks, but he was happy with their work. Next was the window company, and that work seemed to take forever. Tucker had replaced the windows in the basement since they were covered by the porch on the outside, and so he had great sympathy for the amount of work involved in the rest of the house. All of the old windows and frames had to be removed, new frames built and secured within the openings, and then the new windows custom-made in Denver. With fifty-nine windows, it took the company's crew every bit of six weeks. There was a stretch of warm days in January, so masons came to repair the brickwork around the windows and a few places along the foundation.

Having focused so intensely for so long, Tucker took a well-deserved vacation for the rest of the winter.

During the spring months, Tucker worked in the basement. With the construction lights he had hung from the overhead floor joists, the new concrete floor lit up like a showroom. On the floor he marked the locations for the electrical panels, the water distribution system, the furnace, the water heater, and even designated a place that would centralize the wireless router and dish cables for the house. Once he knew the locations of all the busyness that would occur in the basement, Tucker built new walls that sectioned off the different areas, and designated space for the various cables, wires, pipes, tubes, and ducts that would come along later.

He waited for his new helpers before restarting the outside work. Larry Jackson, the high school Building Trades teacher, had visited and was impressed with Tucker's work. He took pictures and presented a slide show to his Building Trades 101 Class. Several students were interested in jobs at the ranch until Larry described the location and the lack of amenities. After that, only two were interested in summer work, a set of fifteen year-old twins.

Tucker met with them and their parents in town in late May, and the twins reported for work the first Sunday of June.

"I'm the handsome one," Tony said. "He's the ugly one."

"At least I'm smart," Tommy said. "He's as dumb as a donkey."

They both broke out laughing.

Tucker gave a little smile. He couldn't tell any difference between them.

Tucker's agreement with the boys was simple: ten bucks an hour for each hour worked plus room and board. Tucker would take them into town either late Friday afternoon or Saturday morning and their parents would bring them back to the ranch on Sunday afternoon or evening. Tucker provided a phone for emergencies, a TV, a DVD player, and a sofa he had bought at a garage sale in one of the dorm rooms that he had cleaned and painted. He installed two new toilets in the men's bathroom of the dorm, which the twins were responsible for cleaning once a week, and hooked up a working sink, vanity, and shower. He put a small electric water heater in the hot side of the water lines. When someone took a shower, it had to be a fast one.

After a guided tour with their parents, Tucker gave the boys paint, rollers, and brushes and told them to each pick a room. When the space had been swept, mopped, primed, and painted, there were two new twin mattress sets ready to be put into the rooms. Tony and Tommy had brought their own sheets, pillows, and towels.

Monday morning brought a cloudless summer day, and Tucker had already moved the tools to the north side of the house by the time the twins finished breakfast.

"This is the deal," he began as the twins sat on the trailer loaded with boards. "Our objective for the next few weeks is to overhaul the two porches on the house. I've measured about one hundred and twenty feet of porch, total, all of it about ten feet wide and covered by a roof. We're going to take down the ceiling under the roof, rip up the floor, clean the ground underneath, repair anything that needs repairing, and then nail down new wood for the floor. I haven't decided on what to use for the ceiling, so we'll wait on it. There's also a gazebo built into one of the corners of the porch. We'll have to treat it special when we get to it."

Anxious to get started, the trio pulled down the ceiling and removed the floorboards one section at a time. Using rakes, hoes, and shovels, they cleared the ground under the porch of tumbleweeds and trash. They also pulled the weeds and spread grass killer. Tucker replaced twisted or rotted joists with new boards.

When the section was cleaned and ready for new flooring, Tucker caulked and fitted end caps onto a twelve foot-long plastic gutter he had bought. When the caulking was dry, he clamped the gutter across two sawhorses and poured it full of paint.

"It would take a long time to paint all four sides of a single piece of flooring and then find someplace for it to dry. Instead of working that hard, we'll put a nail in each end of a ten foot piece of board, then dip the whole board into the paint. We'll lift it out and I'll run a brush down the sides so the paint isn't too thick, and then we'll hang it from the porch's ceiling using strings on each end. We won't care if it drips on the old floor. When the paint's dry, we'll nail it down."

Once Tucker demonstrated the first board, the twins were impressed, wishing that it had been that easy to paint their rooms.

Working assembly-line style, they got the painting time down to one board per minute. By the time they had hung boards from strings all the way around the porch, the first boards were dry. Removing the boards from the hangers, Tucker showed the boys how to lay them straight with the side of the house and tap the groove onto the tongue of the previous board. They used a compressed air nailer to secure the boards to the joists.

Tucker watched as the boys worked. Both boys were fast, cheerful, and kept up a running banter. They lacked several inches being as tall as he, but they were agile and strong. It wasn't hard work, but it was hard enough that everyone was sweating.

It was lunchtime when they were halfway done with painting new boards. Tucker had cleaned the kitchen in the house to make it a useable space and installed a refrigerator from Craigslist, a microwave, a toaster, a coffee pot, and a small freezer. A table made out of sawhorses and a piece of plywood, plus four lawn chairs allowed them to sit down to eat. A new BBQ grill at the bottom of the back door steps served as the center of culinary arts for the main meals. Tucker planned on breakfast being do-it-yourself and had laid in cereal, toast, eggs, breakfast sausages, frozen pancakes, and waffles. Lunch would be make-it-yourself sandwiches, and for supper they would have meat dishes, which translated into whatever could be fixed on a grill.

The boys bolted down two sandwiches apiece plus a half bag of chips. Thirty minutes later, after hauling the old wood to the trash bin, the new floor was begun. Tucker taught them how to stagger the joints, how to finish the edge on the last piece, and how to integrate the sections so that the cut ends were completely covered.

The next day, they reached the gazebo corner, which was more difficult, requiring trim boards cut in an octagonal pattern. Tucker took that over and started the twins on the next straight section as he measured, cut, painted, and installed the gazebo floor himself. Progress was steady.

Tucker couldn't have expected more from his workers. Within two days, they had learned to be quick and efficient without being in a hurry to finish or to quit. After a week, they could be counted on to do the work without supervision, and so Tucker could go to town for more supplies. In the evenings, the twins waded in the creek, played Frisbee in the yard, or played cards on the porch. When Tucker discovered they knew how to play poker, he bought a set of chips and set up Thursday night tournaments for the three of them. Eventually, the evening would darken and the boys would adjourn to the dorm, and Tucker went on his nightly walks, first around the perimeter sidewalk and then through the house.

His loneliness had subsided. He and the boys were doing good work, and the house seemed as endorsing as ever. The days went quickly. He had hired people to work with him before, but they were older and more experienced. And they were obviously on the job only because they were paid, not to learn something. Once the day was finished, the workers went their separate ways to their separate lives and nothing was heard from them until the next workday. Tucker's only influence was to direct the work and write the checks.

The twins were different. They might be a captive audience, Tucker considered, but there was no mistaking their willingness to invest themselves in the house and the ranch. They had no experience against which to measure the situation, and feeling good and doing well was accepted as if it was the ordinary and expected method of work. They knew to do their part to contribute to the success of the experience.

Lynn came out more frequently, showing up on Thursday nights with steaks to grill, or boxes of fried chicken, or pizza, plus new bags of ice and cases of soft drinks. The boys regaled her with news of the week and even taught her poker so she could join the tournaments. Afterwards, she and Tucker walked around the sidewalk and sat on the bench in the lavender garden, visiting and sharing the gossip of the week. He talked about how much he liked having the boys around and how proud he was of the work that they all performed.

Lynn became more emotionally involved with the life that was occurring at the ranch. She might lose most of the poker hands, but she was happy when they were gathered around the table, laughing, joking, eating, and having a good time. It made her feel vital and free, and she could see Tucker's eyes reflect his pleasure in the people who surrounded him. Including her. Her visits to the ranch were becoming the high point of her week.

The front porch and the small side porch were rebuilt and painted in six weeks, including installing sheetrock on the ceiling, which provided the twins an opportunity to learn about drywall taping and texturing. Tucker crafted railings from balusters he had bought at the building store in town, and it only took two days to get them placed and anchored. Afterward, the three painted the ceilings, railings, support posts, corbels, and crosspieces with white, blue, and red. With the white of the roof trim, which had been repaired and painted by the roofing crew, the new white guttering, the white of the new windows, the deep red of the brick, the dark blue of the roofing slate, and the motley appearance of the rockwork around the porches, the Mulvaney Mansion beamed like a lighthouse. The boys were proud to show the progress to their parents every Sunday.

It was a Tuesday evening in mid-July when Tucker looked the house over and declared the outside work officially finished. He and the twins took the next day to clean the workroom and all the tools, to dress the yards around the entire house and dorm, and to straighten up the salvaged wood pile. That evening, Lynn made a special trip to the ranch to help grill T-bone steaks and potatoes for supper. She brought a fresh watermelon and a cake, and they churned ice cream. Tucker presented each of the twins with an envelope containing a two hundred dollar bonus, which sent them whooping, yelling, and dancing into the dorm to store their money away. The boys commented about the strong aroma of lavender that filled the house at dinner, but Tucker had brought in several bunches of lavender stalks to give the smell a plausible source.

It was the next day, Thursday morning, as they were sitting around the table, going over the plans for a deck to replace the back porch, when a knock and a hello came from the front door. Larry Jackson and a young lady walked into the kitchen.

The twins erupted with greetings. "*Hola!* Rose! Hey, Rose, you come to work with us? Rose! Hey, girl!"

"Hey, Larry," Tucker said. "We're done, but I expect that I can scare up some breakfast for you. What do you think of our porch?"

The young lady took the remaining chair and pulled it around to the twins. They began a visit of their own, and so Tucker stood and walked Larry to the back door. It seemed awfully early for a casual visit.

Larry politely refused breakfast, saying that they had stopped at McDonald's on the way out of town. "I am truly amazed," he said. "You did a lot of work there, my friend."

"We did, at that," Tucker answered. "I'd still be pulling up boards if it wasn't for the twins. They make a top-notch crew. I'm glad to have them."

Larry called the girl over for an introduction. "This is Rose Fowler. She's going to be a senior in the fall, and I brought her out to see the house."

Rose smiled and shook Tucker's hand with a firm grip. She was a little taller than the twins, pretty and blonde and Anglo with a slight but athletic build. She had a great smile but seemed a little shy. Tucker assumed she knew the twins from school.

"Why don't you guys give Rose a grand tour of the place?" Larry called to the twins.

That roused them from their seats and the three were soon busy going up and down the stairs. The two men took seats at the table.

Tucker had watched Rose as she got up and followed the twins. She was obviously comfortable with both boys but followed Tony more closely. If she was interested in working at the ranch, she was going to be disappointed, he thought. He had grown used to the twins, and he didn't have any problems communicating with them, changing things at the last minute, celebrating or playing poker with them, or ignoring them otherwise. It was a combination of trust and the lack of opportunity to mess around. He was also remembering the night before. He had seen unrestrained happiness in the boys' reaction to the dinner and to the bonus. It was something that he did not want to lose.

Having a young female around the house would be a game changer.

"It looks like the twins are doing great things. You have enough work for another crew member? You think you could handle a girl out here?" Larry asked.

Tucker was hesitant to reply. "I wouldn't worry about having work that she could do. I don't expect that she can swing sheetrock around like the boys, but I expect that she can handle a nail gun and a power drill. But having a girl wouldn't work. I don't think she'd handle the social life very well."

"From what I understand, you don't have any," Larry said.

"Well, there might be if she was living in a dorm fifty feet from lusty boys without supervision, even if they were friends to begin with. I doubt anybody would be poking each other, but the temptation would be intense. You think the three of them would start anything with each other?"

"Uh, oh, no... I don't think so," Larry said slowly.

Tucker watched his eyes and knew there was something else. It was way too early for a friendly visit and an informal tour. Besides that, the front door had closed by itself while everyone was

[71]

standing in the kitchen. When he heard a couple of clangs from the flagpole cable as they came in, which he hadn't heard in a while, he knew that something was in the works. The flagpole sounding hadn't happened lately, but there was a remarkable correlation between when it did and when something significant was occurring. The house had a remarkable sensitivity to the people who came onto the property, especially if there were some secret in the offing.

It slowly occurred to him what the something else might be. And if it was true, then the house really was remarkable at detecting secrets.

Tucker crossed his arms and placed them on the table, leaned into them, and looked at the man across from him.

"Is she pregnant?"

"Uh, well, a little bit," Larry said.

"Nobody's a little bit pregnant, Larry. You can take her with you when you leave."

Larry grimaced and was silent.

"There's a situation," he finally said.

"You bet there's a situation. I've got a house to rebuild. I don't run a daycare," Tucker said. "And I don't run a home for pregnant teenagers."

"Hear me out, just for a minute," Larry asked. "She only found out a couple of weeks ago, and the news was not well received by her parents or her boyfriend's parents. Quite frankly, everybody's in an uproar. She's Anglo and the boy's Hispanic, and their respective fathers, who already don't like each other for lots of reasons, are vocal about not wanting cross-contamination in the family gene pools. She's between a rock and a hard place, and the mothers are busy holding back their husbands. It's hell if she goes home and it's hell if she doesn't. She was in my Trades class last semester, a good student, and she came to me for help. I just couldn't do nothing. I think that the situation needs a little time to settle down, and then she can start working things out.

"Give me a week. You don't have to pay her, I'll help with the food, and I'll handle the parents. Come on, Tucker. I need some help here."

Tucker's face turned to stone. This wasn't what he did. He rebuilt houses and sometimes hired workers to help. Those workers worked, the work got done, and the workers got paid. But pregnant women…well, he didn't know what pregnant women did. Besides that, he had gotten used to the boys and to Lynn and to the flow of the house activities. A pregnant girl hanging around couldn't help but change things in a bad direction.

"Who's the sperm donor?" Tucker asked.

"A nineteen year-old. Not a bad kid but a dropout with a limited future, I'd say. They dated when he was still in school, and I guess they were having sex then, so everything looks consensual. The boy dropped out last year because his dad made him get a job in Albuquerque. That's where he lives now. With her pregnant, my guess is that the boy will eventually be outta sight, outta mind."

Tucker leaned back in his chair and looked away, disgusted. A good work place was not a refuge. When somebody couldn't work at the same level as the others, was different or had to be treated differently, then people stopped focusing, stopped being mindful of their own work, and started minding somebody else's. Accidents happened, bad work was performed, workers got confused. He had seen the trials and tribulations of unfocused people while working on his dad's crews, and those situations never ended well.

"You're asking a lot. This isn't my business. Why can't she stay with you or another teacher for a week?"

Larry squirmed in his chair. "My wife doesn't think this falls under my job description. She's working a second job already because my salary doesn't allow us to save anything, and she hates the school system anyway. She doesn't have much sympathy for 'pregnant bimbos,' as she puts it. And there aren't any other teachers currently interested in rescuing dumb kids, especially since there's quite a number of candidates."

Tucker understood Larry's position but didn't have much sympathy. Larry was young and new at the school. More experienced teachers had lost any sympathy for their more wayward charges, figuring out that it was best not to be involved. Tucker considered those teachers the smart ones.

But if the girl was here for only a week, maybe it wouldn't be so bad, he found himself thinking. The twins already knew her and so weren't likely to make any moves on her, and she obviously wasn't very far along and so she should be physically okay with the work. She couldn't just hang out, though; she'd have to work. And there'd have to be some new rules, and a new room in the dorm, and a new mattress set, and …

The twins he knew, but could he trust *her*? Would she become a part of the…family?

Tucker realized that it was the first time he had used the word. It had been a long time since he was part of a family.

"If she stays here for the week, what's the danger factor?" Tucker asked.

"What do you mean?"

"Is her father coming after her? Is her father coming after me? Is his father coming after her or me? Is the boy going to show up wanting another poke? You'd better believe that I'm not in the after-hours supervision business, and so what happens in the dorm is going to be up to those staying in it. And if something bad does happen, it's not like calling 911 is going to help us out here. Don't tell me that you're not telling the parents where she is—that would put you in a very bad place and makes me look like a pimp or, worse, a customer. Have you thought about that? I ask again, what's the danger factor?"

Larry Jackson looked scared and depressed.

"Damn it, I don't know! She's just another unremarkable pregnant teenage girl who needs help. And nobody else would do it."

Tucker leaned forward again. "Does she want to be pregnant?" he asked.

"I don't think any seventeen year-old wants to be pregnant, and I don't think she, in particular, wants to be pregnant. She just is. So what's she going to do? Whether she fully appreciates her position or not, I don't know. I doubt it. If the families would quit bitching at her, she could probably manage."

"What about the boy? Does she understand that the sperm donor has rights if she's thinking about an abortion or giving the baby up?"

Larry Jackson looked perplexed. "I don't know. I don't think she's gotten that far."

Tucker looked away, silent. It wasn't his problem, at least for the long term. But maybe he could help in the short term. It was obvious that nobody else was going to, and if she had to hide somewhere, the ranch was about as hidden as she could get. If she had to be here while work was going on, building the deck was straight forward and wasn't hard. He wasn't going to mess with putting a railing on, but if there was another hand to help, maybe a railing could be finished as well.

"Let's go find the kids," Tucker finally said.

He called everyone and they gathered on the shady side of the porch.

"You know she's pregnant?" he asked the twins. They knew.

"You know everybody's pissed at her for it?" They knew.

"You know she needs to hide out for a week?" They knew.

"You know that Mr. Jackson is asking that she stay here?" They knew.

"Do you know it possibly puts all of us in danger if she does stay here?" They didn't know.

He listed the players, gave an indication of who might be wanting to do what to whom, and then asked Mr. Jackson to give his opinion of the situation. Larry stumbled through what he thought but didn't express any fears.

"Rose, what do you think will happen if you stay?" Tucker asked.

She held her head up as she responded. "Nothing. Nobody wants to see me or hear from me right now, and as long as my mom knows that I'm being taken care of, my parents will leave me alone. My parents aren't exactly the warm fuzzy types."

"What about your boyfriend?"

She was quiet for a moment. Finally she said that he wasn't going to do anything that would get his dad any madder than he already was.

"You need to understand that everyone here works," Tucker continued. "We work hard. If you stay, you get to work too, but I'll be mindful of your condition. Have you had a pre-natal class?

"A what?"

"I thought so. The bottom line is this: you're going to feel tired a lot, you may be sick in the mornings, you'll be eating for two people, and the food has to be healthy stuff. You will need regular exercise, good food, and plenty of sleep; this will be true even after you leave. While you're here, I'll make sure that you give yourself the attention that you need. But you still have to work. And I'm not

[75]

talking about cleaning house and cooking. I'm talking lumber, nails, hammers, and saws. Are you okay with that?"

"I can work," she said. "And you don't have to pay me. And Mr. Jackson said that he'd help with the food."

"Well, that's not the way I run things. If you're here, you're a member of the crew. As a member of the crew, you work and I pay you for what you do. Room and board is also part of the deal."

When she nodded that she understood, Tucker looked at the twins for any indication in their expressions that this was a bad idea. They looked something between confused and happy.

"Okay. If she stays here, we have to make sure everything is on the up-and-up and that, if someone questions our arrangement, we are completely innocent of anything they might assume. Specifically, there can be no sex, no kissing—in fact no touching at all—no peeking and everybody covers up to and from the shower. There can be no off-color jokes, and she gets her privacy. For her part, Rose does the work that's expected of her, eats with us, works with us, and takes care of herself. And everybody gets treated with honor and respect.

"And you guys," he said, making sure Tony and Tommy were looking him in the eye, "still get to work as hard as you've been working. Having another person around shouldn't slow you down any or change how well you work." The twins nodded their agreement.

"The decision is mine, but I want the two of you to be aware that it's going to affect life around the ranch. Rose has to agree to be a good worker, to behave herself, and to be a part of the work crew for a week. If she agrees, Mr. Jackson has to make some phone calls to be sure everybody knows exactly what's going on. One week, and then she's gone. What do you think?"

The boys were smiling and Rose was smiling. "Yup, it's all good with us," Tony said. Mr. Jackson nodded his consent.

Tucker still wasn't sure that it was going to be a great situation, even with everybody buying into it. It had been a long time since he'd interacted with a teenage girl. After he had met Rose, as he watched her follow the twins on a tour of the house, he realized that she resembled his own daughter, though Sara had dark hair. She had the same smile and eyes. But Sara wasn't pregnant, which was one factor that would be utterly new to him. Dealing with a pregnant teen would definitely be a whole new experience, and probably one he wasn't going to be very good at.

"This is my decision," Tucker stated one more time to the group around him. "Mr. Jackson has brought a teenager to me who would like to work here for one week. She'll be under the same verbal contract as the other workers: ten bucks an hour for each hour worked plus room and board. She won't go home this weekend, and so I need one of you guys to stay here, for which I will pay you extra. I'm not about to be left alone with her because of what might be assumed by some people.

"I'll go to town this afternoon to buy more food, a new mattress set, a new toilet, maybe two, and another sink. I'll get what we need to plumb the women's bathroom and get us the materials for the deck. While I'm gone, you boys tell her how we do things around here and the rules about the house. Walk her over the property so she can get her bearings, and then help her get a room ready in the north wing—mop and paint. If she throws up at the smell, then you do it for her."

With no objections, Tucker considered that it was a done deal.

Larry Jackson spent the next hour talking to the school counselor, the principal, and the twins' parents on his phone. Both he and Rose spoke to her parents, assuring them that she was doing legitimate work for an experienced builder, and working alongside other teenagers she knew from the high school. They emphasized that Mr. Jackson was participating, and that she was being paid a wage and getting room and board. Larry assured them that the arrangement would only be for a week to let things cool down. No one was told her location, but Mr. Jackson let Rose's parents know he was available as a contact.

It was decided not to speak to the boyfriend's parents or to the boyfriend.

Tucker called Lynn, filled her in on what had happened, and canceled the night's card game.

8

Rose Fowler knew she should feel lucky, but she wasn't feeling lucky. She had been ready to tell everyone to shove it—her parents, Rico's parents, and even Rico. She'd do fine by herself if she could get to California to live with her sister or with one of her aunts. It had only been two weeks since the test revealed her pregnancy, but the flurry of disapprovals from her so-called loved ones had quickly made her sick and tired of having to interact with anybody. Maybe Mr. Jackson was right: if she could just get a week away from everybody and give them time to settle in with the idea, things would be better. But she doubted it.

"So, what are the rules? You can't smoke?" Rose asked.

"No, you can't smoke, but nobody smokes anyway and so it's no big deal. You can't drink alcohol either. He's got lectures on honoring and respecting each other. He's big on that."

"And no drugs. And no trash. Don't let him catch you leaving trash around."

"Especially in the house," Tommy said. "Don't smoke in the house, don't drink, don't throw trash around in the house, don't play loud music in the house, don't cuss in the house."

"You gotta be kidding me," Rose said. "He's got a thing about the house?"

"Oh, yeah. You gotta respect the house, honor the house, listen to the house."

"Are there ghosts in the house or something?"

The twins both raised their eyebrows and smiled, but they didn't laugh.

"No ghosts," Tony said, "but we don't go in the house after dark. It's downright creepy. It creaks a lot, and moans, and…"

"Moans? The house moans?"

"Oh, yeah! I was in the house once and it started shaking a little bit, ya know, and then it let out this long moan. Scared the pee out of me! I was like outta there!"

"We don't go into the basement either unless Mr. Whitby is with us. And doors open and close by themselves sometimes. Mr. Whitby says it's the wind, but it ain't."

"I hate creepy things," Rose said, "so if I'm supposed to do something in the house, you have to do it for me, okay?"

They turned from the path along the riverbank and went up. Tucker had walked the property enough that a well-worn path led from the river along the boundary fence, crossed the road by the gate, went to the bottom of the west cliffs, and turned back to the dorm. They diverted from the path to check out the lavender garden.

"This is totally cool," Rose said. "He must like lavender."

"Must like it a lot," Tommy said. "He's added all of the gravel since we've been here. He works on it every Sunday morning, so there's always something different when we get back from town. And he waters it every night too, so he leaves a bucket under the bench."

Walking around the gravel of the lavender garden, they rejoined the sidewalk and finished the circuit around the property. Getting drinks, the twins unlocked the tool room and pulled out the vacuum, the cleaning supplies, and the painting equipment.

"Which room you want?" Tony asked. "The last one in this hallway used to be a chicken coop and still smells worse than the others, but you can have any one you want."

"Yuck. These rooms are disgusting," Rose said, looking in the first one in the hall. "Is this what yours looked like?"

"Worse. And this is after Mr. Whitby sprayed the ceilings and walls with a power washer," Tony said. "Once we put on the primer and some paint, it'll look okay and smell a whole lot better. It'll be fine, you'll see. Like a Holiday Inn. You'll be okay."

"Mr. Whitby took out the sink in the back so you have to go down to the bathroom if you want water," Tommy added. "He got us our own little fridge. It's in the TV room if you want a drink or something. We'll also need to get your window open so the room cools down in the night."

Rose chose the first room of the north wing. The bathroom was next door, making for a short walk. She hadn't been throwing up, but she was queasy in the morning, and she felt more tired than she could ever remember. Other than that, being pregnant hadn't made a lot of difference. It was a surprise, for sure, and it wasn't what she wanted. Rico had been surprised too but hadn't said anything one way or the other about liking it or not. He hadn't been afraid to have a white girl as a girlfriend, but she wasn't sure he thought their relationship was long-term. They'd had a lot of fun when they were dating, but he'd only used condoms for a while. They were such pains to get on and off, and he was always in a hurry to get inside her and so they let it go after a while. She liked the way he felt without one, and so she was cool with it. He claimed he was careful, and she thought he must have had a lot of practice

His dad was a real jerk and couldn't stand the thought of having a mixed-breed grandchild. He went ballistic when he heard. He never finished school, worked for the county road crew or something, and treated his wife like dirt. Since he was stupid, it seemed to Rose, he figured his kid ought to be stupid too and so he got Rico a job in Albuquerque, which was to get him away from her but also took him out of school. Rico promised to get his GED, but studying was hard for him with his job and all.

Rose was still thinking about going to her sister's in California, but if she was going to stay around, she'd have to figure out what to do about school and everything else. Rico might not want to get married or even be a father. He said that he loved her and would always be there for her, but now it was going to be different, especially because of his dad. Babies messed up everything.

Tony began sweeping while Rose wiped the built-in desks and shelves, the small vanity, and the closet. There was so much solid grime that she finally got Tony to get her a scraper. Tommy worked on the ancient metal window and finally got the bottom portion unstuck. Having refused to open, the window then refused to stay open, and so he used a stick from the workshop as a prop. He used the vacuum to get the dirt and the dead moths out of the bottom of the window frame.

[81]

"We paint everything with a primer," Tony said. "Then you can choose if you want off-white, off-white, or off-white for your interior decorating needs."

Rose laughed. "I'll take off-white."

Drop cloths to protect the floor were useless since it was ugly to begin with, and so Tommy opened the five gallon bucket of primer and used an electric drill and a stirrer to get the goop on the bottom mixed in. He used a paint screen in the bucket to get the paint into his roller, then painted the open portions of the wall while Tony and Rose used brushes in the corners and next to the ceiling. In an hour, they had it all covered and Rose declared that it didn't look half bad.

"We'll let this dry, then come back with the color paint," Tony said. "Let's go to the house and get something to eat."

Rose sat in one of the lawn chairs and watched as Tony set the sandwich fixings on the table. Tommy pulled out slices of bread, put them on paper plates, and passed them around. He opened a couple of sacks of chips and put them alongside the plates.

"What are you and Rico going to do?" Tony asked.

"I guess we're going to get married."

"Oh, girl. Maybe you could just have the baby. Your mom would help."

"My mom is not happy about the baby," Rose said. "So she's thinking I shouldn't keep it, like give it up for adoption or something. And my dad thinks I should get an abortion, real quick like."

"Abortion? Can you kill the baby, Rose?"

"I don't know. I haven't really thought about it."

Of course, she had thought about it. Whether God thought it was okay or not, killing something inside of her seemed like a violation of something—her or the baby or society or life. Something. She didn't know if she could do it. And she was worried that it wouldn't be up to her, that somebody else might get to decide for her, which really sucked.

Rose had been sitting at the table pulling the crust off her sandwich and picking at the thinly sliced turkey. She had been talking, then was quiet, then was tearing up, and now burst into a flood of tears.

[82]

"Damn it!" was all she said, over and over and over, putting her head in her hands and leaning heavily into the table, her shoulders shaking.

"Oh, Rose," Tommy said, reaching over to put his hand on her head. "It'll work out. You just got to keep on doing stuff and taking care of the baby and it'll work out."

"Our momma will help," Tony added. "She's had eight, so far, and so she's an expert at having babies. She'll help you a lot. And Rico's mom'll be the same way. You'll see."

It was another hour before they heard Tucker's truck pull into the side yard, circling until the trailer could be backed up next to where the deck was going to be built. Looking out the window, the twins could see the pickup piled high with a mattress set, boxes that held toilets and a sink, and other cardboard containers. The pipe rack across the top held several lengths of white PVC pipe, and the utility trailer was layered with long boards. On top of the boards was a long roll of something wrapped in plastic.

Tucker was untying straps when the boys piled out and started carrying boxes to the dorm. Rose came out a few minutes later and retrieved sacks of groceries from the back seat.

Tucker had decided that it was a better use of time to focus on the dorm for a couple of days. Rose's arrival was an opportunity to fix up the bedrooms and the other bathroom. He bought a roll of carpet to cut into strips and lay in the hallways for a padded surface from the bathrooms to the single rooms. He'd gotten Rose a mattress set—with sheets, pillows, and towels since she hadn't brought anything except clothes—and new light fixtures for both bathrooms. And he had splurged to buy ceiling fans and lights for the three bedrooms and the TV room.

He bought two toilets plus the plastic pipes needed to get the hot and cold water to the ladies' bathroom. He had cheated with the plumbing in the boys' bathroom, running PVC pipe through the ceiling girders and dropping it down the outside of the walls for the toilets, sink, and shower stall. He planned to do the same thing on the ladies' side, but it was a longer run: out of the utility closet, over the boys' bathroom, through the work room, and into the ladies' room. It could not be finished before tomorrow, and so the kids would just have to make do with sharing the one bathroom for the night.

[83]

* * *

I am interested to see what happens with this girl.

The man is a good man and a good manager. I have watched him as he has made his timetables and his lists. I have seen him when things have gone well, and when things have not gone well. His experience keeps him calm and he always sees his options. He knows how to work, as witnessed by how much I've changed over the last year.

But people are not so easy to predict and are sometimes arbitrary where they should be resolute, and unknown where they should be known. People change. This girl will be different for him. I sensed her when she came in the door. She has an undeveloped mind. There are thoughts hidden inside her that she has yet to discover. She will need more than paint for the walls and a pillow for her head, I believe. The man will have to be prepared for things that do not fit so well into his schedules.

9

It was early Wednesday morning of the next week that Tucker stared at a neat stack of folded sheets and towels and a pillow placed at the foot of Rose's mattress. Rose was gone, leaving the ranch sometime during the night without telling anyone.

The neatness with which she had left things should have told him something. She could have just crawled out of bed, put on her clothes and left everything as it was. Or, she could have wadded up the sheets and thrown them on the floor, hotel style. But instead she had taken time to fold the sheets and towels, make a stack and place the pillow directly on top, fluffed.

He recognized the neatness, but it didn't help him understand.

Tucker and the twins had heard nothing, but tracks behind the dorm indicated someone had paced, occasionally peering into the windows. It wouldn't have been difficult even in the dead of night to figure out which room was hers. The moon shed enough light through the windows to distinguish the disarray of clothes, magazines, videos, hats, and chairs in the twins' rooms from the austerity of Rose's, who was living out of a single suitcase.

She wasn't forced to leave, Tucker surmised, looking at the two sets of tracks, one set following the other, that led down the road and out the gate to a car parked off the side of the road. In the soft dirt, the tracks became well-defined imprints and he knew that the person in front had worn shoes with a waffle sole. The footprint was not large, though, only a little longer and wider than Rose's. If it was a man, he was not very big.

Tucker's assumption was that it was Rico Mares, Rose's boyfriend. She had talked little of him, but the twins had told Tucker what they knew. Given their description of him, he seemed the most likely person that would be able to get her to leave in the middle of the night. How he knew where she was, Tucker did not know.

He hadn't seen it coming, hadn't had a clue at all. Rose seemed happy, was working well with him and the twins and seemed to enjoy the ranch. She had been resolute in eating a good variety of foods, sleeping well, resting when she was tired, and walking her loop around the sidewalk every morning. Tucker told her that good health was important for the health of her child and that she needed to stay fit. She accepted it all as a mature woman, he thought, and enjoyed being special.

Tucker continued to stare at the sheets and blanket for a minute longer, then decided that there was nothing to do. He judged the situation as one in which a member of the work crew had decided to leave. No worker was constrained to stay, but it was discourteous to leave without notice and violated the trust he had shown her and had expected in return.

Tucker would mail her paycheck to Larry after briefing him on what had occurred. After that, he guessed he was done with Rose. He and the twins were back to working on the deck by nine o'clock.

As he and the boys laid the deck boards flat across the joists they had installed the day before, Tucker couldn't help but think about the last week. He tried to remember the conversations, what she had said and how she had said it, and her expressions. He admitted to himself that he was sorry she had left. Instead of corrupting the ranch environment as he had feared, she had added to it during her short stay.

Thursday afternoon of last week, the day she had come, after everything but the trailer's decking material and the carpet had been unloaded, Tucker gave Rose and the twins an overview of how the ladies' bathroom was going to be plumbed.

It was a good break from carpentry work, and he let the twins cut and piece together the PVC pipes for the cold water side as he worked on the pipes for the hot water side. Tucker connected a water hose to the outside faucet so that Rose could wash down the ladies' bathroom and shower room. It had been cleaned before, but almost a year's worth of airborne dirt and dust covered the surfaces. An hour made a good difference, after which she helped the twins uncrate the vanity and sink and set them in their places.

When all the pieces of plumbing had been cut and laid out, they gathered everything into an empty box and set it aside. Tucker would wait to install the plumbing until the next day. He had bought a paint sprayer in town and wanted to spray Rose's ceiling before the twins painted the color coat on the walls.

It was almost seven by the time they quit. Leaving Rose's room open and with a fan turned to high, they grilled hamburgers and ate on the front porch.

Rose stayed in her dorm room that first night, the fan still going. She and the twins hung a sign on the men's bathroom door to indicate when it was occupied.

Friday morning began with breakfast, now more overtly healthy, with fruit and yogurt and a selection of fruit juices. And there was a waffle maker and a hot plate for making eggs, omelets, and browning sausages. Tucker asked Rose to make two walking laps around the longest route of the sidewalk before beginning work each day, starting a daily routine to help maintain her health as a pregnant woman. He also laid down the rule that she would rest whenever she needed, asking her to keep track of her hours and he would adjust her pay to be fair to the twins. He allowed her to start work at nine o'clock, after her breakfast and walk, unless she wanted to start earlier. He and the twins continued to start at eight.

On Friday morning, as she was striding around the sidewalk, Tucker and the twins reviewed the work from the night before, laid out the pipes and fittings, and glued everything together. There was hot and cold water flowing from a new faucet into a new sink on top of a new vanity within a couple of hours. The new toilets were working soon after. There were ceremonial pees in both bathrooms, with simultaneous flushes to commemorate the occasion.

After the plumbing was done, the twins used the spray gun to paint the ceilings in their own rooms while Tucker and Rose worked on her bathroom. A new shower line was piped over, with faucets and a shower head installed; all the old light fixtures removed; and a new light fixture installed over the vanity. Tucker finished the morning installing a ceiling fan in her bedroom.

In the afternoon, all four worked on coating the remaining eight bedrooms of the dormitory with primer, everyone using respirators to keep down the amount of paint fumes sucked into their lungs. Tucker sprayed the ceilings of the rooms and hallway as the others worked on the walls. The next Friday, they declared, would be a painting day to put the color over the primer in the remaining rooms. They would then focus on painting the two bathrooms.

Rose was happy. Tucker saw it in her eyes, her smile, and the relaxed relationship that she had with the twins. She knew them from school but was a year ahead. It seemed that the twins knew all the girls at school, regardless of their classes. It was an overdose of extrovert personality times the power of two that made everyone connect to the brothers, Tucker assumed. He could well imagine that the boys were the movers and shakers of the high school social network.

Rose showed no resentment at the loss of a social life, and didn't blink when she no longer had cell service or the internet. Tucker thought she was happy to be out of touch, happy not to hash and rehash her situation with friends and other online contacts.

Tony and Tommy decided to both stay that weekend, and Tucker took everyone to Tucumcari on Saturday afternoon to see a movie and to eat out. Sunday was the work in the lavender garden, which all three teenagers helped, out of boredom, and then the trio went exploring along the riverbank and back into the far canyons. Tucker could hear them laughing as they waded in the shallows of the river. Meanwhile, he read, worked on his spreadsheets, and wrote emails.

Monday was a good day, using strings to mark the positions of the deck supports, digging the footings for each one, and then setting the treated posts in cement. Tuesday, the timbers were bolted in, the joist hangers nailed on, and all the joists cut and placed. Rose earned a reputation for her expert handling of the impact drill, driving long screws into spacers between the joists. Everyone was proud of the work.

Then, on Wednesday, she was gone.

In retrospect, her sudden disappearance took Tucker's breath away. He hadn't realized that he cared that much.

After making the phone call to Larry, Tucker and the twins returned to working on the deck. It was not hard work but required concentration. "All we need to do," he told them, "is lay out the planks, line them up, cut them to length where needed, and screw them down." The ends of the boards were left hanging over the edge, waiting until all were in place to be cut cleanly and in a straight line.

The job went bad from the beginning. Cuts were made in the wrong places, screws broke, and planks ended up with curves and had to be taken off and repositioned. It was as if everyone had lost their coordination. Anger, flaring tempers, no smiles. It was the first time Tucker had seen the twins mad at each other. They seemed to be fighting over who should take the blame that Rose had left.

When Tucker wasn't paying attention and fell off the deck, landing with a thud three feet below where he had been standing a split second before, he'd had it. Picking himself up out of the dirt, he called the twins together.

"We're done for the day. Put up the tools. We're going to town."

He figured that the twins had earned the right to a TV that had broadcast channels. Radio Shack had all the equipment he needed to split off from his satellite dish on the trailer. They stayed for an early supper at Chili's, which was followed by a run to Walmart. By seven, the twins were arguing over the channel changer and Tucker was walking his nightly rounds.

When he first met Rose, she had reminded him of Sara, his own daughter, who was a little younger than Rose when she died. Sweet, strong, loving, and beautiful, she was a duplicate of her mother but had the efficient and orderly mind of her father. What would he have done if she had turned up pregnant? How strong would his love have been?

He wasn't sure he knew the answer to the first question. But he knew the answer to the second. His love would never have wavered. His daughter would never have stopped being his daughter, and the child that she brought into the world would have been loved without reservation. He would never have broken the family because of anything that either his wife or his daughter had done. Family, home, was everything. And he would have done everything to support her, no matter what.

Of course, he thought to himself, that was the standard answer for loving fathers. He wondered if reality would have been harder if the father of the baby had been a marginal boy. He couldn't see Sara messing around with anyone she didn't respect, but then she probably, like Rose, wouldn't have been thinking about getting pregnant if she had. If Sara had been in the same position as Rose—uncertain boyfriend, unknown future, hard-to-overcome bad start—maybe he would have had a less than honorable reaction. Could he have condoned a marriage with a man he didn't like? Could he have loved a baby born from a bad relationship?

He missed Sara and Jennie, and he certainly would have missed Jennie's wisdom if Sara had become pregnant. It had been hard enough being a single parent with a teenager; he was sure he would have struggled more if she had grown older. In spite of the moral quandaries that he considered, he could still see in Rose the possibility of how Sara might have been as an older teenager, her native intelligence and self-assurance overlaid with teen self-doubt, youthful angst, and her need to be surrounded by a strong family. Rose was a glimpse of things he had once loved, of a life he once shared, he realized, and he was sorry she had decided to leave.

Tucker kept walking until he had finished the loop. After that, he called Lynn. He knew that she would want to know that Rose was gone, and he also knew that he wanted her to know. He canceled the next night's poker game. He didn't think anyone would be up for it.

The next day was better. Without the shock of Rose's leaving, without each of the three looking up to make sure she hadn't reappeared, the work got done. By late Thursday afternoon, all of the planks were down and screwed in. The steps Tucker had built to the backdoor would be adapted to the new deck. He'd work on that the next day while the boys got back to painting the color coat on the dorm rooms. He expected that Friday would be a good day.

Then Rose came back.

But she was not the same, and she was not alone.

10

After their Thursday night dinner, the twins brought the chairs to the front porch and relaxed as they watched the sunlight crawl up the faces of the cliffs across the river. Tucker strolled along the sidewalk.

When he had reached the foot of the cliffs across the front yard, a car engine's whine from up the canyon invaded the quiet. It was a small engine, so Tucker knew it was not Larry or Lynn.

The flagpole cable clanged once against the pole, then again, as clear as a doorbell. Tucker slowed in surprise, then stopped. When Rose initially appeared the week before, the cable had sounded, and now it was sounding again.

He watched intently as a small compact drove up to the house. He did not recognize it, but when he saw Rose limp as she stepped out of the car, he started thinking about how he was going to find Rico and tear him into pieces. He cut across the yard towards the front of the house.

As he aimed in her direction, Rose helped a man get out of the back seat. Tucker's mounting fury subsided when he recognized that, if this was Rico, and he was sure that it was, the young man was probably not responsible for Rose's limp. His face was bandaged and he winced with pain as he did his best to stand upright.

By the time Tucker reached the front walk, the driver had gotten out and was helping Rose situate the young man against the front step's railing. The woman was inches shorter than Rose, thicker, fifty-ish, and Hispanic. She moved as if in a hurry. Or as if afraid, he thought.

Tucker surveyed the arrivals but said nothing.

Leaving the injured man as Tucker came up, Rose moved across the walk to stand in front of him. Her face was swollen on her left side, a darkening bruise around her eye socket and forehead. Her lower lip had been cut and was held together with a butterfly bandage. Her eyes were deeply red and ran with tears. She put her hands on his arms and gently laid her head on his chest.

"Please help us," she said quietly, then broke into sobs. He said nothing but encircled her with his arms.

The young man was Rico, as Tucker had guessed, but he wasn't what Tucker had imagined. He had an image in his mind of what a hot-blooded, irresponsible, high school drop-out, chop-shop junky, stud loner looked like, and Rico wasn't it. He was shorter than Rose by about an inch, even if he could have stood up straight, but it was his body type that was most out of sync with Tucker's image. Rico was not athletic, not tall or skinny, not dark or angry looking. He was, in fact, soft, rather pudgy, and had a childish face. The woman who had stepped from the car and helped Rose was almost a carbon copy of the man who was gingerly leaning on the stone railings of the steps. Tucker assumed she was his mother.

Rose sniffled and rubbed the tears from her eyes, then recited the events of the last two days.

It was past one in the morning, two nights before, when Rico had come. Watching from the darkness, he found her room. After an hour of talking, he convinced her to leave. He wanted them to marry and be a family. He would be a good husband, he had told her, and he would do his best to ensure that their future was full of happiness. But they needed to make their convictions known to their parents, he had told her. It was the honorable thing to do.

He convinced her that they should do it as soon as possible, and the two lovers slipped away in the dark and headed to the car he had left up the road. They found a pull-off and slept in the canyon until daylight, then drove into town. They talked to Rose's parents on Wednesday. It didn't go badly, but there was only begrudging support. Her dad had resigned himself to no abortion, and the mother was cold, still considering adoption a good choice. It wasn't until noon today that they went to Rico's house. His father's shift did not end until two o'clock, and that gave them time to talk with Rico's mother. She was the most sympathetic to the situation and was welcoming of Rose, but she feared what Armando Mares would do when he came home to find the "blonde whore" who carried his son's "mistake." Resolute, Rico knew that confronting his father had to come sometime, and he wanted it to be over.

Which was also what his father thought. But Armando had a different ending in mind.

The conversation had been brief. When the swinging started, Rico was the first objective but the major target was Rose. From her description, Tucker understood that Armando had decided to kill the baby within her by savaging her body enough that nature would reject the fetus. A do-it-yourself abortion. It was more than the mother could stand and she jumped into the fracas. Armando was no more concerned with her welfare than the others, and so she took his punches and kicks as she covered up the girl while Rico did his best to grapple with his father.

The neighbors heard the screams and called the police, at which time Armando ran for the back fence. He had a five minute head start, and he had friends. He was gone.

Rico's ribs hurt like crazy, and he had bruises on his arms and face and a cut above his eye. Rose had been able to shield her baby but the kicks had gone to her back and thighs and one to her face. Rico's mom, Consuelo but called Connie, showed only a bruise or two.

They were taken to the emergency room and an afternoon of treatment had gotten them dismissed. Rico was the most serious, suffering three cracked ribs, bruised muscles, and busted knuckles. He now had a fully wrapped chest, making it hard for him to breathe, while bending over was impossible. Riding the rough country road to the ranch had been agony. Rose was bruised and sore and bore the visible wounds on her face. Connie needed only painkillers.

Armando was officially a fugitive, but the family feared every moment that he would reappear. He had not finished the job, and his anger, according to his wife, would last a long time.

The three of them agreed not to return to the Mares' home, and they were afraid that Armando might also lie in wait at Rose's parent's house. Rose knew of only one place where comfort and protection were assured, and she was now there and in Tucker's arms.

"Mrs. Mares," Tucker asked after the story had been told. "Will Armando come here?"

She answered quickly. "No. We didn't know where Rose was this last week, or where Rico was, and we told no one today that we were coming here. Mando has family in El Paso and Mexico. He'll go there, at least for a while."

Tucker looked at the damaged people on the front step.

"Okay," he finally said. "It's too late to go to town tonight, and so I'm going to pull my queen mattress out of the trailer and put it in the dining room for Rico and Rose. It's going to be a painful night for both of them, but it's softer than the floor. Rico's mom is going to sleep in Rose's room, and I'll sleep on my floor. Tomorrow, I'll go to town and get mattresses and bedding and more food. Tony, you and Tommy work up two more rooms in the morning, one on your side for Rico and the one next to Rose's room for his mom.

"We have two new rules," Tucker said as he looked from face to face. "I'll put a chain and a combination lock on the gate. If you go out, you lock it behind you; if you come in, you lock it behind you. If anybody feels any danger, if any vehicle shows up that you don't know, if you see a stranger anywhere on the property, you go into the house and lock the doors. Do you understand?"

Heads nodded.

"I repeat: go into the house. The house will protect you."

The twins, silent now, and seemingly embarrassed to stand healthy and whole in front of the others, helped carry the few bags from the car and then decided to drive Connie's car back by the woodpile. Energized with a plan, they moved the car, then covered it with tarps from the workroom and added pieces of lumber on top to disguise it.

Rose and Connie helped Rico struggle up the stairs and into the dining room, where Tucker was already dragging his mattress. He put on a clean set of sheets, then watched from the hallway as they struggled to right their ship in a vicious sea.

What to do? It had been a long time since he had dealt with fear. He was used to risk—construction always involved risk—and Tucker knew how to handle risk. But fear of someone else? Fear so great that you actively guarded against it with locked gates, and remained on edge because of the danger, and constantly watched for some blow that might be coming? It had been years since he had known that sort of fear, but he already felt a knot growing in his stomach.

Connie had said that Armando wasn't coming, that no one knew they had come to the ranch. But the last time he was told that no one knew anything, Rico had shown up like he had an invitation and a map.

Love can find a way, obviously, but so too can evil always find a way, Tucker thought. So he did a last check on Rose and the Mares family, stopped to talk with the twins, who had no familiarity with being terrified, and went to his trailer. He checked his pistol, strapped on his gun belt and holster, put extra clips of ammunition in his pocket, and went into the cliffs.

Fifty yards behind the house, in the cliffs close to the ranch gate, the stoneworkers from Ohio that Cyrus Mulvaney had brought to the ranch had discovered a large crack at the bottom of a cliff face. Leveling a space around the crack as a work area, they set up scaffolding, brought their hammers, chisels, wedges, and pry bars, and created a stone quarry, using the crack to help slice the cliff into manageable pieces. The definition of patience, they chiseled, hammered, pried, and broke out the large stones needed for the foundation. Later on, they rendered smaller pieces for lintels, thresholds, capstones, and other cut stones that were needed.

Tucker now sat in the quarry on leftover stones. He was hidden in the deep shadows cast by the strong moon. If someone came down the road, he'd see them. If someone crossed the gate or the wire fence, he'd know it. If someone came from upriver or from downriver, he'd be able to watch them along the riverbank. If someone approached the front of the house or the back of the house or the dorm, he would see them.

The knot in his stomach had gone away because he was now active and had a plan. He was not frightened, but he was deliberate. He knew that he had entered a world in which he was at a disadvantage. He did not hate, did not abuse, did not see life as cheap, and he was not a natural predator. That made him not as powerful and not as reckless as the inhabitants of the world where those qualities were admired. He was not especially concerned with the aspects of combat for he was smart and armed, which would count for a lot. But being without predatory emotions, he knew he would be slow to react and slow to be aggressive, a disadvantage in battle.

Tucker sat, apprehensive, as his gaze moved from the road to the river to the house to the dorm to the gate to the road. As he watched, he set his thoughts free.

He had told the twins about Cyrus Mulvaney and the house, including the sordid details of the kidnapping, the suicide, and the crazy wife. He gave a general history of the rest. Most of the house's history was in the context of what he could point to in the house—the coal room in the basement, the VA wiring, the dorm, the linoleum floors.

But he didn't tell the twins that the house was alive. He didn't show them the breathing, didn't have them listen to the heartbeat, and always blamed the wind if the flagpole ever clanged or the doors ever swung open or shut by themselves. Both boys still picked up on the less dramatic signs of the house's spirit, and so they had decided on their own that the house was haunted. It was enough to keep them cautious but not alarmed. Tucker decided that, with as many years as the house had stood without substantial witnesses of supernatural happenings, it was probably smart enough to be discrete with playful teenagers and would know to resist flagrant exposure.

In fact, it had been months since the house had done anything exceptional beyond an occasional clang now and then and the scent of lavender. After the noisy machinery had finished last year, there were long days of relatively quiet work, and all the new work, especially replacing the windows, brought what seemed like an even greater absence of action on the part of the house. Tucker thought at first it had possibly gone to sleep, but he decided instead that the house was just content, like a dog lying in the sunshine.

That was okay with Tucker. It was like having a satisfied customer.

What would Lynn think about the recent turn of events? Of Rose? Of Rico and his mom? Of this new episode of fear? He wished that he could talk to her, wished that she was beside him on his lonely rock in the deep shadows. It had been years since he had a female friend, and longer than that since he had encountered a female for whom he had felt stirrings of passion. He wasn't sure that this was the case here, but she was more and more on his mind. He was tired of being alone, and the days were always brighter when he knew she would be coming. But he also knew that he should stop thinking about her.

Had it been thirty some-odd years since Jennie died? And then six years alone with Sara? It wasn't that he didn't value a woman's friendship, but the pain of what he had done, the utter condemnation he felt because of his actions, prevented any significant relationship with someone new. He wasn't stupid—he had not stopped Jennie's heart and he had not pulled the trigger to kill Sara—but his specific actions had led to those events. He had felt responsible for their deaths then and felt responsible now. When all the feelings were assessed, there were pieces of him that no longer existed, pieces that would have allowed him forgiveness, pieces that would have allowed him peace.

What woman could live with a man who had pieces missing?

After Tucker had watched over the ranch for a couple of hours, a large owl swished down from above, glided over the small backyard, and swooped up to the copper ornament on the roof's peak. The bird gently landed, settled his wings, and sat motionless in the moonlight.

That was the first bird Tucker had seen sitting on the roof. Maybe the house really is asleep, he thought.

The presence of the owl convinced Tucker that it was both late and that the ranch was secure. Owls were quick to spook, and if it was content that all things were as they should be, then that was good enough for him.

He left his perch in the quarry and descended the slope to the back of the house. He was tired, but the idea of sleeping on his floor was not inviting.

He headed to the front of the house, then walked down to the garden.

He found the birdbath empty, so he took the bucket from under the stone bench and made a couple of trips to the river to refill it. He often watched the garden from the front porch, and birds were constantly bathing themselves in the shallow water.

After scooting the pail back under the bench, Tucker sat. He stretched his back muscles and rubbed his eyes and face and yawned. There had been no noises from the house as he passed by, but he could imagine the useless night ahead for Rose and Rico. Their pains, as well as their despair, would keep them awake. And sorrow. Abuse was always sorrowful, and knowing now that Rico's father not only refused their relationship but was violently committed to ending it, would bring thoughts of running away, of leaving completely, of doing something, anything, to escape. Tucker could see Rose and Rico lying together tonight but feeling miles apart.

There was little Tucker could do for them beyond offering refuge. How long would they be here? How long could they hide? His thoughts returned to fear, the basic life-robbing awareness of having to guard yourself against someone out to hurt you. Such a young age! They should both be enjoying the last of their teenage years but instead were fighting a war.

What's the mother going to do? Connie had barely spoken a word. She couldn't go back home, and he didn't know if she worked in town or not. Life had changed for all three of them, he guessed, and the next few days would have to be muddled through before they found a path forward.

He wondered why Rico's father, Armando, would be so intensely against Rose and the baby. There had to be something more. It was one thing not to want an interracial marriage and a mixed-race baby, but he suspected something else. Rico was an only child and was like his mother. That could be a possible source of the dislike. Maybe Armando had always wanted a son who more closely matched the father, someone big, strong, and definitively male. Tucker was betting that Rico not only looked like his mother but that his temperament was more-or-less identical. That would have made the son look soft, weak, and feminine in Armando's eyes.

Well, no matter. Now, they were all within his purview. Now, it was going to matter who did what to whom. And who threatened who. And what happened tomorrow and the next day and the next. He was now a protector.

Tucker suddenly shuddered with a hot flash. It wasn't fair. All the things that he could do well, all the talents that he could bring to bear on problems. Yet, he had failed when Jennie and Sara needed protection the most.

Now it was Rose. With or without the others, he saw in her the vulnerability of the young. Defiant but stupid, really, unequipped and inexperienced, exactly what a teenager should be. They were supposed to be protected until they became equipped, became experienced, until they were capable of carrying on by themselves. Until they grew up.

Rose needed him. Rico wasn't enough, Connie was only an observer, and her parents were estranged from the situation by choice. So Tucker was needed, right now, as the foundation that she could rely on. He didn't want that. She had no idea who she was dealing with, of how unstable he could be, how unreliable his level of protection might become.

Tucker leaned forward, his elbows on his knees and his head in his hands. He took several deep breaths and found himself shaking. He was so damned tired of being alone.

Tucker weaved back and forth on the seat, losing control, feeling overwhelmed. He jerked with a spasm and slid down to the ground, his hands scraping into the gravel.

He wasn't good at this, he thought, as tears ran down his cheeks. He didn't want to find out, again, just how *not* good at this he was.

The sound of the crash came back to him, the car slamming into the railing and rolling down the embankment. He hadn't felt that drunk, and he ignored his good wife's pleadings. But he was drunk—drunk on alcohol, on childish pride, and on foolish arrogance. He was so drunk that he didn't come around until Jennie's body had been wheeled down to the morgue. He missed her last moments. He missed his only chance to say he was sorry.

After that, it was only Sara and him. She was ten when Jennie died. The years sped up after her mother died, and it seemed that she was sixteen overnight. He should have quit and taken her away, but he didn't. Maybe it was in compensation for Jennie's absence, but he became caught up in his work. His foolish pride returned and he gave himself over to the idea of greatness. This brought on a high profile court case, then money, then fame. And then the man he had defended turned on him and there was another trip to the morgue, another missed chance to say he was sorry.

He and Sara had been placed in a world in which he was at a disadvantage, and he had been too slow to save her. He had traded justice for money, and thereby, he had earned being alone.

Now there was another girl, another daughter in his keeping. She could not understand why he did not want to be her protector. She didn't know that he would fail.

Tucker shuddered and sobbed, releasing too many years of carefully monitored emotions, carefully restrained memories, and carefully orchestrated control.

* * *

I listened as he wept.

He is correct—I have been enjoying the attention that he has given me, celebrating the life that has come back to me. I feel strong, renewed, even though much rebuilding remains. I have reveled in my newness, sloshed in my fullness, and enjoyed the pride of a new shine.

Tonight, however, I realize that I have been neglectful.

I have been a house of tragedy and sorrow. I have been inhabited by people whose pain seemed never ending, whose thoughts and dreams were consumed by their struggles and whose desire for life ebbed and flowed. I have seen defeat, surrender, and I have watched Death crawl under bed sheets and steal the hearts and minds of the innocent.

I have also seen humility and acceptance, people for whom the smallest of victories brought them to new places and to new peace. Sometimes it lasted, sometimes not. But hope was strong in many, and I learned that hope can sustain people when other means fail them. Those who have no hope usually die.

But what of those who do not hope because they are sure about the outcome?

I have thought many times about the dancing man who gave me life, the one whose memories I hold. When he gave me his charge, he was certain of the future—she would come and he would return. He knew it as fact. He had only to wait for these actions to take place. His mind and heart were firm. But what happened? Did she die? Did he die? What was in the future that he had not imagined?

And what did he do when he saw that the future was different from what he had assumed? Did his fact turn into hope? Or despair?

This man who is rebuilding me, he believes that he has failed in such a way that forgiveness is not available to him, that he is eternally cursed. Because of what he did or didn't do, the future was changed. Did he believe that his future was fact? That it could not change without him? Or that it changed only because of him?

The future belongs to no being. Why did he think it belonged to him?

There was a time that the nuns were here, alone. I had watched them as they ministered to ones who suffered, but I found it as interesting to watch them after all the patients had left. After years of being in close contact—every day, every night, every minute— with people who suffered in one way or another, they were suddenly unconstrained. Whereas they had been bound, they were set free.

And they felt guilt.

They felt that, if they no longer suffered regularly with those who were suffering, then they were not sufficiently faithful. Their condition was beyond the need to rest their tired bodies after so arduous a life. It was as if their faith had always been displayed in their works; and so, without works to demonstrate their faith, they felt they had no faith.

The man in charge of their community came to speak with them, and he helped them understand that their work had changed but not their faith. "You should not allow the past to judge your present," he said, and he encouraged them to find different ways to demonstrate their faith. He encouraged them to hope, to think beyond what had been their past and to see their present as the context in which they should live.

Tonight, I listened to this man as he knelt on the ground suffering his guilt. I had not understood why I found him to be devoid of happiness, to be so continually resistant to the woman. Now I understand that his is a far more difficult problem than loneliness or grief. It is a problem in the fabric of his soul.

This man has doled out punishment for himself, punishment for sins that he considers unforgiveable, for which there is no redemption. It is his clinging to the past that constrains him in the present and prevents him from having hope in the future.

Many people who suffered within my walls wanted to have sinned so they could feel that their sins had brought on their suffering. They wanted to have earned their pain so that they could deserve their recovery. They sought guilt because, without it, they could not understand why they suffered.

This man wants to be punished. He wants no hope of redemption because he cannot cancel the consequences of his sins.

I have been neglectful. I have grown blind and dull, not seeing that I can act, that I should act. It is time to pay for my rebuilding. I need to rebuild him.

He should let go of the past. He needs to revitalize those emotions within him that he considers missing. And he needs to love again, freely.

The powers from the dancing man—I remember them. I remember his thoughts, his prayers, his handiwork that was revealed in the smoke that engulfed me. The dancing man was a shaman, and he used his powers in the spirit realm to bring about change in the physical realm.

When he put his hands on my threshold, I received those powers as well. I will use them to heal this fine man. It will not be easy, and the path will not always be clear for it is a difficult thing to work with a man's soul.

11

Armando never showed. Larry Jackson kept in contact with the Las Vegas PD, and they reported that Armando seemed to have left town. The police said that it wasn't unusual for family arguments to become battles, but when the word got around that he had been kicking a pregnant girl, even his friends seemed to bid him good riddance.

After a day or two, things at the ranch slipped into a routine.

Tucker's two-person work crew had turned into a five-person family. Rico was almost immobile, and so he required constant care and feeding. Rose became protective of him, spending about half of her time with him rather than working, and Connie stuck with them because she was the mother-in-charge, taking to the role like a willing hen. The twins were no longer the definers of the ranch's social life and retreated to a subservient role, regarding Connie as a substitute mother. It ruined their attitude as employees, Tucker thought, and they now sought approval from her instead of him.

After a few days, Connie formally asked Tucker, on her behalf as well as Rico and Rose's, if they could continue staying at the ranch, bargaining the cost of groceries and running the kitchen in exchange for his hospitality. She had quickly closed her and Armando's bank accounts and moved the monies into safer places. It was several thousand, so she was confident she could make it last for a good while.

She confided to Tucker that she wasn't yet thinking of divorce, but living alone felt better than living with an increasingly abusive husband. Plus, the potential of having a grandchild brought even more of her mothering instincts to the situation and she found it hard to imagine Armando being a good grandfather to a child he had tried to kill.

The sudden manifestation of a family living in close quarters wasn't a comfortable arrangement for anyone. Tucker noticed that the conversations were awkward and that Rico and Rose felt embarrassed to require such obvious protection.

The early work done on the dorm paid off. Other than buying yet more mattresses, more carpet, more fans, and more food, Tucker and the twins had Rico and Connie installed in their rooms in less than an hour. Those who were able spent the next three days on the bathrooms, spraying primer on the ceiling, painting the walls, cleaning the floors, and erecting stalls around the toilets. Tucker hung six more ceiling fans, one each in the bathrooms and in Rico and Connie's rooms and two more in the hallways.

However their circumstances might evolve, Tucker grew to understand that nobody was thinking about leaving. He was not shy about his authority and could ask them to leave, in a nice, courteous way, after they had all healed and were mobile. And he was sure that they would leave without disrespect or resentment. But he couldn't do it. It wasn't a problem of authority or courage. It just would have been wrong, he decided. They needed him. He knew that this response was the right one, and so he tolerated the lack of progress on the house as best he could.

It was his nature to get work done, to have a clear plan that progressed step-by-step, and to have measures in place that allowed him to gauge progress. With a family in residence, though, there were always interruptions, schedule changes, the inconvenience of working around people, and the occasional emotional upheavals between Rose and Rico.

Tucker lectured himself, and it even took a visit to Lynn in town to talk through his frustrations. He had to readjust his goals, his daily expectations, and his priorities. He had to rethink his role. And the more days that went by, the more adjusted he became and the more he accepted his role. He, in fact, decided that the situation was probably more or less permanent. A family had come and that family was going to stay, regardless of what had been planned.

And that presumption changed everything.

The dormitory was okay for housing teenagers during the warm months, but Rico and Rose posed a situation that Tucker hoped would result in a long term relationship. If so, they needed real accommodations if they were going to have a real marriage. Connie reminded him too much of his mother to imagine that a one room boarding house approach was appropriate for her. And he foresaw that the ranch would be covered in snow within three or four months and the dorm would be unlivable. The bottom line was that everyone needed to live in a place that had real rooms, real beds, real insulation, and real heat.

They needed a real house.

A meeting followed this realization, and Tucker laid out the new work objectives for the next few months: a working kitchen with a real stove, a big refrigerator, an ice maker, a freezer, a dishwasher, countertops, and shelves; a big bedroom for Rose and Rico; a bedroom for Connie; and a bathroom with a working sink, toilet, and shower next to the bedrooms. A washer and dryer, baseboard heat to keep the spaces warm, real wall plugs to replace the extension cords, and real lights to replace the temporaries. And every time an outside wall was redone, insulation had to be pushed into every opening.

It seemed like a simple list, but there were some fundamentals that couldn't be done piece-meal. Electricity couldn't be put into a few rooms without installing the electrical panel for the whole house; hot and cold water couldn't be put into the kitchen and bathroom without installing the central water distribution system for the whole house; and baseboard heat couldn't be put into a few rooms without installing the boiler for the whole house. To get any one particular room finished and functional, Tucker had to spend seventy percent of the cost to finish all of the rooms.

It wasn't the way he liked to work, and it grated on him that his house building had become a list of forced requirements. The work was now driving him instead of the other way around. He remembered his premise when he had bought the house: it was to be his long term project on which he could spend as long as he wanted. Before Rose and the others had come, he was succeeding. Now, everything had become urgent and he was not happy.

Lynn came out a couple of times, but he could tell that she wasn't happy either. There was now more drama at the ranch than she had at work, and it made her hesitant to visit. The twins still played cards on Thursday evenings, but the tournaments had drifted off the schedule and it stopped being a natural time for her to come by. It was also much more expensive providing pizza for seven than four. Tucker resented most that talking with Lynn never produced easy conversations anymore.

But with the change in the work plan, Tucker accepted his responsibility and poured his energy into the schedule. There was no time to waste if he was going to get the house livable before winter.

The contracted items were scheduled first. The electric company would move the electrical hookup from next to the trailer to the main panel in the basement, and a thousand-gallon propane tank would be installed and gas lines run to the basement and the kitchen. A Las Vegas company would install a new propane boiler in the basement, run the heating pipes to all the needed locations, and then baseboard radiators would be installed in every room on the list after the sheetrock was done. And, finally, a plumber would set up the water system.

While the contractors were busy, Tucker decided that his own work crew should focus on redoing the kitchen. It was the daily hub around which everyone revolved, and they needed that hub to be as functional as possible.

The twins, Rose and Connie helped Tucker remove the baseboard around the bottom of the walls, the doorway facings, and the crown molding around the ceiling. Everything else in the room was destined for the trash bin.

As Tucker and Tony and Tommy balanced on tall sections of rented scaffolding, the ceiling plaster and lath was whapped, jarred, pushed, pulled, pried, and tugged off the ceiling until nothing remained on the joists. Connie and Rose filled large plastic trash cans with the rubbish, and the twins alternated hauling them to the trash bin. Rico was still not able to bend, and so he ran the shop vacuum as the others swept and shoveled.

Finished with the ceiling, Tucker left the twins to strip the walls and Connie to clean while he and Rose laid out the shape of the kitchen on the library floor. They placed chalk lines to match the kitchen's dimensions, then marked the openings for the sink, the refrigerator, the freezer, the dishwasher, and the stove. With Rico using the miter saw and Rose handling the nail gun, Tucker built two-by-four tables, without tops, that fit the lines on the floor. He also built legs for a kitchen island. Once the kitchen walls were rebuilt, the tables would be placed in the kitchen and Tucker would add plywood on top of the legs to create countertops. After the plumbing was ready, the sink and the appliances would be moved in and hooked up. It would be a fully functional kitchen when they were done.

It was the second week of August when the kitchen was completely stripped and cleaned. Only the pantries remained. We're making good time, Tucker kept telling himself. The electrical panel had been hooked up, and the propane as well. The heating and air conditioning company had brought the boiler and the water heater, connected them to the propane and to the old flue, and set up all of the powered valves to control the distribution of hot water for heat. Tucker would give them a call when the walls were finished, and the workers would then return and run the pipes from the valves to the radiators in each room.

Tucker thought that he had two more weeks, maybe, of the twins' time. They had made all the difference during the summer, and he was not looking forward to their leaving. He hoped they'd be back the next summer. He left them getting the two pantry rooms ready for taking down the plaster while he went to the basement, starting Rico and Rose on the electrical.

"Mr. Whitby," Tony said, "did you see these?"

Working on the wood trim around the doorway to the storage pantry, Tony pointed to the door trim on the right side of the pantry's opening. Starting about three feet from the floor, notches had been cut into the wood. Irregularly spaced, they went up both sides of the facing, the notches along one side for more than five feet from the floor while the notches on the other side quit at about four feet.

Tucker looked at the notches, faint because of the layers of paint applied through the years. He thought for a minute, then surprise registered in his face.

"Good grief. These are marks to track the height of children as they're growing up."

Tony grinned. "Yeah. My mom did the same thing for all us kids. Even did it on the kitchen door facing, just like this. But she

[107]

used a pencil. She would have laid us out if we cut chunks out of the wood."

The others gathered around, looking at the marks and running their fingers across the notches. Rose brought a measuring tape. The top mark on one side was five feet four inches, while the other was four feet two inches.

"Wait a minute," Tucker said. "When were there children in this house? You think these could be from the Mulvaneys? Remember the story? The father hung himself and the mother disappeared? The boy who was kidnapped by the Indians was ten and the little girl was six. How tall would they have been? Connie, how tall is a ten year-old boy and a six year-old girl?"

Connie shook her head for a moment, then guessed that the marks could be about right. "The boy is tall for his age, if he's only ten. The girl too."

"Uh oh," Tommy said. "Look at those."

He pointed to the top of the door facing. There were two more marks, larger notches than the others, one mark a little below the top of the doorway and the other an inch or so above it. "They were giants if those are the same thing."

Tucker held the bottom as Rose ran the tape to the other two marks. "One's six foot five inches," he said. "And the other is six foot nine inches. Those marks don't make any sense. Somebody was just fooling around. Anyway, if these notches are really the marks of the Mulvaney family, that was a hundred and forty years ago. I want to make sure that we get that piece back in place without messing it up, so be careful as you take it off."

Tony slipped the pry bar in the crack along the wall and lightly tapped it with a hammer.

The board flew off as if it had been spring-loaded and hit Tucker in the face.

"Oowwwoo," he said, grabbing the board. The board left a welt on Tucker's forehead, right between his eyes.

He was still grimacing as he handed the board back to Tony. "Well, I hope they all come off that easy."

Everyone laughed but didn't notice the clanging of the flagpole.

With the kitchen being demolished, the grill was moved from the deck to the covered side porch where it was surrounded by boxes of various kitchen supplies. With a cooktop burner to one side and a new griddle for pancakes and toasted sandwiches, it served for almost all the meal preparations.

Thank God for Connie, Tucker thought. He hadn't realized how little effort he and the twins had put into cooking. It wasn't that Tucker was lazy about cooking, or even lacking in talent. It was that his attitude was rather Spartan: food was fuel. It's what you put inside of you so you could get back to work. That made most meals quick and plain, and unfortunately, uniformly boring.

Connie had taken over the cooking with a vengeance. She wasn't one to watch from the sidelines, and if Rose and Rico were working, and the twins were working, and Tucker was working, then she was going to be working too. She had increased the amount of food being bought each week, which was fine with Tucker. He never questioned her expenses since she was swapping the cost for her family's rent, but he knew the weekly cost had to be considerably more than what he had been spending.

It also hadn't taken Connie long to refuse the idea of a sheet of plywood and folding chairs constituting a table. She retrieved her dining table and chairs from her house, first setting them up in the dining room, and then moving them to the basement when the kitchen construction started. It was difficult cooking upstairs and carrying everything into the basement, but the absence of dirt and dust more than made up for the inconvenience.

By the end of the day, which was Thursday, Tony and Tommy had removed the woodwork from the pantries, and they would finish removing the shelves in the morning. The next day being Friday, finishing and cleaning up would put them about ready to go home for the weekend.

In the basement, Tucker sketched out for Rico and Rose how the electrical in the house worked, showed them how the main panel would be wired for different electrical circuits, explained how the black, white, and bare wires would be run to the various electrical boxes and then combined to power the various fixtures. He then walked them through the kitchen space, indicating where the different electrical boxes would be placed for the lights and plugs.

That was enough for the day, and everyone had learned never to be late for supper when fajitas were being served. Once supper was begun, it took only twenty minutes for everyone to clean their plates.

Whereas July had been like an oven, August cooled off, afternoon rains coming once or twice a week. Rose had begun walking in the evenings as well as the mornings, so, with Connie cleaning up from the meal, she and Rico started around the sidewalk. Tucker went for the path along the river. The twins gave up on their card game and sat in the lawn chairs watching the river, telling jokes, and laughing.

Tucker thought about skipping his walk for the evening—the welt on his forehead still stung like a hundred little pricks on his skin. But his force of habit was stronger than his pain and he even stood along the bank of the river longer than usual, eyes closed, smelling the grass.

It was an hour later that people wandered back to their rooms in the dorm and Tucker started his nightly house walk-through. The pain on his forehead had slacked off, but he was still conscious of the bump. This made him a little distracted, a little bit more casual about walking through the rooms, and it wasn't until he was on the third floor that he smelled smoke.

The house was on fire.

He rushed downstairs and out into the yard, yelling for the others to come, to hurry—help! The twins were first on the scene, watching Tucker as he frantically pulled the water hose into the house. He directed them to the third floor. "Find the flames! Where's the smoke coming from? Rose, get the fire extinguisher from the workroom. Connie, go to the basement. Look for flames! Rico, find the fire!"

They all ran like crazy. They all searched like crazy.

But they found nothing.

And they smelled nothing.

Tucker hurried from the first floor to the third floor to the second floor to the basement to the third floor to the kitchen to outside, looking at the roof, the gables, and the windows.

And he found nothing.

It took almost a half hour for Tucker to calm down, requiring him to start at the third floor, go to every room, feel every wall, touch every ceiling he could reach, and then repeating this for the second floor, then the first floor, and finally the basement.

Nothing. No smoke, no flames, no fire.

The others had returned to the dorm some time before. Tucker saw their puzzled expressions. The twins were even cracking jokes about bringing in smoke jumpers to land on the roof. It made him a little embarrassed that he had been so frantic, but he knew that they had no idea how fast a fire could consume a house.

He finally sat on the porch and tried to regain his composure. In spite of there being no fire, Tucker knew there had been something. But it was little comfort if the fire, in fact, did not exist; denial was not a virtue he admired. He did convince himself to buy fire extinguishers for every floor and a bigger one for the workroom.

He finally yawned, got up, and headed for the trailer.

He smelled smoke again. Struggling to keep from leaping for the hose, he urgently followed the smell, straining to differentiate it from the surrounding odors of wood, sawdust, paint, food, grill, plaster, and the other strong scents in the house. Frantically sniffing, he quickly walked up the stairway to the third floor where the smell of smoke was the strongest.

He could hardly stand not to rush away, not to shout for help, not to repeat his actions of an hour before. He resisted, however, finally coming into the third floor bedroom that was above the library on the first floor.

He forced himself to stand still, close his eyes, and wait. He smelled the sweet, pungent odor of juniper and the strong scent of *piñon*.

What the hell?

The timbers of the house were ponderosa pine and fir, and most of the floors and trim work were oak and mahogany. And every piece of wood in the house was a century from being strongly scented. It was no house fire that he smelled—it was a campfire. And it was strongest in that room.

"Samuel!"

Who said that? Tucker glanced down the hallways and stairs, then through the window to the dorm below. There was no movement that he could see and all the lights were out. Who would be in the house now?

Returning to peer out the window, Tucker found a wall and slumped down, shaking his head.

What in the hell is happening to me?

He knew he was tired, and searching for fire within the house had drained what little energy he had left. But he didn't think he was going crazy.

"Samuel! You need to be up!"

Tucker's head jerked up. It was a real voice. Somebody was calling up the back stairway. The voice was loud and clear but he didn't recognize it. Who could it be? He was entirely confused. He tried to get up but his legs didn't respond. He leaned forward and put his head in his hands.

He felt exhausted. And the smell of the campfire was getting stronger.

Tucker felt his remaining strength drain from his body. He shook his head, stretched his neck muscles, bent his back, and slowly collapsed onto the floor. His eyes closed.

Wisps of smoke drifted up from the cracks in the floor, made little innocent swirls in the air, and soon slid over Tucker's body.

"Samuel!"

12

"Samuel! You need to be up! It's a special day!"

Sam Mulvaney hunkered deep into the cool of his sheets and tried to imagine how a cow might be trained to milk itself. He finally yawned, stretched, and turned his head to watch a ray of sunlight slice across the blue and yellow flowers in the wallpaper across the room.

The best time of the day was the early morning, the moisture in the air making the smells coming from the kitchen downstairs even better. Another hour and the sun would be hot and harsh, drying the air to only a whisper of moisture, and carrying only the smells of dust, sagebrush, and juniper trees.

Sam crawled from his bed, stretched again, slipped his shirt over his head, and then pulled on his overalls. He had to wear the shirt. If he didn't, his shoulders would be covered with freckles by afternoon. Struggling into his boots, he heard the clanking of pans downstairs.

Father had let the cook go at the beginning of the summer, and Mother had taken on cooking for everyone, though most of the ranch hands had been smart and followed the cook. Mother was a better cook now, but her meals in the beginning had been a challenge some of the hands couldn't abide.

Sam ran his fingers through his hair in front of the mirror—an unruly mop of bright red hair just like his father. From beneath the hair, a tall, thin, light-skinned boy with freckles looked back, ten years old today. He yawned again.

Milking the cows was his first chore every morning. The ranch hands had already been up, roped their horses out of the corral, saddled, breakfasted, and moved on with the ranch work for the day. That left the barn empty except for the two milk cows, and they'd be making a racket if Sam were late. From the two, he would get a whole bucket of milk, enough for breakfast and lunch and for making a couple of pounds of butter. They'd be ready for another milking in late afternoon.

This was Sam's chore every morning, every afternoon, every day.

He hurried more than usual. The party wasn't until afternoon, but he felt the need to get his chores out of the way. He wanted it to be a special day, from the first minute to the last. Being this far from the other ranches, and it being his birthday only once a year, he didn't want to waste a moment.

"That's a good boy," his mother said as he brought the bucket in and poured the milk through a cloth strainer into the big crock. "It's a special day! You're already ten years old! I expect that, by next year, you'll be up with the hands and herding cattle like a grown-up. But for this morning, I'm making special pancakes."

Oh, no, Sam was thinking. It wasn't that she didn't make them right, but either the lumps were the size of his thumbnail or the batter was so thin that the pancakes broke to pieces when they were flipped. He preferred eggs because it took more effort to ruin eggs. He'd have to make sure plenty of butter and honey was on the table.

Lucy, as usual, was talking a blue streak. Four years younger than he, her chores were few and would be done with Mother. Lucy had the same red hair as their father, but hers was long and always more manageable. She and her mother loved to spend hours combing and braiding her hair, turning and twisting it into different styles.

"Okay, it's time. Come over here, birthday boy!"

Sam stood with his back against the door facing of the pantry. Mother held her largest butcher knife delicately balanced on his head, holding it flat, trying to mush down the unruly hair so she could measure directly over to the facing. She nicked it, moved Sam from underneath, and then sliced a notch into the wood.

"You forgot to subtract for my boots," he reminded her.

She became flustered, then put another notch about an inch below the first. "Oh, that will do. You're getting so tall!" She found a pencil and wrote August 10, 1870 next to the notch.

Far above his new mark, almost to the top of the door, Sam could see his father's mark. Sam had asked him to stand there, to hold the knife as Sam stood on a chair, still having to reach up to put a scratch into the wood at his father's height. Father then put him on his shoulders so he could cut a large notch into the door facing.

Sam considered how far he had to grow to match his father. He was already a head taller than all of his friends, just as his father was taller than his friends, but Sam still thought he wasn't growing fast enough. He wanted to be able to ride with the hands, to learn how to rope horses and cattle and, especially, to hunt antelope up on the plains. He'd already been using the small rifles, but Father refused to let him fire the Sharps.

"Your father's working in his study this morning, so you two make sure to keep everything quiet," his mother said, waving a spoon as it slung drips of batter across the floor. "Samuel, move the cows upriver to fresh grass. We need to get them fattened up before the cold comes. After lunch, I'll bake the best birthday cake you've ever seen and we'll get the house ready for the party."

Sam had to admit that the pancakes were better than usual. Mother had taken Lucy to the thickets across the river and gathered almost a whole pail of raspberries. Mixing those with the batter, and getting the thickness good enough, the pancakes had come out fine. Still dripping a generous amount of honey on his stack, he considered that this breakfast was a good start to his special day.

When Sam had finished his pancakes, he got the cows out of the barn and started up the road. He was soon flicking the end of a rope against the two waddling rumps ahead of him. The air was still and already losing its freshness. He breathed deeply as the road swung by the river, watching the busyness of bees as they hovered in and around the wildflowers randomly sprouting from the tall grass. He loved walking along the banks of the river when the smells of the grasses and reeds hung strong and wet in the morning air.

Sam caught a quick movement from the corner of his eye, but before he could turn, a rough hand stuffed a wad of something in his mouth and a muscled arm looped a rope around him that held his arms tight against his body. Before he even had time to react, two men had him hog-tied and shoved into the grass beside the road.

He could see them clearly—two deeply tanned men with paint on their faces, chests, and arms. They wore no shirts but had deerskin leggings and breechclouts fringed with tassels.

They were Comanches, the most vicious Indians in the Territory, Father had told him. Sam tried to yell out but the gag almost choked him.

The two men ran up on the last cow and quickly cut its throat. Before the cow was barely on her side, her bag was cut off and was held aloft as a prize. The braves juggled the bag to their mouths and gulped as much milk as was left in the udder, the white juice mixing with the red of the animal's blood as it ran over their faces.

Sam watched in horror as the cow on the ground still trembled. One brave hacked deep into the hindquarter of the cow, ripped back the hide and cut several strips of meat, putting strips in his mouth and throwing some to his partner. The soft skin of the stomach was slit and a long piece of gut fingered and yanked from the belly. Long enough to encircle the buck's waist a couple of times, it was cut, wrapped around him, and tied. The Indian would eat the gut as he rode, Sam had been told, squeezing the innards of the intestine into his mouth until the whole length was consumed.

Satisfied, the two young men gave a string of shrill calls and whoops and shot their arrows into the cow and toward the house. One of them grabbed Sam around the waist and half-drug him to horses tied in the bushes next to the canyon wall.

Sitting him upright behind the biggest buck, the other brave tied one of Sam's feet with a leather strap, ran it under the horse, and tied it to his other foot. His hands were bound the same way around the waist of his captor. Sam realized that this made it impossible to escape; if he slipped to one side of the horse or the other, he'd hang under the hooves and be trampled.

The second Indian quickly straddled his horse and a race was on. The horses charged up the riverbed.

Sam's hands were soon hurting from the rawhide around his wrists, but his legs hurt worse. His thighs rubbed hard up against the Indian saddle, which was more like a pack saddle than a western saddle, and it was only a couple of hours before the tough fabric of his overalls tore and his skin was smeared with blood.

The shield held by the brave was in constant motion, and it was scraping Sam's arm raw, but falling to the side or slipping back over the rump of the horse filled him with a fear that overwhelmed the pain of his body. Sam held on tight.

He was being stolen—kidnapped—and there was not one thing he could do about it. The ranch hands had told him stories of Indians stealing children, taking them back to their camps, torturing them, roasting them over fires, and eating them alive. The images raced through his brain, and any remaining composure he had gave way to panic, then to desperation and despair. Sam screamed through his spit-soaked gag and sobbed between the jolts of pain.

The two bucks rode for hours, driving their horses viciously in and out of the canyons, onto mesa tops, and out into the high country foothills. Sam could tell that they changed directions repeatedly. Once, they stopped and set fire to the tall grass around them, riding ahead of the flames as the smoke covered them and the swirling wind currents destroyed their tracks.

By dark, they had reached a deep ravine far to the north of the ranch. Below, five or six other braves squatted next to a string of horses. Sam's bonds were cut and he was thrown to the ground. A horse had been killed and cut open, and a fire had been built. Hunks of meat were wrapped around sticks and held above the fire, the bubbling fat dripping into the flames.

In a few minutes, the liver of the horse, half-burnt, was given to Sam, and he hungrily bit off chunks and swallowed, hardly waiting to chew, and then he vomited. A few minutes more and the band of raiders remounted their horses. Sam was shoved onto one of the stolen ponies, his legs retied around the belly of the horse and his hands around the neck.

The Comanches drove their horses harder than before. Day after day, night after night, the band of raiders dashed across the land, stopping for only a few hours of sleep. Sometimes they headed toward the sun, sometimes away, sometimes back across the land from where they had come.

The land changed from mountains to vast stretches of grassland, flat and empty, with no trees, no rivers, no mesas. Only grass. A sea of tall, dry, yellowish-green grass that ran to the horizon, with long, slow, ocean-like waves as the wind blew over it.

Once on the plains, the hard-riding group made longer stops to eat and sleep. Sam was viciously hot, hungry, thirsty, tired, and sore. Being strapped to the horse had tortured his muscles to almost uselessness. Only his fear continued to force his hands to hold on. His back, shoulders, and arms were long sunburned through his shirt, and large blisters had come and gone under the straps of his overalls. He cried from the pain. He could feel the heat constantly on his forehead and knew that freckles covered his entire face.

Every so often, the raiding party stopped, dug a shallow hole in the ground and filled it with stalks of dry grass that were then set alight using steel and flint. Handfuls of greener, wetter grass were thrown into the flames to make a thick, black smoke. Using a blanket to cover and then uncover the column of smoke, individual puffs billowed high into the sky. Soon after, other Indians appeared on the horizon to join them, usually with horses but sometimes mules, and sometimes with other captives—white, brown, black— all children. Within a week, more than a hundred braves were pushing upward of three hundred horses and mules across the empty plains. Among them were strapped a dozen small faces.

While they halted for the night, Sam tried to talk to the other children. They were mostly from Texas, but some were from the Indian Territories and some from the Territory of New Mexico. They were as young as seven and as old as twelve. Two or three spoke Spanish, a little of which Sam had learned from the ranch hands. Several spoke German, which he recognized as the language the store owner in Las Vegas spoke who sold his mother material for dresses.

All of them talked in frightened whispers and tired tears.

Where are you from? How old are you? Anybody coming after you?

Don't know, but pretty sure the army's coming; my family's coming; my father's coming; won't be long; they're right behind us.

But Sam thought that, except for the youngest, they all knew that there was no hope. No one was coming. Their capture had been too quick, the Indians too fast, and the country too hard.

Nobody ever caught the Comanche.

A week later, or perhaps two, the sea of grass abruptly halted on the rim of a wide canyon, far wider than what Sam had ever seen and several hundred feet deep. Rimmed by high cliffs of sandstone, the rugged canyon had appeared out of the north and broadened into a wide gash through the flat plain around it. A small stream wound back and forth down the center of the canyon. The canyon cliffs around Sam's family's ranch were uniform in color, but these canyon walls were striped with reds, whites, browns, and tans.

As his pony was led down a steep, narrow, dusty trail, Sam saw teepees scattered up and down the canyon floor in both directions. Women, men, and children of all ages were bustling about. The teepees had various symbols drawn in yellow, red, and black, and painted shields decorated with feathers hung around the entry ways. Scattered among the teepees were quivers full of arrows, long bows, hatchets, long guns, hides stretched across forms for drying, huge buffalo robes, and blankets. Ropes were strung between poles, dripping with what Sam thought were strips of meat.

As the warriors worked their way down the trail, the canyon echoed with shouts and yells and whoops. As they were finally riding between the teepees, people touched the braves as they passed by, calling out in excited voices, slapping their thighs in congratulations. Sam was soon yanked off his pony and separated from the others. He could see other children that were white-skinned like him, but they were wearing breeches and moccasins. They silently looked at him as he was hustled through the camp.

His overalls, shirt, and boots were taken, and Sam was immediately thrown into the stream. The dirt of almost a month's worth of travel was scoured from his skin and hair by three squaws. They were not gentle and his skin burned under their scrubbing.

From the stream, he was brought, still naked, directly before the Chief of all the Comanche in the canyon. The old man ran his hand through Sam's thick red hair, already dry and frizzy.

His hair was his everlasting gift from his father, Mother used to say. Not one man in a hundred has hair like this, Father used to say.

The Chief held Sam's hair tight in his hand, shook it, then turned him back to the squaws. They herded him away. Outside the Chief's teepee, he was given a set of breeches and several pair of moccasins. After he had pulled the clothes on, the squaws began swatting him with sticks, forcing him to join in the common labor, gathering wood and water, carrying blankets, tending the fire, beating the dust from buffalo hides, rolling and unrolling blankets— all under a constant barrage of a language he did not understand. If he was caught doing nothing, they beat him even more.

There was no time for any tears, no one to cradle him or to give him hope. He could barely breathe, and he wished that he could find some corner in which to curl up and cry, to let go and scream, to bury his face away from the reality of being forever taken from his family. But there was no time that they were not watching him, were not brutalizing him, were not constantly punishing him out of thinking whatever he was thinking.

He stopped thinking as much as he could.

The afternoon of the next day, in a broad meadow, a ring was created by circling ropes around poles. Sam was sure the captives would now be roasted and eaten as in the stories the ranch hands had told him.

Steady drum beats filled the air, and he and the other boys, in their turn, were pushed into the middle of the ring to meet Indian boys of similar size. For Sam, this meant boys older than he was. Each meeting was a fight, and the crowd cheered and laughed as Sam was twisted, turned, thrown, punched, kicked, and wrestled while he cried, yelled, and blubbered. Bloodied and dirty beyond recognition, he was drug from the ring and thrown into the stream to wash himself.

That night, the Chief spoke to him. Sam used what Spanish he had learned at the ranch, and the Chief knew enough that they could make each other understood. The fighting in the ring was not punishment, but training, the Chief said. Sam was no longer white—that was in his past. Sam was now Comanche, and he was expected to learn the ways of the Comanche and become a warrior. The Chief had watched him, he told Sam. Sam had done well enough in the fights, but it was his hair that was the omen the Chief desired, a good sign. Sam now belonged to the Chief's family.

He was no longer a captive; he was a son.

13

Tucker slowly opened one eye, then the other. He blinked and took a deep breath.

Every part of his body felt like it had been pounded with hammers. Woozy, nauseous, unbalanced, Tucker tried to stretch his muscles but almost passed out in the attempt. It was like his body had been twisted and strung over a board, then raked with a fork. The inside of his thighs felt like raw meat. He tried to look at his legs but couldn't bend his neck to look down.

He attempted turning on his side, but pain shot up his shoulders and neck. Finally, without moving, he directed his eyes through the window above him where the canyon cliffs were lit by soft daylight. The sun was not yet directly on them. It had to be early morning.

Why was he on the floor?

He managed to rotate his head enough to see more of his surroundings.

The wallpaper.

He watched a glowing patch of sunlight as it appeared on the wall. It grew, narrowed, and focused, until a sharp sliver of bright light cut across the dirty flowers of the wallpaper.

The boy. The Comanche.

His mind coming out of a fog, Tucker began to remember. The images became more distinct, the colors filled in, the smells more vibrant—of sweat, blood, and terror—and he could now hear the noises of the encampment along the river.

He blinked hard to clear his eyes, gave them a good rub, and coughed. He'd never had such a vivid dream. And sleeping on a bare wood floor was a torture he hadn't experienced in a long time.

Tucker twisted his head and found the aches and pains significantly less. Struggling into a sitting position, his thighs did not hurt as badly. Carefully, he rolled onto his knees, put a foot out, and stood up. The aches and pains that had bound him to the floor a few moments before were fading away.

Pans were rattling downstairs, and so he carefully held onto the wall as he found the door, stiffly walked through the doorway and cautiously stepped down the stairs. Connie was busy cooking on the side porch. He paused to watch her, then went down the stairway into the basement. The four teenagers were already surrounding the dining table, yawning with bleary eyes, waiting.

"Hey, boss. We thought maybe you'd died. You almost missed breakfast, amigo!"

Tucker found a chair, plopped down into the seat, and pulled up to the table.

"You would not believe what I did," Tucker said. He related his sleeping the night in the third floor bedroom and repeated the dream as much as he could. He didn't tell them about smelling smoke again.

"Dude! You been working too hard!" Tommy said as everybody laughed.

Tucker was still confused as he recited the dream. How did he know all that stuff about Indians? He remembered the stripes on the faces of the Comanches, even the color of their horses. And the view from the canyon rim—where was that?

Connie appeared and set a plate of three pancakes in front of him.

Tucker smelled the aroma, and then used his fork to test the texture and to play in the butter Connie had scooped on top.

"Do you have any honey?"

Connie grimaced as she rummaged around in a cardboard box that held various bottles from the kitchen. She found the honey and put it on the table. Tucker squirted a load on top of his stack and attacked the pancakes with an unusual degree of hunger.

"We need to start working on our schedules," Connie said as she sat down. "Somebody's going to have to take Rose to school every day."

Tucker stopped eating his pancakes as a rush of reality overcame his memories.

Damn. How did he forget that? How did he not remember?

Not only would the twins soon be leaving, but Rose needed to go back to school. And Rico. Tucker had forgotten about him too. Highlands University in Las Vegas offered classes that would get Rico a GED by December. The classes met twice a week, Tuesday and Thursday evenings, so Rico would have to go into town twice a week. Rose had to go every day, and somebody would have to take her and bring her back. Tucker was not only losing the twins, but losing Rose and Rico as well, at least for some part of every work week. And Connie was going to be on the road a lot.

He'd be the only one dedicated to working on the house.

Tucker went to the trailer and got his calendar. He returned and sat at the table. Moving his plate to one side, he flipped open his large format calendar to August and looked at the date. Today was August 10th, a Friday. He had written notes in all of the calendar's spaces: when contractors were starting or finishing, material delivery times, messages about preparations and tools. He flipped to September, October, then November. He was thinking about what he had expected in terms of work, starting dates, ending dates, and notations about the weather.

He wasn't going to make it.

"Tucker!" Connie said.

He looked up. All eyes of the people around the table were on him.

"Mama," Rico said. "You need to get this guy to take a break."

The twins were laughing. "Man, you didn't get any sleep at all, dude! You need to go back to bed. Get some shut-eye, man!"

Tucker sat back in his chair, embarrassed.

Connie laughed. "Okay. Well, let's see if we can talk about schedules. Rose needs to go to school starting next week."

"I don't need to go back to school," Rose said. "I can make it just fine."

She pulled a magazine from her lap, laid it on the table, and opened it to a half-page advertisement. It was one of Tucker's construction magazines, and the ad described a company's training courses for becoming an interior decorator.

"This is what I want to do. I don't need to go back to school. I can get a GED like Rico and be taking these courses online. I could get a job in six months."

Rico remained still but the twins crowded around as Tucker and Connie read the ad.

"I really like doing the stuff that we're doing," Rose said. "And I've really liked talking about how the house is going to be decorated, the paints and colors, curtains, furniture, and lights and stuff. That's what I want to do. If Rico can learn enough here to get a job in town, then I want to be able to work with the contractors, too, helping them making their houses pretty."

Tucker sat back in his chair. "I think interior decorating is a fine career, and I know that contractors value people who do it well. But you need to know math to figure quantities, and history to understand styles, and science to know materials, and English to talk well to customers. You're not going to school just to spend time until you don't have to go anymore. You're going to learn how to get knowledge and learn how to use it. And you're going so that you can compete with other interior designers. If they look, sound, think, and speak better than you do, then they'll get the jobs and you won't.

"You're going back to school," Tucker said emphatically. "We'll get you there and get you back. And Rico's going to have his GED by Christmas. These are not negotiable. Just like a house has to have a good foundation, people have to have a good foundation, and that's being educated. You have to be intelligent to be successful."

Tucker not only stated the case with conviction but he allowed no discussion, and so Connie started writing out the schedule as Rose sat back with an expression of defeat.

Rose needed to go every day. That was an hour into town and an hour back. If someone took her, came back to work, then returned for her, that accounted for four hours out of each day. But Tucker usually averaged one trip into town every week for supplies, and so he could get her there at least once a week. Connie went to get groceries and to do laundry once a week, and Rose would be able to drive on her own in a few months. Rico needed to be in town on Tuesday and Thursday evenings and so could drive twice a week, dropping Rose at school in the morning, going to the college to study during the day, attending his classes in the evening while Rose did her homework in the Highlands library, and then the two of them would come back late.

Tucker also wanted Rose to find a pre-natal class and made it a rule that she start regular visits to the doctor's office. He assumed her parents had insurance.

They worked out a complex schedule over the next half hour, which accounted for everything except working on the house. It was painfully obvious to Tucker that rebuilding work would be cut back by more than three-quarters of the summer level. There could even be a time period during the week when no one—no one—was actually working on the house.

Tucker sat at the table with his chin in his hands, glum. He stared at his calendar trying to figure out how he had missed it all. His calendar was useless. There was no way to get the house ready to be occupied before it got cold. The twins and he had worked for a week and only gotten the kitchen to the bare walls. It would take, what? Four to six weeks to get the plaster down in the other rooms? Then electrical, plumbing, insulation, sheetrock?

"What we going to do today, boss?" Tony asked.

Tucker lowered his head into his hands. What to do at all?

"A party," Tucker said quietly.

Everyone was looking at him again.

Tucker raised his head and sat back in his chair.

"A party. He never got his party."

Rose didn't understand. "He who? What party? What are you talking about?" The twins were laughing again, and Connie was shaking her head.

Tucker finally looked at the people around the table and smiled. "Today is August the tenth. This is Sam Mulvaney's birthday. Remember the story? He was kidnapped on the morning of his tenth birthday, just like in my dream. His birthday party was going to be that afternoon. He never got to have his tenth birthday party and so we're going to have it for him. While you guys are stripping the shelves out of the pantries and getting everything cleaned up, I'm going to town to buy us a birthday cake, a real birthday cake with real frosting, some candles, and some ice cream. We'll have a party this afternoon before Connie takes the twins back to town."

After Tony and Tommy erupted with even more laughter, everyone shook their heads and went about business.

And, right after lunch, they all had a birthday party.

It was a nice, quiet party, not at all what Sam Mulvaney would have wanted.

After Tucker had wished Sam a happy birthday, they all gathered around to blow out the ten candles. The back door to the house suddenly opened and a gust of wind swirled through the basement, snuffing the flames from the candles as if Sam himself had leaned over and blown them out.

The door swung back and closed by itself.

14

It took the weekend and two days of exhausting himself before Tucker gave up. He had thought that maybe by working weekends and evenings, he might be able to get the schedule back on track. But what he had done just emphasized that, if the schedule was totally dependent on him, it would never satisfy the sheer volume of work that needed to be done. Getting the rooms deconstructed, cleaned, electrified, plumbed, insulated, sheetrocked, taped, textured, painted, and heated with all of the fixtures, appliances, and furniture in place would clearly be impossible before the weather turned the house into an ice cube. It would take at least two months more than what he had anticipated.

There was no hope.

Connie, Rose, and Rico needed to move back to town. That was the only way for them to have the decent living arrangements that they needed. He was hoping that Connie would be okay with that. It had been more than a month and Armando hadn't reappeared. With the police still hot to find him, Tucker thought that she and the others would be out of danger living in her house.

He considered it a fact that no one could live in the dorm during the winter. Rico argued with him, but Rico had not experienced the dorm when it was cold. He had no idea how much Tucker had to run his heaters on a cold day just to be able to work in the single room workshop. And even if it was heated, winter in the dorm would be impossible for Rose. She'd been sick every morning for the last three weeks. Even if she felt better the rest of the time, the confined space, the inconvenience of the bathroom, and the lack of amenities like a personal TV, rocking chair, recliner, constant room temperature, and company would be, in a word, miserable.

Tucker remembered what it had been like for Jennie when she was carrying Sara. The key words were "consistent comfort and family support," and that wasn't offered by a facility that resembled a penitentiary. Rose had a March delivery date, which meant she would be living in the dorm during the last trimester. Jennie would have booted him out of the house if he had even suggested that pathetic level of accommodation. Besides, what would they do when the baby came?

School began the middle of August. In fact, the twins had gone home after Sam's birthday party, consulted with their parents, and came back the next week for only a single day, long enough to gather their stuff, clean the rooms, and give their parents one last tour of the work they had done. Tucker gave them another cash bonus and guaranteed them a place on the work crew for the next summer if they wanted it.

Rico and Rose got registered and their schedules finalized. Rico started his evening classes two weeks after Rose started her senior year at the high school. He had also signed up for an on-line electrician's course that he could take at the school's computer center, starting whenever he wanted. He'd be gone all day on Tuesdays and Thursdays, and Rose would be gone every day.

"Connie, I'm sorry," Tucker said one morning. "But the three of you need to plan on moving to town." He had waited until Rico and Rose had left for school.

Connie didn't seem surprised. She had been in charge of the weekly schedule and knew that work on the house had slowed considerably.

"Do we have any options?" she asked. "Can the work be done at night? Can you hire someone else? Can I pay for more help?"

She continued with more ideas. He was surprised how much she did not want to move and assumed the fear of Armando must be stronger than he had thought. He also guessed that she wanted to keep Rico at the ranch. She didn't want to put him back into contact with his old friends. Besides, Rico had never had much of a father, and Tucker was acting not only as a boss but as a mentor.

"I've worked on the schedule as much as I can," Tucker replied. "There's just too much work. It will take us a month or more to remove the plaster at the rate that we're going, and it will be getting cold in the dorm by the time we're finished. All the work after that will take a couple of months and we'll be December before anybody could even consider moving into the house."

Connie looked sad. She obviously liked the ranch. He hadn't thought about how different life had been for her.

"How about this," she said. "Let's get Larry Jackson's building class to come out on a Saturday and take all the plaster down. We could provide lunch and drinks. He could probably bring a couple of dozen kids. They'd have a great time, and when they leave, you'll have all the plaster down."

Tucker was shocked at the idea. "Are you kidding? I can't imagine giving hammers and crowbars to a mass of teenagers in an open field much less inside a real house. It could turn this place into a war zone."

"You are too mistrustful," Connie responded. "They'd be fine. Kids can manage if you just let them. Larry would earn respect, the teenagers would like working, and they would get done in one day what would otherwise take weeks."

It took a few more minutes of mulling it over, but Tucker was finally convinced that it might just work. Proposing it later, Larry was enthusiastic about the request. He confided to Tucker that he felt stuck only being able to talk about building practices and that he'd love to have some excuse for his students to actually grab hammers and beat on something. It took a couple of visits to work out the details.

In addition to targeting the pantries, dining room, the two upper bedrooms and bathroom, Tucker included the first and second floor hallways, the back stairwell, plus the big bedroom that was directly over the library. That would give them an extra bedroom if they needed it in the winter. After it was all finished, the whole back of the house on the first and second floors would be available for living on a full-time basis. They would drape plastic across the openings to the rest of the house to keep the heat inside the finished areas.

Early on the second Saturday of September, a bus full of teenagers pulled up in front of the house, followed by a half-dozen cars.

Several parents had asked to join the effort. The rumors of what was going to happen at the house had spread from the twins to their friends and their friends' families. The adults felt they were missing out on something, and so Larry started getting phone calls. By that point, Tucker was happy for anyone to come. He was more worried about the house staying quiet.

He hired the twins for the day and put them in charge of work crews to pull down the plaster and lath. Other students worked at getting the broken plaster out of the rooms. The week before, Tucker and Rico had removed a window from the dining room and a window from the bedroom above it, then built plywood and two-by-four chutes from the windows down to the ground, the chutes sloped so that the broken plaster rubble would slide straight into trash cans. Full trash cans would then be emptied into the trash bin and returned to the chutes. This strategy greatly decreased the amount of work needed to get trash to the bins, and it lowered traffic in the hallways and stairs.

Rico was sufficiently healed from his cracked ribs to take on his share of the work. He was definitely his mother, in both body and temperament: friendly but shy, naturally kind and patient, and unsure of his authority. He was hesitant to do anything that he hadn't done before. He was also sensitive to surprises, being startled if someone came up behind him, and he grew anxious when he knew that Tucker would be checking his work. In spite of that, he, like Rose, had taken a liking to the construction business. He was envious of electricians after he found out their typical salaries, and he was now hoping to learn enough from Tucker and the on-line courses that he could earn an electrician's license. That would give him the potential of a real job, of working for real money.

With Rico increasingly involved in the rebuilding work and becoming less dependent on Rose and Connie, the quality and quantity of work had gotten better in the last weeks of August. Though the efforts needed to live day to day consumed most of the spare time, no one seemed resentful of working on the house. Tucker, as well, had grown accustomed to the family activities.

They would do what they could do, and he was satisfied with the progress.

That left Lynn. Things weren't going so well.

Tucker didn't understand. He was working as hard as he could, and he was more than benevolent with the people at the ranch. He was more than generous with his money, time, and patience, and even the house had been exceptionally quiet. But Lynn seemed to come less often, and she remained fewer minutes when she did. What was he supposed to do? He missed her, that was clear, and he wished that he could give her more attention, but the schedule demanded that even his weekends had been sucked into the rebuilding efforts. Friends were supposed to recognize the obligations and sacrifices involved in one's life, and so he didn't understand her reaction.

At least he got her to help with the high school plaster party. She even seemed enthusiastic and volunteered to get Larry's wife to help. That was a hopeful sign.

And so the day finally arrived.

After the bus full of teenagers pulled up in front of the house, things couldn't have gone better. The house was so significantly different from people's ordinary houses that working inside was more entertainment than drudgery. Other than the rules of the house—no cussing, no smoking, no trash, no loud music—Tucker had few constraints, allowing anyone to go anywhere on the ranch. Accepting that as a gesture of trust, everyone was careful, worked with their gloves, protective glasses, and masks on, showed enthusiasm in accomplishing the goals for the day, and still had enough casual time to wander through the house, visit the river, and check out the ranch in general. The trash bin was overflowing by mid-afternoon, and the rubble from the trash cans was dumped directly onto the ground. Tucker and Rico could clean it up when an empty bin was delivered.

The adults worked like they were having fun. Two of them were so enthusiastic about the modern plumbing system that Tucker had them installing the plastic-like tubing, called PEX, into the kitchen. The PEX tubing carried the hot or cold water to the fixtures from the water outlets in the basement. Thirty minutes later, two other men were hammering in electrical boxes and running wires between them. Tucker asked Rico to work with them to make sure it was correct.

Larry was also a standout, helping the teenagers as needed, regulating who was doing what, shifting people between the different activities as they tired, inhaled too much dust, or got bored.

Lynn and Charlene, Larry's wife, who worked at Walmart during the week, came in the late morning. Together with Connie, they hosted a sandwich buffet for lunch, kept a steady stream of snacks and drinks flowing during the afternoon, and then put Tucker on grill duty for a hamburger and hot dog feast after the work was done. They moved the dining table and chairs up from the basement and into the front parlor, trying to keep it as far from the work space and its dust as possible, but making it readily available to the workers.

Tucker declared the work finished at 5:30, but he was still watching parents pull electrical wire and the PEX tubing thirty minutes later. The work in the bedroom over the library was left incomplete—the plaster on the walls had been taken down but the twins had not made it to the room in time to attack the ceiling. He thought it was better not to start something that could not be finished, and so they wrapped up the work by getting the scrap down the chutes and into the rubble pile.

Finally getting the parents to cease, and before stoking up the grill, Tucker wanted to show everyone what he had discovered. He had found it in August, after the twins left.

Without the shelves, the storage pantry was a surprisingly large room. Looking over the room, imagining the plaster being removed and the new electrical wiring being put in, Tucker noticed a few loose linoleum tiles. He used his knife to slide around the edges and, one by one, pried them off the floor. The wood underneath was not the same flooring material as the kitchen and other rooms. Widening his removal of squares, he found that a rectangular piece of flooring in the center of the room had been cut out. Different boards, not even flooring boards, had been placed into the rectangle as if someone had patched an opening.

Along the right side of the room and under the counter was another patch of the same kind, maybe two feet wide and extending from inside the doorway to halfway across the room.

Tucker got his tools and went to work. In less than thirty minutes, he had removed both patches, opening two sizeable holes in the floor.

He found the cistern. It had always bothered him that he had never found the massive reservoir that would have been used to store water for the house. And he also found more evidence of Sam Mulvaney.

"Before we begin eating, let me speak for a minute," Tucker said to the noisy crowd of teenagers. He asked everyone to gather in the kitchen, which was a tight fit. The teenagers nonchalantly plopped down on the floor, whereas the parents found leaning against the walls more feasible.

"I'm sure that Mr. Jackson has told you the history of the Mulvaney house, and you've probably seen more pictures than you were interested in. I want to show you something you haven't seen—a secret room." That got their attention; everyone stopped talking.

"I didn't know this room existed until I found it in August, and I promise that everyone will get a chance to go into it and see up close what I'm about to tell you. But I have a question first. How did people keep their milk cold in 1868?"

Someone finally said, "Ice."

"That's right," Tucker responded. "The predecessor to the refrigerator that you have at home was called an icebox, an insulated container in which a block of ice was placed on one side and the other side contained the milk, eggs, and butter that they wanted to keep cool. You've probably all seen one in an antique store or museum."

Tucker walked in front of the storage pantry and pointed to the back wall. "In a Victorian house in the 1860s, there would have been an opening in the back wall of this pantry that was covered by an insulated door on the outside of the wall. The carpenter would have built an insulated box around the opening on the inside, which had the two compartments, one for ice and one for the foodstuffs. Periodically, maybe every day or maybe every other day, early in the morning, an ice wagon would pull up in front of the house and the ice man, using ice tongs, would take a block of ice around to the back porch, open the insulated door of the ice box, and slide the ice inside. He never needed to go into the house.

[133]

"That's how the ordinary house in St. Louis worked. But how did Cyrus Mulvaney keep his milk cold? There was no ice man to come to his house. An 'icebox' was useless to him."

Tucker leaned over and lifted a sheet of plywood he had laid across the storage pantry floor, revealing the two rectangular holes. The teenagers stood and crowded around, elbowing each other as they strained to see the floor.

"Below the big hole in the floor is the cistern. A cistern is a big, big jar in the ground, maybe eight feet high and eight feet in diameter with a round bottom and an opening that got smaller toward the top, just like a jar. Masons built it out of bricks and then covered the bricks with a thick layer of cement on the inside to make it waterproof.

"All of the water used inside the house came from the cistern. Either a bucket was lowered into the water and drawn back up or a small hand pump was mounted above it and the water was collected as it came out of the spout. The cistern was filled by rain water, by taking water from a stream, by laying a pipe into a spring, or by pumping water from below ground using a windmill.

"The water for this house finally made it into the cistern by coming through an underground pipe. It's right there," he said, pointing back into the hole. "That means that Cyrus Mulvaney either had a spring or a windmill. The water came out the pipe and ran into the inlet hole of the cistern. The cistern, by the way, has an overflow hole just like your sinks at home. When the cistern filled up, the water would run through the overflow hole into the waste pipes of the house.

"Now, Cyrus Mulvaney did an inventive thing with his cistern. He had the masons put a big cement lip around the top that started several inches below the inlet hole and stopped a couple of inches above the hole. The water from the pipe would run into the lip and create a little pool several inches deep before the water ran into the cistern."

Tucker moved back into the kitchen area. "Cyrus Mulvaney kept his milk cold by running cold water over it. A servant would lower a bottle of milk from above and put it into the water flowing around the lip of the cistern. When the family was ready to drink it, they would pull the bottle of milk up. It would have been cooled to the temperature of the water."

Lynn squeezed into the doorway and waved at him, pointing at her watch to stop lecturing and get the meats on the grill so supper could be finished before it got dark. But Tucker had one more item to convey.

Tucker retrieved a cardboard box from the kitchen floor. He asked for their attention one more time, promising that supper was just a few minutes away.

"When I found the cistern, I found something else." The group quieted as he opened the box and took out five small pieces of wood. About five to seven inches long and two or three inches wide, the wood looked like cut-offs from the pickets of the small fence out back. A couple were more crude, but all were primitive. Narrowed at one end or both, perhaps by a pen knife or a saw, they all had short, well-used, round pencils projecting out of the surface. Three of them had remnants of paint, and four of them had square pieces of brittle cloth pressed down around the pencils.

Tucker held them up to the crowd. "I found these in the lip of the cistern. If my guess is correct, these are a child's play boats, complete with sails. I believe that Sam Mulvaney, Cyrus's young son, made them so he could play in the water that flowed around the cistern's lip. I'll pass them around, but be careful with them. The last time they were played with was about a hundred and forty years ago."

There were oohs and aahs from the people in the room as each person took one or passed one along. Tucker asked for them to be returned to the box, then finished his presentation by pointing out the larger access hole to the side and the built-in ladder. Everyone was welcome to climb down beside the cistern and look at the arrangement of the pipe and the lip. He had rigged up lights so that people could see.

Lynn hustled him out to the grill. All the teenagers and parents had formed a line in front of the pantry. Everybody wanted to go down into the hidden room.

It took an hour to get everyone fed and on their way home. Tony and Tommy wanted to stay and called their parents to come get them the following afternoon. Larry finally got the rest of the students on the bus, waved goodbye, and took off on the adventure of dodging potholes by headlight. Charlene followed him with

Lynn close behind, which disappointed Tucker. He had hoped she would stay after the others had left.

Once everyone was gone and the food was put away, those staying at the ranch sat on the porch, resting and feeling the cool of the river.

Tucker lined the boats up on the porch railing.

"I've been wondering about the cistern for a long time," he said to the porch-sitters. "After I found it, I went to the basement to see why I had not figured it out before. It was right in the northwest corner of the basement all this time, but they had built a wall around it, a wall that looks just like the foundation walls. I never made the connection that it wasn't a part of the foundation.

"I also looked inside the cistern. I lowered a light down through the hole, and it's quite a mess. I don't know when it last held water, but there're a lot of bones of creatures that crawled or fell in. I expect several mice lost their lives to that hole. And, by the way, don't think about going down inside the cistern itself. You would use up the oxygen very quickly and suffocate."

He reached over to a little boat, picked it up, and turned it around in his hand.

"I was thinking about Sam and his boats. *Treasure Island* wasn't written for another ten years or so, but I'd like to think that Sam dreamed as he played, maybe of pirates and sailors, maybe of canoes and frontiersmen. These little boats, these pieces of wood with pretend sails, until I brought them up a few weeks ago, hadn't seen the light of day for almost a century and a half. I hope that the last time they were bobbing up and down in the water, Sam was a happy little boy."

15

Lynn knew that Tucker wanted her to stay.

She had used the excuse that she was tired, but she wasn't *that* tired. The ranch had just turned into more of a burden for her than the good place it had been. It was bad enough when Tucker was falling in love with a haunted house—and vice versa she guessed—but then to have a family move in and take over, well, that was downright irritating. It was a lot easier being jealous of only the house.

She understood that Tucker hadn't asked for any of it, his new housemates or their problems, that it was a collision of unfortunate circumstances. And she knew that the decision to rebuild the house to accommodate everyone during the winter was in fact the opposite of what he wanted. He wanted them to move back into town, and she wished they had.

Oh, well, she thought. She was just griping. Driving on a country road after dark always made her bitchy.

She really liked Connie, and she had enjoyed working with Charlene. But Rose had flat-out become a pain in the ass. Tucker, of course, never noticed short-comings, but today Rose had captured some of her friends and was giving them personal tours, which kept all of them from doing work. And she was always talking about how "they" were fixing up "her" house, and about the colors "she" was choosing for "her baby's room" and "her" bedroom. Lynn knew the girl's attitude could be attributed to being young, pregnant, and isolated, but it still pissed her off.

She knew Connie was becoming annoyed with Rose too. Not that Connie would ever say anything, but life had been hard enough for her with an abusive husband. Suddenly gaining a live-in princess-in-law was more tolerable, but it still wore on her patience.

Tucker should appreciate me more, Lynn thought, cutting the wheel to miss a pothole. The schedule is everything! Getting the house ready for snow is everything! Getting the utilities in is everything! How about Lynn being everything?

Maybe it was that the first half of the summer had been so good by comparison. She loved coming out on Thursday evenings, having supper, and then playing cards. It was so much fun listening to the quick banter of the twins and hearing them laugh. It livened her up. Tucker had been different too. He was relaxed, happy with how the work was going, and didn't feel the pressure of a rigid schedule.

She'd spent a lot of time thinking about her and Tucker. She had grown to like him a lot, and maybe even more than like. He might be some years older, but he was a good, strong, smart, consistent man. He was talented, dedicated, easy to be friends with...she could think of a dozen descriptors. He even had money, obviously, so she didn't have to worry about that side of things. She was in no rush to be in another marriage, and maybe not even in a full relationship rather than this halfway thing they had. But she wouldn't avoid a real relationship either, if the right man was interested.

Which Tucker didn't seem to be, and that was something she kept trying to work around. He still had his hang-ups from the past, and his refusal to allow himself to think about emotional attachments was now definitely irritating. But damn! She thought it was time for that man to face up to things. She had a lot to offer. He obviously struggled with being alone, and she could help with that. She just didn't understand. He seemed convinced that he had to stay unattached for the rest of his life, but he refused to explain why.

Lynn turned onto I-25. She had been following Charlene, who was following the school bus. They both sped up and passed the bus, and Lynn was now getting close to her exit.

Maybe ice cream would help more than a glass of wine, she thought.

She knew she shouldn't be so hard on Tucker. He was a good man in a bad situation, and he was handling it as best he could. She just wished she'd move up on his list of priorities.

16

After the intense work of the plaster party on Saturday, Sunday was a relaxed day. The twins helped Rico and Tucker thoroughly clean the demolished rooms, return all the tools to the workshop, and take off the lower trash chute and store it until spring. They still needed the upper chute for the unfinished work in the spare bedroom. The four also made a concerted effort to clean the bathrooms; the twins had learned over the summer how much more they should appreciate their mother.

The twins' parents came in the afternoon and both boys repeated Tucker's lecture on iceboxes and cisterns and play boats, and then gave a guided tour of the hidden room below.

The household meals for the day consisted of leftovers. Rose did not feel good, so she stayed on the sofa in the basement. Connie rested with a book down on the riverbank, then came back to the house to watch a movie with Rico.

Tucker read on the porch for most of the afternoon. Between chapters, he found himself thinking about the day before. He was unusually impressed with the teenagers. As soon as he could carry a board by himself, he worked for his dad, and he always worked hard. He never felt that he shouldn't work or that it was someone else's responsibility for making him work. Tucker didn't think such an attitude existed much anymore. Modern society seemed to have taken away personal responsibility, turning everybody into dependents who weren't expected to work. That's one reason he was so happy with the twins. They worked hard every day and understood that they earned their pay. Fair pay for fair work.

And the teenagers at the plaster party had also worked hard, and seemed to enjoy it. That was a good sign. Maybe he was selling their generation short.

Finally admitting that his book wasn't that interesting, Tucker retrieved the box of boats. He examined each one, slowly running his fingers over the edges, straightening up the sails, pushing the little masts harder into their holes. He had built toy boats as a young boy too, and the best time to play with them was after a heavy rain. He and his brother would sail their boats on the puddles in their back yard, imagining them on voyages of adventure, danger, and daring. Or sometimes they were lazy riverboat captains on the Mississippi with Huckleberry Finn. Once they played U-Boats in the North Atlantic and sank all their boats with big rocks. They didn't float so well after that.

The air was clean and cool as Tucker began his walk. He had been busy since his dream about Sam's kidnapping, and hadn't dwelt on the dream, its reasons, or meanings. He had not forgotten, however; in fact, he had thought about it every day. Tucker actually knew quite a bit about the Plains Indians: how they lived, how they fought, and how they died. While remodeling a house in Austin, he visited some of the historical museums and parks of Texas, giving him some idea of the landscape. And he had even read personal accounts of children being kidnapped by the Indians. So maybe his mind put those details together with the story of Sam Mulvaney and produced his vivid dream.

That's what he had decided at first. It was the reasonable explanation. Now, after thinking about it more, he had a different idea. It had to be connected to the door facing.

The door facing had been touched by Sam, and then Tucker had touched the same door facing more than a century later. He was convinced that the physical contact created some sort of psychic connection between him and Sam. It wasn't rational to think that way, but after all, he was living in a house that was alive, why would he think that his explanation had to be rational?

But even an irrational explanation didn't answer all his questions. The smell of smoke hadn't occurred in the dream. Where did it come from? The others had not smelled anything. Had he imagined it? And he heard the voice before he was asleep. How did that work? What caused him to fall asleep on the floor?

Why had the dream of Sam Mulvaney come to him in the first place? And what about the pains when he woke up—without question the same kinds of pains that Sam experienced during his kidnapping?

Without answers to any of his questions, Tucker's mind had come to one, hard, irrevocable decision.

He wanted to dream again.

He wanted to go back to that canyon, back to watching Sam.

Would it happen? Could he lie down again on the floor and find another dream waiting for him? Could he force it to happen?

He hadn't thought it possible, but then he found the little boats. The boats could be the key—something Sam had touched that now he could touch. If what he thought was true, the toy boats should be able to get him another dream.

And now was as good a time as any to find out.

It was late, and Rico, Rose, and Connie had returned to their rooms. Tucker watched around the corner of the house until all the lights were off. He took the box with the boats to Sam's room.

He lay down on the floor, finding it harder than he remembered even with a blanket folded under him. Taking each boat from the box, he placed them in a line beside him, then lay back, fully extending his body.

He kept glancing at the doorway, wondering what he would say if anyone walked in. He reminded himself that the others never walked around the house after dark, but still, he'd feel pretty stupid if someone did.

He lay quietly, trying to not think too much.

Time passed. Nothing happened.

He tossed his watch across the room to keep from checking it.

More time passed.

Maybe he should move or something. Maybe he needed to whack himself in the forehead with a boat.

He finally reached over and picked one up. It was cold to the touch, as if it had been taken out of a freezer. Tucker didn't understand. How could it be cold?

He balanced the boat on his chest and reached for another. It, too, was icy to the touch. He laid it next to the first boat, then lined all of them from his chin to his belt buckle, each one bewilderingly cold. He felt the cold soaking through his shirt and could now feel his fingers getting stiff.

He soon felt cold all over. He would have at least squirmed a little to get his circulation going, but he had become tired. So tired, he could hardly move.

The aroma of smoke came to his nose, the pungent scents of juniper and *piñon*. He relaxed and inhaled, filling his lungs, coughing as the dryness hit the back of his throat. Slowly, but surely, he lost consciousness.

No one was awake to hear the clang of the flagpole.

17

"Samuel! You need to be up!"

Sam woke with a start. He had felt the softness of the sheets as he snuggled deeper into them. The bright dagger of the sun was cutting across the wallpaper of his room and the dust was glittering in the morning air. The pots and pans were clanging on the stove in the kitchen, and he smelled the pancakes as he remembered the tastes of honey and cool milk.

But when he opened his eyes, the only light came from smoldering embers in the middle of the teepee, and the smells were only of dull smoke, dirt, body stink, and buffalo hair. The faint glow made shadows around the humps of squaws and children buried under the mounds of robes and wool blankets.

Sam was cold. Every morning he was cold. Every evening he was cold.

Winters were the hardest times. The Comanches molded themselves to the rhythms of nature, so when nights were longer, they slept longer; when it was colder, they stayed inside more; when food was scarce, they did not eat. What they had stored for the winter months never seemed to last long enough, and so Sam was always hungry and he was always cold.

And more time in darkness meant more time to remember.

He had a new father and three new mothers he held in high regard, and even loved, but in the long winter nights, he remembered his first father and mother, the tall man with red hair like his, the pale woman who made the pancakes.

Had it been two years? Or three years? Sam tried to remember. Where had they been? There were violent snowstorms in the canyons of the Palo Duro the year he was stolen. Then they traveled across the Llano, the wide plains of north and central Texas, into the southern mountains of the New Mexico territory. In the spring, they moved their encampment to the Canajin valley and ranged with buffalo for the summer. Now they were camped somewhere in the eastern plains of Colorado.

Three? Two and a half. He had lived as a Comanche almost two and a half years.

Rolling over and drawing the buffalo robe around his head, he could feel the thick matting of his hair.

Red Hair, some called him. Hair of Red Clay, some called him. Head On Fire, some called him. He had grown proud of his hair, though it had taken a while for him to get used to having it braided into ponytails.

Sam had his hair and his body from his father, something the Comanche could not have given him, could not take from him, nor could they possess it themselves. He was as tall as any man in the village, even though he must only be twelve. Thirteen? No, a half-year past twelve. In the summer, he would be thirteen. He no longer knew the day but he remembered the August moon.

He never had his party. And he wished he could measure himself against the doorframe.

Spring would come eventually, then the summer and the fall, and it would all be good. Winter was part of the cycle and the cycle never stopped. Indians knew how to wait, how to be patient. But it was difficult not to spend time thinking, and Sam thought mostly of food.

Except for the hungry times, it was a lot easier being a Comanche boy than a white boy. No chores. Those were for women and girls. They took care of the fires, the cooking, the drying of meat, the skinning of buffalo, horses, and deer. They made the clothes and hauled the water. He remembered how much they had swatted him with sticks in the beginning, how much the work was constantly hard and long. But he gradually joined the other Indian boys and became a Comanche brave. He never carried water again.

Braves practiced riding horses and stealing and shooting arrows and making fire and fighting. The older men taught the tactics of battle—the signals, the formations, the planning of war.

Sam learned to make his own bows and arrows and to ride against his enemies, leaning to the side of the horse and firing his arrows under the horse's neck. He learned to track buffalo, deer, antelope, and elk. He knew how to call turkeys and how to lay traps for rabbits and squirrels. He learned how to survive if he was ever left alone.

Every day was filled with playing games and chasing ponies and wrestling with his brothers and playing jokes on the older men. He practiced being grown up.

Of course, he was the son of the Chief and it mattered that he was the son of the Chief.

It wasn't all fun. Sometimes, his Chief sent them on raids long distances and he was away from the camp for many weeks, sometimes riding days before he could rest. They traveled from the mountains into the plains, from the plains south into the white settlements, from the settlements across the mountains into other mountains. They stole horses and mules to trade to the Comancheros for iron to make arrowheads and lance heads, and to trade for guns and ammunition, knives, blankets, and beads.

Once, they made war against the soldiers from the forts. He was not in the battle but kept the spare horses.

He hadn't killed people, yet. He didn't think that he'd like killing people.

But the stealing was fun. He was one of the best, and already had stories of sneaking through darkness into ranch corrals, smearing horse manure on himself, slipping catches from gates, and leading horses away. He always imagined the surprise when the settlers woke the next morning.

It mattered how many horses and mules you stole. It mattered that you did it well.

And then there were the buffalo!

Sam smiled and felt pleasure in his heart. The herds were scattered and hard to locate, but when a trail was found, the whole village followed the buffalo. Every brave in the village spent a day painting himself, his shield, and his horse, working on his bows and arrows, and sharpening his knives and lance.

When the hunt began, there would be hundreds, maybe thousands of buffalo as far as he could see into the distance. He would mount his horse and ride alongside the herd, reveling in the sounds, the smells, the excitement as he rode as fast as the wind. He would come closer and closer to the hairy beasts, hear them loudly snorting through their huge noses and thundering with their giant hooves, and then watch as one buckled to the ground as his arrow found its heart.

Sam would whoop and shout and go at them again. When it was over, when the women had cut all the meat and harvested the hides, everyone would feast and dance and celebrate.

It mattered how many buffalo you killed. It mattered that you did it well.

Sam laid another stick on the coals, pulled the buffalo robe over his head, and went back to sleep.

18

Mondays were always hard. Rose had to be at school by eight, and so she and Connie had to leave by seven. Connie normally got up comfortably at six, but getting Rose up after the weekend always took additional effort, especially since Connie demanded that she have breakfast. Hopefully, it would stay down, but if it didn't, Connie would bring something for her to nibble on during the ride to town.

Rico learned to stay in bed if it wasn't his day to drive. Otherwise, he only seemed to get in the way of the two women. Connie got him up as they were leaving, and she pounded on Tucker's trailer door on the way to the car. Rico and Tucker would take care of themselves, but without speaking for neither was a morning person. The work day began at eight.

Today Tucker did not respond to Connie's pounding, but that was usual. He replied in grunts if he replied at all. He was slow and ponderous when he got up, clearly moving against the grain. He became suitable for public display only after he had found his rhythm, which usually took two cups of coffee.

But when he was a no-show at eight, Rico was surprised. Tucker was never late. At eight-fifteen, he banged on the trailer's door but there was no answer. Opening the door, he found the trailer empty and the bed not slept in.

The construction lights were still plugged in when he had come into the kitchen. That was unusual too but it wasn't his responsibility, and so Rico did nothing. At eight-thirty, thinking that perhaps Tucker had begun work early, he walked through the house.

Rico found him on the floor of the third floor bedroom. Tucker was curled in a fetal position, wrapped in a blanket, shaking and shivering, taking short breaths as if he were freezing. Rico awkwardly pulled him upright, then helped him to stand. Tucker was as warm to the touch as the sunlight coming in the window, and yet the man's teeth were chattering too much for him to talk.

Rico struggled to get him downstairs, and then went after another blanket, wrapping it around Tucker as tightly as he could.

"It's seventy degrees in here, amigo. What's going on? What happened?"

Tucker stuttered out the words, pulling at the blankets. He related the dream: the fire, the shadows, the smells, and the cold. The thoughts of Sam were drawn out and detailed, and Tucker finished with a description of Sam in the buffalo hunt, whooping and yelling, the feelings of victory and joy bursting from him.

Rico listened, but Tucker was not sure he believed the details of the dream.

Tucker struggled up, yanked the blankets around him, went to his trailer, and crawled into bed. He lay there for the rest of the morning.

19

The Mulvaney Ranch visit by Building Trades 101 was judged a success at the high school, spawning an article, with pictures, for the following week's edition of the school's newspaper. It was well-written, fun to read, gave a short history of the house, reiterated the events of the day, and included a sidebar about the discovery of the old cistern. A parent liked the article enough to send it to the editors of Santa Fe's daily newspaper, *The New Mexican*. The editors liked it as well, especially the history and possible haunting, and decided that it was worth a story of its own. They called ahead, and a couple of days later, a reporter and a photographer came out to the ranch.

Tucker did not trust the public press, but he knew that it was often worse to refuse their advances than to go along. He compromised and accepted their request, then decided to be off on a buying trip, leaving Rico and Connie to field questions. He also asked Lynn to sit in on the interviews, thinking that she would like the publicity. She also knew the most about the house's history. Tucker's absence was to the newspaper's advantage. Between Rico and the ladies, the reporter had enough for a novel by the time they left.

A Sunday edition of *The New Mexican* came out a couple of weeks later with a full page of pictures and a lengthy story in the "Local Color" section. Tucker enjoyed the articles, and the pictures were excellent. There was nothing that wasn't already public knowledge: the story of the Mulvaneys, the history of the mansion, the adventure of rebuilding a Victorian house, the involvement of the local high school, the generosity of the owner, blah, blah, blah.

But when he read their names and a description of where the house was located, he felt a twist in his gut.

If Armando could read, he would discover that his family was living with an innocent old man on an isolated ranch several miles from any kind of law enforcement. The story was an invitation for something bad to happen.

Tucker was going to stand guard with his pistol that night, but decided he was being paranoid. Armando might be in Mexico, and if so, he would never see *The New Mexican*. If he was closer, it might be days or weeks before he got an issue. Or, even if he was in Las Vegas, he might not even look at the newspaper. There were too many factors of uncertainty, and Tucker thought he'd look pretty stupid acting like the town sheriff waiting for the villain to show up.

Connie and the others weren't concerned, and so Tucker let it go. There was work to be done.

The next big item was putting up new sheetrock in all the rooms, and Tucker had decided to forego the huge effort it would take he and whatever helpers he had, and hire a contractor to do it. He called around Las Vegas and Santa Fe and found a sheetrock installer who could provide a work crew close to the first of November. There would be several workers, and they would bring all the sheetrock, lifts, scaffolds, ladders, and tools. They estimated four days to do all of the rooms. All Tucker had to do was watch— and of course pay. As soon as the sheetrock was up, he'd bring the HVAC guys out to finish installing the baseboard radiators; they had already run the pipes from the boiler through the floors and ceilings to the locations of the radiators. By the middle of November, even if the finish work in the rooms wasn't complete, they would have real heat in the house. They could move in if the weather turned cold.

Rico was doing well with his GED courses, and he had found more on-line courses for electrical training. After Tucker let him practice on the basement, putting in plugs and lights, Rico was no longer so jumpy when he was on his own. He designed the new circuits for the upstairs rooms, drew the diagrams, set the boxes, and pulled the wires. Tucker was impressed.

[152]

Meanwhile, Tucker spent his time with the plumbing. The new kitchen sink was in a different place than the old one, the new sink in the island had no existing drain pipe at all, and he had forgotten about the little sink in the butler's pantry. The dishwasher needed a new drainpipe, and he needed to add a drainpipe upstairs for the washer and dryer. With the new design, either the old plumbing was in the wrong place or it didn't exist at all. It took cutting through the cast iron pipes in the basement and integrating new PVC fittings before Tucker was able to construct a system that worked for everything.

He also added walls inside the extra bedroom upstairs for a new bathroom and closet. That would make the room a nice suite for visitors.

Rose grew more baby bump every day. Her morning sickness had subsided and she was able to balance school, travel, and Rico sufficiently that she could help Connie most evenings with pulling the PEX tubing for the hot and cold water. Connie rode herd on Rose about exercise and eating, and the girl was a regular at the clinic in town. She visited with her parents at least twice a week, and they had visited the ranch a couple of times since summer.

"So, life sounds pretty good," Lynn said as she and Tucker sat inside his trailer. Supper was finished and the others were watching a movie. She'd brought a bottle of wine, sneaking it into the trailer before she joined everyone for supper.

"Things are definitely going well," Tucker replied. "It's the second week of October and the insulation is done, the plumbing almost done, and the electrical all laid out. Rico and I finished removing the plaster in the bedroom upstairs, so it's ready for the ceiling lights. If something doesn't slow us down, we'll be ready for the sheetrockers with a couple of days to spare."

"So, what are you not telling me?"

Tucker frowned. "You know, I thought psychologists were supposed to be shrewd and perceptive, but I'm beginning to think that realtors have them beat. You always seem to know when I'm not telling you stuff."

"You betcha," Lynn said with a small laugh. "It's just that you're such an honest guy that you can't hide anything. If I remember right, you really stink at poker too."

Tucker laughed. "Well, as a matter of fact, poker is a form of wealth redistribution for me. Bluffing is not in my blood."

His face softened and his eyes grew serious. "Let me show you something we found yesterday."

He went to the closet and brought back two items. The first was a cigar box, old and dull, marked up on the outside and dirty.

"I told you that Rico and I took down the plaster in that upper bedroom? That's the bedroom ceiling that we didn't get to during the plaster party. When we were pulling down the last of it, we were close to the outside wall. Before I pulled on the last piece, I looked up and these were stuck between the floor joists."

Lynn opened the cigar box. It was a collection of kid's playthings: four or five coins, bird feathers, a broken pocket watch, a pocketknife, a few stubby pencils, a few marbles, and some pieces of chalk. Folded in the corner was a Confederate ten-dollar bill. The inside of the box was covered in pencil marks and chalk dust.

"This was beside it." Tucker handed her an arrow.

It was an authentic arrow with bird feathers tied on the shaft. Tucker pointed to the animal sinew that had been used as thread. The notch had been whittled out by hand, with sinew wrapped around to keep it from splitting. The arrowhead was a piece of rough iron, cut and hammered into a thin, sharp-edged, triangular blade inserted into a split in the shaft and also secured with sinew. The shaft was rough but remarkably straight, with small streaks down the side where it had been scraped and burnished. The shaft had bands of blues, reds, and yellows painted in various places.

"This can't be real," Lynn said. "Indians used flint for arrowheads."

"Not the plains tribes of the mid-1800s. By the time the West was being invaded by waves of foreigners, the Indians had learned that iron made better arrowheads than rocks. When you hear of Indians burning settlers' wagons, it wasn't for fun. They were burning the wagon wheels so they could carry off the big rings of iron around the outside of the wheel. They'd use forges, hammers, punches, and gouges to cut the iron into the shapes they wanted, like arrowheads, lance heads, tomahawks, and knives. When they sharpened these tools and weapons, they were far superior to flint."

"Wow." Lynn slowly twirled the arrow in her hand, looking closely at the colored markings. "This is really something."

"I couldn't guess how these ended up between the joists, and so I went upstairs. We were directly below Sam's room, right below the window where the old radiator had been located. I looked at the floor. Whoever had run the pipe for the original radiator made some kind of mistake that, I guess, damaged the floorboards. Three of the boards had been replaced, but they didn't nail them down.

"Sam must have discovered that, by pushing and pulling, he could remove those boards. That made an opening in the floor big enough for a secret hiding place."

Tucker held up the cigar box. "His dad probably had plenty of these around the house. Sam took one, filled it with his private stuff, slid it between the joists, and then put the boards back."

"And this," he fingered the arrow, "he probably got from a ranch hand, or he found it, or maybe he got it as a souvenir from his father. It was a prized possession, I'm sure, and he kept it with his box."

Tucker slowly rotated the arrow in his hand. Lynn waited.

"A very interesting thing happened to me last week," Tucker finally said, with an impish smile. "I had a dream."

"You've told me about the dreams," Lynn said. She didn't know what to think about his dreams, except perhaps that he really needed a vacation. She figured that the house had to be involved, which just complicated any understanding she might attempt.

"Yeah, but this one was my own while in my own bed." Tucker looked up at the ceiling, then looked back at Lynn. "I was riding a horse across a prairie. Grass everywhere. Riding smooth, sitting tall on this fine looking pony. Pretty soon, I was hunting buffalo."

"Buffalo? You mean a real buffalo?"

"Oh, not just one—thousands. I was riding this horse, riding like all get out right next to a herd of thousands, and I mean thousands of buffalo stretching for a mile or more as they thundered across the prairie. The ground was shaking something fierce, and I had a lance in my hand as I rode right next to these huge animals. They were snorting and thundering, and I leaned over toward them, my lance pulled back, my arm ready to throw. My horse was snorting and jerking around as I threw the lance, which went right through the skin and deep into the shoulder. This gargantuan buffalo stumbled and jerked and rolled over, and then other buffalo were tripping over the dead one. I turned my horse away from the mess and slowed down, whooping and screaming and yelling and throwing my hands up in the air…"

Tucker was standing up, waving his hands and jumping up and down. He stopped and let out a big breath. Lynn was silent and wide-eyed, amazed at the man in front of her.

"I did it. I killed me a buffalo. It was remarkable." He sat back down. "It was so real. It was the greatest feeling I've had in my life. I woke up sweating. I was probably yelling too. It's a good thing the dorm is as far away as it is; I probably would have gotten the whole bunch up. It was absolutely thrilling." He sat back and folded his arms across his chest.

"I'd do it again, if I could. For that moment in time, I felt really, truly, vitally alive. It's like I'd found a new drug. I'd go back there in a blink of an eye if I could."

"Wow," Lynn said in a subdued voice. She'd never seen much emotion from Tucker, especially passion. It was not like him at all. It was, in fact, a little scary. "Sounds like a great dream."

"Oh, it was a great dream. But I didn't tell you that there was a scene where all the Indians were getting ready for the buffalo hunt. They were painting their horses and their faces and putting markings on their lances, arrows, and bows."

"Okay," Lynn said. "You realize, of course, that this dream sounds exactly like your last dream about Sam?"

Not hearing her question, Tucker unbuttoned his shirt and pulled it back to expose his chest. "Look at this."

"OH MY GOD!" Lynn said as she collapsed in laughter. "What did you do?"

"I don't remember doing any of it," Tucker confessed. "And I couldn't have told you where my old shoe polish was before I went to bed, but in the morning, there it was, right on the table. I used up the whole can. It doesn't wash off either."

He buttoned his shirt.

"So, did I, in the middle of the night, get up and paint stripes all over my chest? I guess that I did. Thank God I didn't paint my face."

Lynn was wiping tears from her cheeks and struggling to keep her laughter down.

"So," she said, regaining her composure. "Are you worried about this?"

Tucker poured himself another cup of wine, sipped, then leaned forward, his elbows on his knees. "The first of Sam's dreams came after I got whacked with the door facing. It was the dream where he was kidnapped. I woke up with terrible aches and pains, as if I had been riding a horse bareback with my hands tied. The aches and pains lasted about five minutes.

"The second dream came after I had found the little boats from the cistern. Sam was in a teepee in a winter camp, and he was really cold. I woke up freezing, despite the fact that it was September. I went to bed and continued to be freezing for most of the morning, wrapped up in every blanket I own.

"I have this theory that I haven't told the others. I seem to be able to access these dreams by touching something that Sam touched. The first trigger was the door facing. The second trigger was the boats that he played with."

Tucker looked into her eyes. "If my theory is correct," he said as he held up the cigar box and arrow, "I can now have two more dreams."

Lynn's face hardened and she frowned. "I don't know about your theory," she said, "but I'm not sure that it's a good idea to test it, *especially* if your theory is right. You might be playing with fire here."

"I want to go back," Tucker responded. "I *want* to go back. I have new objects, a cigar box and an arrow which, I have no doubt, belonged to Sam Mulvaney. He touched these, and now, so have I."

He finished the wine and put the cup on the table. He looked at Lynn.

"I'll bet I can take one of these, go to Sam's room, lie down and put the object on my chest, and have another dream."

"Oh, honey, you are not listening to me. I don't care *if* you can do it or not. I don't think you *should* do it. You may be putting yourself into a situation that's going to get you into trouble. Just let it go."

"Rico and Rose are staying the weekend with Rose's parents," Tucker continued. "I guess her parents are facing up to the inevitable, and so they're trying to make amends. That leaves Connie here in case something goes wrong."

Lynn argued more, but Tucker was resolute.

"Saturday night. That's when I'm going to try it. I want to be Sam again. I want to feel the way I felt. I want to kill another buffalo."

Lynn tried to change his mind, but he was stubborn. She could only half believe that all of the dream stuff was real, herself. She blamed his aches and pains on sleeping on a hard floor all night, and that his freezing episode was because he had caught a chill. Those explanations were far simpler than mystically inheriting wounds experienced by somebody in a dream.

She finally gave up; Tucker was firm in his intentions to dream again. Lynn had to go, and she left him with a last request that he stop experimenting with what he didn't understand.

She didn't understand his desire to do it. Tucker Whitby was as anal as they came when pursuing a goal. Disciplined, strictly procedural, control oriented, and a rule freak. Now he was thinking he could do something completely outside the realm of reason or reality. He thought he could control dreams.

But her real feelings were deeper. She was tired of her visitor status in the house and with him. Tonight was an excellent example of the fact that he didn't listen to her, that what she said or thought or felt didn't matter. She didn't understand these dreams, but the fact that they were causing Tucker to become part of life a century and a half ago made her afraid, not curious. She had told him that, repeatedly, but her words fell on deaf ears. She was becoming more of an observer every time she came to the ranch.

Over the last year and a half, she had watched him become "involved" with the house. That was spooky enough, but he never let it get out of hand. He was always sensible about it, if you can call dealing with a living house sensible, and the house's activities had been relatively benign albeit otherworldly. Then Rose, Rico, and Connie moved in. That threw Tucker off his game, but he adjusted to their presence. However, the family brought a whole new dynamic to the house. Rose, in particular, became the major determiner of the social climate. Lynn knew that it wasn't just because of Rose, but Tucker changed from a relaxed, careful builder to an embattled devotee of making the house livable. Weekends, holidays, any spare moment he had, he was working. He was still sensible but focused to the exclusion of everything else.

Now it was the dreams. Lynn had no idea what was going on and could not imagine what was bringing them on, but Tucker was now obsessed with the life of Sam Mulvaney. The life of the boy in the dreams pulled him in, and he, day by day, was devoting more energy, more time, and now, more deliberate effort to participating in that boy's life. His episodes had stopped being dreams; they had become scripts for Tucker to follow. She saw it in his eyes and heard it in his voice as he described the buffalo hunt.

He wanted to *be* the boy.

She thought he was crazy for even desiring it, but, as little emotional energy as Tucker had been devoting to her, now almost nothing came her way. Maybe it was time for her to get out.

She was still thinking about all the things that were going wrong and that could go wrong as she pulled away from the house and headed back to town. She couldn't help but think it ironic and sad that Tucker had bought a haunted house because of his curiosity. Now, his curiosity was leading him to be the one who was haunted.

After Lynn pulled away, Tucker set out on his walk around the property. When he returned to the house, he started up the front stairway as he usually did, then stopped. He was hesitant to go upstairs.

He reversed his steps, cautiously, as if he hoped that no one had noticed.

Sam's objects were causing his dreams, and Tucker hadn't considered the house being involved one way or the other. But, on this night, he didn't want to go upstairs, and specifically, he did not want to go into Sam's room. Maybe he was afraid he'd have another dream. Of course, that's what he wanted, he thought, but he wanted to be ready when it happened. Arbitrary dreams, uninitiated dreams of Sam, now gave him pause. Maybe he was afraid that he'd find a reason that he couldn't dream again. Or maybe he was afraid that visiting Sam's room too often would use up his opportunities to become a dreamer.

Or maybe he was just tired of walking through the house. He'd done it every night for almost a year and a half. Maybe he needed a break. It seemed as if the house was doing okay by itself. Tucker walked to the trailer. Saturday night. That would be perfect. Tucker felt a shiver of excitement. Buffalo!

He had finished brushing his teeth, remembering how nice it was to have Lynn to talk to, when the phone rang.

"Hey, this is Larry. I thought you should know. Armando's back."

20

Connie was a habitual early riser, and as the sunrise streamed through the dorm's hallway windows on Sunday morning, she knelt next to her bed saying her morning prayers. Then she heard the screams.

She found Tucker writhing on the floor of the third floor bedroom, holding his face and screaming as if his eyes were being ripped from his skull. Across the floor were scattered the contents of the cigar box. A piece of chalk crunched under her feet as she rushed to kneel beside him.

He was screaming, sobbing, huffing, and garbling his words. Not knowing anything else to do, Connie half-dragged and half-assisted him to the dining table downstairs. She shoved him on top of it, then pulled his hands away from his face.

There were no marks anywhere on his face. No bruises, no redness, no obvious injury of any kind. Yet, Tucker strained and pulled at her hands, craning his neck in agony and then sobbing at her futile efforts to ease his misery. She finally wet a towel, made a compress, and gently laid it over the left side of his face. It seemed to stifle his pain, and he shifted into deep moans as he shuddered, witless and suffering as if blind.

Connie called Lynn, who seemed to be there in an instant. They thought about taking him to a doctor in town, but it would have been pointless. What doctor could treat the symptoms of an injury that hadn't happened? A wound that didn't exist?

"What if he's gone crazy?" Connie asked.

Lynn shrugged, but her face showed that she had thought of it.

Using pillows and blankets, they made as much of a pad as the table allowed, and they built cushions around him so he would not fall off. They'd give him an hour, then take him to town for help if there was no change.

A few minutes later, Tucker spoke, his voice shallow and his words halting as he fought back tears. He clutched the compress against his face.

"I killed him, I killed him," Tucker cried, lashing the air with his arms. Lynn held him down, giving him assurance.

Tucker finally quieted, his eyes clearing. He took several deep breaths and looked at the two women leaning over him.

"It was no dream," he said. "I was there. It was me."

21

The name Halverson meant nothing to Sam. That the Halverson family had found hard times in Minnesota and moved to Kansas to start a new life meant nothing to Sam. The fact that Nathaniel Halverson had taken his savings, sold the family home, and sunk all of his money into traveling to Kansas for two hundred acres of relatively good land in the southeast corner of the state meant nothing to Sam. Their ill-timed arrival during a warm winter that left the land dry and barren during the spring and forced Mr. Halverson to take a job with the local feed store, leaving his wife, his young son, and younger daughter alone at their tiny cabin meant nothing to Sam.

But the three horses in the corral next to the house meant everything to Sam.

They needed horses. Raiding deep into Kansas had stretched their resources thin. The Army was building in the plains—more men who were better equipped and more anxious to kill every Indian they saw—and they attacked any Indian camps they found, slaughtering men, women, and children. There was no longer a desire on the part of the white man to negotiate or pacify; the soldiers' job was now to exterminate. This made the Comanche raids more difficult and dangerous.

Sam needed another horse, a big horse if he could find one. He had already ridden two, one being a horse he had raised on the Llano. But the long rides and the vicious speed the Indians required to run from their enemies had exhausted his horse and they had killed it for meat. The horse he had now was quickly failing as well. It had been pampered in a white man's corral and given food that the prairie did not grow, and so it did not have the stamina of an Indian pony. It became weak and slow and would soon join the other horse as food.

Sam and several other warriors were still three weeks away from their camp, and they needed horses. This way of waging war had become the pattern. In past years, they raided to find horses, mules, children, guns, ammunition, knives, rope, cloth, blankets, and other possessions that fed their community, allowing them to grow their families and providing them with trade goods. They would run a herd of many stolen horses, adding to them as they raided along the frontier. But the strategy had changed. Now they raided only for what they needed at the moment, and for revenge, to have an outlet for their anger and hate, to make the new settlers across the countryside fear the Comanche. They wanted to hurt their enemies.

And everyone had become their enemies.

In past years, a raiding party would find an isolated ranch or farm and wait until night to steal the animals they wanted. They were thieves, racing from the scenes of their crimes so fast that their victims had no chance of catching them.

Now they were concerned with blood as much as bounty. They attacked homes as soon as they found them, striking fast and with savage fury. They not only stole wantonly but killed as many as possible, maliciously and with a rage they hoped would spread the fear of the Comanche far and wide. They wanted revenge for their own wives and children whose bodies had been left for the crows and vultures.

And they wanted the people to leave, and so they burned their houses and barns, leaving no doubt that the Comanche were brave warriors who were not afraid of their enemies. They were the rulers of the plains. Rulers who wanted no neighbors.

Today, it was Sly Wolf's turn to lead the raid. He watched from the side of the cabin, assessing the task before them. Sam was to his left, a hundred feet away, working his way around the corral. Fighting Bird, two years younger than Sam, held the horses behind a thicket of oak bushes.

Sly Wolf fit an arrow in his bow and yelled as he rushed the door. Sam leaped onto the porch about five feet behind him, his knife drawn. As the door was thrown aside, Sly Wolf's arrow found the woman, and she had two in her before she could cross the room. Sam was on her twisting body as Sly Wolf swept the cabin for more enemies.   Sam yanked her dark hair back as she fought him, grasping wildly as she screamed in pain. He slid the blade under her hairline, cut fully against the skull, then made a final cut to give him a full hand of hair. Her blood squirted over his hands and legs and splattered on the floor. Sam tucked her hair into his waist belt and started his search of the cabin. Sly Wolf was not as satisfied. He ripped her dress from her as he gave in to a fit of lust and his desire to punish these invaders of their land.

Sam did not watch. He was moving through the cabin looking for guns and bullets, knives, anything that would help them in their dash for home.

He found an unopened door.

Sly Wolf had been too concerned with the woman.

Not hesitating and with his knife in his hand, Sam put his thickly muscled body into the door with all his might, smashing it back against the wall as he sprang on the first live thing he saw.

It was a young boy, quaking with fear as he backed into the corner of a bed. Sam grabbed him by the throat and quickly ran the knife through his heart.

He only noticed the boy's red hair as the body convulsed onto the blanket under him.

There was a fearful cry and he found a younger girl cowering beneath her brother. He pulled his knife out of the still jerking body and grabbed her, ready to kill.

Lucy.

The memories hit him hard and unmercifully.

Lucy.

The girl's soft face, her long bright red hair, her beautiful blue eyes.

Sam remembered his mother and Lucy, singing and laughing as they combed each other's hair, pulling the comb with long strokes, making long braids that were then tied with ribbons.

He heard the music of the piano as his parents danced. He was dancing too, holding Lucy's hands as she laughed and giggled and swung her feet. They waltzed behind his parents as the door to the porch was opened and they swept out, swept out into the night like a

[165]

cool breeze, turning and stepping, and then turning again as they both laughed.

The little girl squirmed and screamed as Sam continued to hold her, mesmerized by her looks and by his memories.

He could smell the morning as Lucy held the big spoon in the pancake batter, making a mess, trying to stir. On some mornings, she would go with him to milk the cows, feeding them handfuls of grass that she had pulled from the riverbank as he labored to get the milk to hit the bucket. She was always laughing.

He dropped the child back onto the bed. He couldn't breathe. Rocking back on his haunches, he stared at the screaming girl, then at her dead brother. The boy was about Sam's age when he had been stolen.

Sly Wolf found nothing of value, but tied the woman's blue gingham bonnet on his head, leaping and dancing as he pranced around her quivering body and past the bedroom door where Sam hovered. Sam knew that, within a few heartbeats, Sly Wolf would be throwing the lanterns on the floor, splashing the liquid across the room, and setting it on fire. Sam knew that Fighting Bird had already tied the horses in the corral together and was driving them into the forest and toward the hills beyond where they would outrun their enemies.

Sam grabbed the little girl around her waist and ran through the door, leaping over the flames crawling up the walls. Coming to the horse that Sly Wolf held, he swung his leg over as he grabbed the reins and was already flying into the forest before the little girl was settled in front of him.

Past the forest was pasture, then farmland, then grassland, and then the prairie. They had scouted the path and had planned their escape. They rode for their lives.

Sam did not follow the path. He left the others and rode to where they had scouted another farm. Galloping at full speed, he headed to the main house, braving the screams and shouts that came from within. He dropped the girl on the porch and then hung to the side of his horse as shots rang out.

Sam had slid back up and laid into the neck of the horse to urge him faster when he felt a ripping to the side of his face. His eyes blazed as an explosion of pain seared across his temple like fire had been touched to his head. Seconds later, blood was running down his face and into his mouth and nose, slinging onto his breast. He yelled, then fought his voice back.

Pain was ordinary, pain was life, to be lived with and then pushed inside.

Sam gritted his teeth and raced for the prairie.

22

The pain of the injury slowly subsided, but the darkness that remained in its wake frightened Lynn. Tucker was the most consistent, steady, emotionally stable man she had ever met, and she loved him for it. But in the hours after his dream, he was remote and sad, almost overwhelmed with remorse.

He killed the boy without a thought.

He scalped the woman while full of hate.

No mercy.

Raw savage.

He repeated the phrases in occasional outbursts, sometimes lucidly and sometimes through sobs as if his heart was being torn in two.

I guess he never expected that, Lynn thought. He only expected to kill buffalo.

She went home in spite of Connie's pleas to stay, then came back the next evening. Tucker had improved. His face no longer hurt and he had ceased repeating those same phrases. He sat on the porch wrapped in a blanket and never said a word, like a man stunned.

Without him ever seeing her, Lynn left and did not come back.

Rico and Rose listened to Connie retell the dream, discussed it, and talked about the other dreams. They analyzed each one, searching for patterns or meanings. Rose refused to believe in ghosts, suspecting that Tucker was secretly using drugs. She went back to the decorating magazines she had bought in town. Lynn had brought more documents that detailed the history of the house and

Connie and Rico talked about the Mulvaneys repeatedly, thinking that the stories might tell them if there was a curse on the house. Perhaps they had awakened a beast inside the basement that now prowled for victims. Or maybe it was that each of the found objects was possessed by the ghost of Sam, who haunted the next person to touch it. Or maybe it was the ghost of Sam's mother, stuck in between worlds, searching for a spirit gateway to find her final resting place. Their speculation relieved the tension, even if they didn't actually provide believable explanations.

On the morning of the third day, Tucker got out of bed, showered, came to breakfast, laid out the plan for the day, and was installing switch boxes in a bedroom by eight. He had no problems remembering the dream, but the aftermath was put aside. He was ready to work.

Rico had made considerable progress in the two days that Tucker was absent, anxious to show that he could do it alone. Tucker was impressed and told him so. He worked with Rico to install the can lights in the kitchen, and then they set the boxes that would power the future under-cabinet lighting. Tucker finished connecting the drain for the prep sink in the island, and ran the electric wires for the plugs in the two pantries. The bedrooms and hallways took the normal number of plugs and lights, with a few additions for wall-hung TVs, wall sconces, and a plug along the top of each mantle. The plugs and lights in the bathrooms and the nursery were installed. Every major room was wired for a ceiling fan.

After the focus on the details, every room was cleaned until not a single errant nail could be found.

Larry Jackson's warning about Armando had caused Tucker alarm for a bit, but no encounter had occurred. After the initial phone call from the police, who had heard of Armando's presence in the community from newly arrested prisoners, no more official information was provided. Rose talked to the twins at school, and an informal network of spies was sent out, checking various places around town. Armando didn't seem to be afraid of the police and was seen in a couple of bars, and then he disappeared after a week. People guessed that he had gone to Albuquerque.

While it was possible that he was in town, Connie drove Rose to Las Vegas every day, using the time to visit with friends and reconnect with her church groups. If Armando was going to come back into their lives, she wanted to be his first contact and so she made herself obvious and available. Tucker guessed that she wanted to be the first line of defense.

And, he reasoned, she thought that if Armando found her first, part of his anger would be spent on her, leaving the others to suffer less.

23

It was early on the first Monday of November. Tucker sat on the porch, his heavy work jacket buttoned to the neck and his cup of hot chocolate steaming in the cold air of the morning. Cradling his drink, he watched the contractor's crew carry the big grey panels of sheetrock into the various rooms. They had already unloaded the mechanical lifts needed for raising the panels to the ceilings, several sections of scaffolding, several long extension ladders, and boxes of tools. Tucker had left the heaters going all night to take the edge off the frigid air inside. He smiled as he took another sip.

By the end of the day, the crew had installed the sheetrock on the ceilings in half the rooms and finished the stairwell ceiling and walls. They were on schedule to be finished on Thursday.

That night at dinner, Tucker announced that the grand move from the dorm to the house would start two weeks from Saturday. During those two weeks, they had to tape, bed, and texture every wall and ceiling, reinstall the trim work around the floors, doorways, ceilings, and windows, and then prime and paint every surface. Installing all the switches, plugs, and light fixtures would be done after that, and hooking up the plumbing would be last. The HVAC people would return periodically to connect the heating pipes to various baseboard radiators and turn on the heat.

They all agreed that the bedrooms would be the first to be finished, the kitchen next, then the hallways. At Tucker's request, the bathrooms would be last. He wanted to teach Rico and Rose about tile, which Connie admitted to not having good enough knees to do. Good tile work was all about being careful, and he did not want to be rushed. Continuing to use the bathrooms in the dorm would be fine in the interim.

Tucker would buy a queen mattress set for Rico and Rose and a regular mattress set for Connie, who had earned every ounce of her comfort. He wouldn't buy more furniture until people had settled in. He gave Connie and Rose a budget for sheets, blankets, pillows, bedspreads, curtains, rugs, and other needed items. They had already been working on the paint schemes for each room.

For this week, while the sheetrock was being installed, work on the rest of the house would be on hold. Everyone could relax, go to school, get ahead on their homework, watch their movies, and read their books.

Everyone was happy to get the time off, but the move wasn't all benevolence on Tucker's part. With the work being done by the sheetrock crew and the others focused on their own doings, Tucker could sneak back to Sam.

He had to dream again. This time he did not have a choice.

The pain following the last dream had been real. He did not deny it. He remembered the days of slowly decreasing agony and the deep remorse that remained after the dream, and so he did not take his decision lightly. He certainly no longer believed that he would only find buffalo hunts and happy times. It wasn't that he had grown comfortable with his murdering the little boy and the scalping of the poor woman, but he had convinced himself that it was a dream. He may have felt it was real, but it was not.

Whatever justification was needed, Tucker found it. It wasn't because he wanted to dream again—he *had* to dream again. Like he had told Lynn in the trailer, he was addicted to the dreams as if to a drug. He was not an escapist, but he now had an uncontrollable compulsion to go back to that world—a world alive with smells, colors, textures, volume, and emotions of a life so unlike his own. He was the only one who could do it, so it felt like a calling to which he had to respond. On the other hand, his mind kept reminding him, he had never felt so alive. Wasn't that why he had bought the house?

The timing for another dream seemed good. If something in the next dream put him out of commission for a day or two, that would be okay. He was willing to risk it. The sheetrockers knew exactly what they were doing, and the radiator guys had everything prepared for when they returned. If there were any questions, Rico could answer them. If there were any problems, Rico could take care of them.

Tucker would not tell Lynn. She'd be furious with the idea, and it seemed like she was trying not to be involved anymore, anyway, and so not knowing should suit her.

He would use the arrow, which worried him. If chalk and marbles had brought him savagery and murder, what would an instrument of war bring?

Tucker stayed on the porch that evening, watching the canyon, the river, and the stars as they materialized out of nothing. He waited until late, making sure everyone was asleep, then went to Sam's room using a flashlight.

Tucker got to his knees, rolled over into a sleeping position, and shivered as he touched the cold floor. He pulled a couple of blankets over him and tucked the edges beneath him. He stretched out, laid the arrow on his chest, and waited.

But he could not sleep.

He felt the dull points of his bones making contact with the hardness of the floor. He should have more sense than to try to sleep on a bare floor in a cold, dark room, in November, he told himself.

Two hours went by, maybe three.

Tucker felt his mind drifting, wondering what time it was, still debating whether it was going to work or not. Then, barely noticeable at first, a thin mist of smoke leaked from beneath the baseboard. Creeping along the floor, thickening, making little swirls, the smoke swept around the room with what air currents there were, then snuck up the sides of the blanket. Tucker jerked as he realized he was being engulfed, but then yielded, closed his eyes, and took a deep breath.

24

There were the storms in the Palo Duro, and then living in the snow of the southern mountains, then in the valleys of Colorado. They came back to the canyons east of the big mountains the winter after that, and then moved north of the Arkansas for the buffalo before fleeing back to Texas. They had wintered in the canyons of the Llano twice after that.

Six winters meant that he had been a Comanche for seven years.

Sam was still years from being a grown man, but he was already the tallest Indian in his village by a foot, and he had never met any Indian even as tall as his shoulder. His body matched his height. He was strong, thick and broad-shouldered with powerful muscles covering his chest and arms. He was lithe and athletic, quick and deadly, his hands and feet as large as a grizzly bear's paws.

No one had ever seen a warrior like him. Two full braids of red hair hung down his back, though he was known to unbraid it during battle and let it flow in the wind as a sign to his enemy. He was Red Hair, giant of the Comanches, savage warrior of the nations.

Seven years and he had become a Comanche warrior that others feared. In the plains, the ranchers and settlers kept looking over their shoulders to see if Red Hair was coming. At the Army forts, officers asked specifically of Red Hair's whereabouts. Towns even posted warnings when a raiding party included a giant Indian with red hair.

His heart, his enemies said, was a raging storm. His eyes, they said, were the eyes of a wild animal. His mind, they said, held no mercy.

Sam sat quietly on his horse as he peered out over the valley of teepees that stretched out before him, and he tried to remember. Pancakes, milk, taking the cows to grass, being taken.

Times had changed. The land now swarmed with white settlers like ants over spilled blood, and soldiers seemed to be everywhere. The tribe roamed in smaller groups and seemed to always be on the move. There were no good times anymore.

After a battle, even when the actual battle was a hundred miles away, his people would pack up and move, evading those who would seek the remnant of the once strong tribe. Even if they won the battle, they still scattered before their enemies could reform. They constantly searched for land where they could hide. The Comanche used to steal children so they would grow up and replace the braves and squaws who had been killed. Now they no longer stole children because they weren't expected to live long enough to become adults.

The Llano Estacado was the only land that no white man wanted. The flat grass plains and waterless reaches offered nothing easy. So the Comanche lived along a riverbed here, a valley there, or in the side canyons of the Palo Duro. There were caves in the south that they sometimes lived in, and intricate canyons north of the Canadian. They moved often and warily. They had become a sneaking people.

His Chief, the father whom he loved, had died two years before. Wrapped in a red-striped blanket and lifted upon a platform of poles, his horse and dog killed and placed below him, the Chief now dwelt with his ancestors.

The tribe wept, then moved on.

Sam, then still a young teenager, was adopted by the medicine man of the tribe, another man of honor who had respected the Chief. The shaman took him as a son and taught him things the others could not comprehend. The shaman believed his red hair was a sign that the boy could see into the shadows, could hear the voices in the wind, and could feel the trembling of the ground. Over the next two years, Sam grew powerful in ways that had nothing to do with his body.

The new Chiefs were not like the old Chief, a man of honor and of war. They tired of fighting and did not have the spirit to continue. So they allowed the white man's Indian agent to come among them and negotiate a treaty. And part of the treaty, as they had known, would be the return of captives who had been stolen. Even Red Hair must be given back to the white man.

Sam hated the whites. They killed the old Chief and his two wives who had served as Sam's mothers. They killed his friends. They brought war into the villages. It seemed that all that was precious to him had been taken away by the whites, and they had dishonored all those he loved.

When Comanche villages were found, the soldiers attacked without mercy, killing the old, the young, the men, the women, and then hacking their bodies to pieces. In response, Sam killed *their* men, *their* women, and *their* children, captured their horses and mules, stole their possessions and burned their houses. They were not his people. They had no honor, no integrity.

He was not white.

He was Comanche.

But the new Chiefs were jealous of the great warrior Red Hair, and they resented the medicine man moving so quickly to lay claim to the boy. Among themselves, they thought it better that Red Hair leave the tribe. A treaty would do that for them.

When the Indian agent came to declare the treaty done, the tribe began the long, slow walk to the reservation near Fort Sill in the Indian Territories. Any captives held by the tribe traveled two miles farther, to an Indian school run by the Dutch Church. They would reside there until they could be claimed by their families.

Red Hair resisted for a long time, running through the vast distances of the Llano and hiding, but the threats mounted from within his own tribe, and then from the neighboring tribes. One day, full of sorrow for the death of his people and expecting his own death to be soon, he turned his horse toward his enemy at Fort Sill and rode through tall gates that slammed shut behind him.

Red Hair—the great Comanche warrior—slid down from his horse into a world as strange to him as the other side of the moon.

25

Tucker lay in his trailer bed loosely covered by the sheet, unmotivated, sad and confused, and feeling old. His mind shifted from one idea to another, from one scene to another, from one dream to another, over and over. Images of the Mulvaney boy, his growth from young boy to young man; Tucker's memories of the house, how it was alive, and how it revealed itself to him; and the ever-present Connie, Rose, and Rico. Was it *a* family? Was it *his* family? It ought to be Connie's family, Rose being a daughter-in-law in fact if not on paper. But they're not here by choice, he told himself. They were only boarders, and boarders don't make a family. Work in exchange for rent, money in exchange for work. They were refugees from a real home.

Like him. He was a refugee too. Just a guy passing through.

Maybe the house was tired of refugees and so it was scaring the beejesus out of him and the others to make them leave. Tucker thought about hooking up his trailer and pulling away, wondering what it would be like to be free again.

He heard her walking outside before she gave a strong knock, opened the door, came in, then leaned against the wall with her arms crossed.

"Well, here you are again," Lynn said.

Rico and Connie had found Tucker sitting in Sam's room on Tuesday morning. He was just sitting, leaning against the wall, the blankets wrapped around him. He was doing nothing, saying nothing. He didn't seem to be in pain nor be experiencing any horrifying memories. He just sat and looked at them vacantly, as if he were somewhere else.

Once found, Tucker got up from the floor, thanked them for their concern, and went to his trailer. He did not tell them the dream from the night before, and they did not ask. That was yesterday. After he entered the trailer, the contractors were told that he was ill and unable to come into the house. When there were questions or problems, Rico sat in the trailer with Tucker, discussed various answers or solutions, then carried the messages back to the workers.

Tucker had found a hole and crawled in it.

"Get up," Lynn said suddenly. "You look like hell and you stink. Take a shower, get your clothes on, and meet me outside." She turned and went out the trailer door, not even bothering to shut it.

Tucker's eyebrows furrowed. Was she mad at him? But he had been through another dream and he thought she'd take it for granted that he would be out of commission for a little while. And she should really want to hear about his dream.

Slow and disgruntled, he got up, took a shower, made himself presentable, put on his jacket, and walked outside.

Lynn was leaning against the porch. "Let's go," she said, and started to the front of the house. She weaved in between the big trucks of the sheetrocking crew and walked down to the lavender garden. Tucker followed obediently.

"You've neglected the garden," she said as she reached the bench, next to which several bags of mulch were stacked. Rico had helped her unload them. Two pair of gloves were to the side of the stack.

"Lavender is a bush-oriented plant, and they'll fare better in the winter if you spread mulch around the bottoms. And you've let the weeds take over."

She threw him his gloves. "Let's get to it."

It was cool, but the work was intense, and neither of them talked or slowed down. They cut the mulch bags open and packed handfuls of mulch in and around the root systems of each bush. They pulled weeds and combed out tumbleweeds, steadily moving through the rows until every row was cleaned and packed. It made an immediate and significant difference in the garden's appearance. After Lynn had gathered the ripped plastic of the mulch bags and stuffed it into a garbage sack, she wiped her brow and sat on the stone bench. Tucker started to sit beside her.

"No you don't. You sit on this," she said, turning the water bucket upside down and setting it in front of her.

Tucker looked at her with a little disgust coming to his face, then sat on the short bucket, his knees sticking up to his elbows. Man and woman faced each other.

"Now," Lynn said, "tell me about your dream."

Tucker tried to tell it well. He got all the facts right, but when he tried to express Sam's dismay at being betrayed and how he felt as he finally surrendered, how he slid off his horse in great sadness, it came across lame and flimsy.

"Okay," Lynn said. "Now I want to know about this garden. Tell me why lavender is so important."

Tucker was surprised at the question. "My wife liked lavender, like I told you. She chose that color as the primary color of our wedding and decorated all the tables at the reception with the blossoms."

"Not roses, like everybody else?"

Tucker colored a little. "Not roses, like everybody else. She didn't particularly like roses."

"So, what happened to her?"

"Jennie was her name, if you're interested. She died in a car wreck."

"Tell me about the car wreck."

Tucker felt silly. He hadn't told anyone the full story, and now he was having to do it under interrogation.

"I got drunk at a party. I refused to let her drive. I missed a curve, went over a guard rail, rolled the car several times, and killed her. She was dead at the scene. I didn't come out of my stupor until after she had been taken to the morgue."

That was it. He could have said more, but he wasn't feeling like it.

"I'm sorry," Lynn said, softening her voice. "Did you go to jail?" she asked without emotion.

Tucker didn't like this at all, but he continued. "No. I was a lawyer in a big practice. You can get away with anything if you're a lawyer in a big practice."

Lynn tightened her lips. "You were a lawyer? That must be where you got all your money. Well, okay then. Do you think you were responsible for your wife's death?"

"Yes. I was responsible for her death." It seemed pretty simple to him.

"Okay. Tell me about your daughter's death."

This was going to be a little bit more difficult, Tucker thought, but she asked, and so she was going to get it.

"I was a trial lawyer in Washington, DC. I went to law school at George Washington, graduated at the top of my class, and then went to work for a hotshot firm inside the beltway. I was good, consistent, hardworking, and they liked me. I was especially good about knowing the law.

"I married Jennie in 1970, and we had a daughter in 1972. Her name was Sara, named after my grandmother, if you want to know. Ten years later, Jennie died. I kept my daughter with me and she became the center of my life.

"But I was ambitious and desired to be a great and famous lawyer, and so I asked for bigger clients and more public trials.

"My biggest case came in 1988. The son of a congressman had stabbed a whore to death in the back seat of his car. There was no question that he was guilty, but I wasn't paid to prosecute. I was paid to defend. He was mentally disturbed, and everybody knew it. He had actually met my daughter at some halfway house that she was interning at, and even she agreed he was crazy. I got him off on a technicality, some little glitch in the law that I had found. Justice wasn't my concern, and so he walked out of the courtroom a man who only needed counseling. And I got a bonus that was five times my salary."

"That's a pretty nice bonus," Lynn said.

"Yeah. Gave me a taste of real money. Two weeks later, the man I had helped set free broke into my house and killed my little girl."

Lynn wasn't expecting that. She stared at him, horrified.

"I knew he was crazy when I defended him," Tucker continued in a matter of fact voice. "Crazy as a loon, and I told my bosses so. He was a very dangerous man. He had taken a knife and ripped that whore from her crotch to her neck because he wanted to play nasty and she wanted out of the car. He killed her because she refused him, and he killed her because he enjoyed it.

"And when he was standing in my kitchen with my daughter in his hands, a gun pointed to her head, I knew that my sins had come

[184]

home to me, that I was being punished for exchanging justice for a bag of coins."

Tucker took a deep breath.

"I almost made it across the room in time, but I wasn't fast enough. He pulled the trigger and sent my daughter to heaven, where her mother was waiting. And the man was smiling as he did it. I got the gun away from him, beat him with it, and then I took a kitchen knife and slit him the same way he had done that whore."

Color drained from Lynn's face. She covered her mouth with shaking hands.

"The congressman wanted no publicity, and so he pulled enough strings that I wasn't even charged. The news was buried on a back page of the newspaper and I got to spend time in a nice, little institution for the mentally disturbed. Once I was out, I left the firm, which was okay with my bosses because offering to defend a client with a damaged lawyer was a difficult sell.

"It was okay with me too. I no longer liked the people I worked with, no longer wanted to be a lawyer. I kept having dreams of the guy smiling as he killed Sara, and so I stopped being interested in what the law said."

Tucker sounded worn out and embarrassed at finally telling his past.

"I went back to doing what my dad had taught me to do. I worked on a construction crew for a while, then went out on my own. First in Washington, DC, and then Austin, Fort Worth, Lubbock, and now Las Vegas, New Mexico."

He looked at her with no expression.

Lynn struggled as she stood up. "And now you want sympathy?" she asked as she looked down at him. "You want me to cry with you over the things you think you did? You want me to hover over you and feel sorry for you when you've wasted thirty or so years of your life feeling guilty? You're a damned emotional cripple dragging a ball and chain around—suffering as if it were penance for your sins. What I can't figure out is why you're content to be that way. Do you feel better for it? You like being punished? Well, buddy-boy, you screwed up, just like everybody else screws up. But most people move on and you didn't."

Her voice was raised now, and she pointed at him with a shaking finger, tears streaming down her cheeks.

[185]

"You want me to wait for you to come around? Well," she said more quietly, her whole body shaking now, "I'm not doing it. Go off and be a damn Indian for all I care."

Lynn turned and left. It was but a half-minute before the black Yukon was peeling out of the yard.

26

After Lynn's outburst, it all came apart.

Tucker thought he and Lynn were having a private conversation, but he glanced up to see Rose and Connie watching them from a second story window. Even without hearing all the words, they had a good idea of what was being said. He heard later from Rico that Connie had stopped at the realty office the next day and Lynn told her about his wife's death, the daughter's murder, the treatment center, and his acceptance of the guilt involved. She finished with a long list of Tucker's problems.

Then Rose got a gun and started shooting up the countryside.

It happened on Tuesday of the next week. The sheetrocking was finished and the rooms had been cleaned. Tucker was labeling various pipes in the basement when Connie called down to him. Rico had taken Rose to school, and so it was the first time in a couple of weeks that the ranch was quiet.

Connie led him to the lavender garden. Stopping close to the concrete bench, she took his arm and kept him looking ahead as they walked to the river.

"Don't turn around," she said, handing him a small mirror. "Look at the cliffs."

Tucker held the mirror close to her shoulder and tilted it until he could see above the house. There was a man peering over the canyon rim. Tucker took a deep breath, then moved the mirror along the rocks. He saw no one else.

"I saw him yesterday when I came down to the river," Connie said. "I thought maybe it was a hunter or something, but he came back today. I saw him when I was taking the garbage to the trash bin. You can't see him from inside the house."

Tucker looked intently at the figure. "Is it Armando?"

"No. Not big enough."

The man disappeared as Tucker watched in the mirror.

He and Connie walked back to the trailer. Tucker spread his topographic map on the kitchen table. He remembered that the map had shown some kind of dirt road on one of the mesas, and he found it on the map but the road stopped at a watering tank that was a short distance from the curve of the mesa above and behind the cliffs. There was an incline between the two elevations, but the topo lines were relatively wide apart, indicating that it wasn't a steep slope. That made it an easy hike to get from where the road ended to the rocks above the house.

The primitive road led to a county road that joined with the highway about fifteen miles west of the ranch. There had to be at least two gates along the way, he thought, and it was all private land. It wasn't likely that someone would accidently end up above the house. Whoever it was had been there on purpose.

Tucker waited until evening, after the dining table was cleaned from supper, to tell Rico and Rose of the mysterious visitor. He showed them the map and described what he and Connie had seen.

"The ranch is a great place to hide when no one knows you're here. But if somebody wanted to shoot at us, we'd be sitting ducks. They could even throw a rock and probably do some damage. Do you think you need to move back to town? At least you'd have the police for protection."

"Is this your attempt to get us out of here?" Rose asked.

Tucker was confused. "What?"

"You want us to leave, right? Why don't you just tell us to leave? Or maybe you ought to leave. You move to town and leave us here. I'll bet Lynn would share her bed with you."

Rico looked confused as well.

"How about you going after this guy, instead? Why don't you get your bow and arrow, ride your horse up the cliff, and go get him. That should be easier than shooting a buffalo, right?"

Tucker sat back with a blank expression, but Connie was turning red, her eyes narrowing.

"It's a big question anymore whether you want to finish this house or not," Rose continued, spitting her words out. "Go spend some more money—it seems like you've got plenty—and you won't need us at all. It's not like you need us anyway. Big guy, big money. Taking care of all us poor people."

"What are you doing?" Rico finally blurted out.

"He's your friend, right?" she said to him. "And your meeentor?" She sounded the last word with Rico's accent, an insult that obviously stunned him. "Can't you see he's using us? He moped around in his trailer for a few days, twice, while you took care of things. He wasn't even needed. And this dream stuff... Oh, sure, that little boy is so pathetic, having to be an Indian and all. Maybe he was better off with the Indians than living in this dump."

Connie jumped up, grabbed Rose's arm, and roughly ushered her into the kitchen.

Tucker and Rico sat stunned while Connie laid into the young woman with a tirade of scorching words in the next room. While the barrage of words continued, Tucker leaned forward on the table, gave Rico a shrug, rose, retrieved his blanket, and went to sit on the porch.

It wasn't only Lynn who was calling his hand, he thought. He had lost everybody someplace along the way. Even if ninety-five percent of Rose's words were stupid and wrong, she must be expressing some grain of truth that the others felt. They had lost faith in him. While he was keeping his eye on the schedule, while he was focusing on the contractors and the work, and while he was dealing with Sam's dreams, his crew—his family—had stopped believing in him. He no longer had credibility.

He heard shouts coming from the side yard and a series of pistol shots.

Tucker launched out of his chair and dashed down the porch, leaping over the end rail, and then sidling along the foundation until he could see what was going on.

Rose was in front of the dorm firing a pistol at random points on the rim of the cliff above her. She was screaming, yelling, crying, frantically waving the pistol in the air.

Tucker came up behind her, and grabbed the pistol from her hand.

"Where did you get a gun?"

[189]

Rose whipped around. "You think I can't get a gun if I want one? You think I can't defend myself? You've got another thing coming, Jack! I can fricking well defend myself, and don't you think I won't!"

She was stumbling around as she yelled out the words, crying and blubbering. Rico had rushed out of the dorm and was now holding her; Connie watched from the doorway. Rose allowed Rico to lead her back to her room.

Tucker unloaded the pistol, pocketed the shells, and slid the gun into his pocket.

He stood for a while, looked around, meandered around the grass, and then went to his trailer where he put the pistol in the gun safe. He sat down at his kitchen table and stared at the trailer's interior.

Where had he gone wrong?

After several minutes, he reached into a cupboard behind him and removed a deck of cards. He dealt the cards out on the table, making several piles, running his fingernails along the edges of the cards so they were perfectly on top of one another. He then straightened the piles with each other, lining them up so they were perfectly horizontal to the edge of the table.

He gathered the cards, shuffled them, and repeated the process. It wasn't a game. Sometimes there were more piles, sometimes less, sometimes up the side of the table, sometimes along the bottom, and sometimes randomly spaced.

Each time he'd straighten the cards in each pile, line the piles up until their alignment was perfect, gather them, shuffle, and start over.

He had lost Lynn. He had lost Rose. He had lost the family that had come for his protection, and now they were being spied on by an enemy even as the whole business was falling apart.

Damn. He did not understand why it had all gone to hell, and he plainly did not know what to do to make things better. He wasn't even sure he could. He regretted most what Lynn had said. Had he wasted his life missing his wife and daughter? Had he talked himself into more guilt than he deserved, or, at least, hadn't his penance for thirty years been enough? He felt stupid. He felt small. He couldn't believe that he was that far wrong in his assessment of his fault, but he wondered why Lynn could hurt him so easily with her accusations if he hadn't been utterly wrong all along. Couldn't she see how he had failed? Couldn't she see how he had earned everlasting punishment?

He kept dealing the cards, straightening them, lining them up, and gathering them up again.

What also bothered him was that the house and the property had now been under a significant threat by an unknown person on the cliffs above the house for two whole days.

And not once had he heard the flagpole make a sound.

27

Tucker stood at the window and stared empty-mindedly as the first big snow of December began covering the front yard with a layer of white fluff. Forecasts called for a half-foot or more in the Canadian River canyons. The mountains west of Las Vegas were already blanketed with enough snow to last until spring, but the eastern plains and canyons had yet to remain consistently cold enough to keep snow on the ground.

He pulled a chair to the window in the darkness of the library, wrapped a blanket around his shoulders, and watched as the snowflakes drifted through the light from the kitchen window and the window of the upstairs bedroom.

He listened to the sounds behind him: Connie shifting pots and pans in the kitchen, constantly chattering with Rico, while Rose worked on a roll of dough that would become a loaf of monkey bread for breakfast.

The kitchen was completely finished, bright and fully equipped, and it fairly hummed as the center of life in the house. That had been his solution to the trials and tribulations of November. After a long night of playing with his cards, he had decided that too much of the work in the past months had not produced a final product. It was work done to prepare for more work. It satisfied him to check things off his To-Do list, but it left everyone else unsatisfied and frustrated. His crew needed to see results from their hard work.

It was also his conclusion that his family still felt like they were in hiding, living in shacks, eating in stark circumstances, and acting as refugees. The emotional strain was high, and although the builder's life more or less suited him, the isolation from town, in combination with Rose's pregnancy and the threat of Armando, had worn the Mares family thin.

Early the next morning, Tucker began work on the kitchen. It took two weeks to finish the walls with drywall compound, to replace all of the trim around the doors and windows, paint, hook up the lights and plugs, and install the plumbing. They moved in the table leg units built in August and Tucker cut and fit countertops that gave Connie at least three times the space for food preparation. The new sinks, faucets, stove, refrigerator, and dishwasher gave preparing the meals a whole new level of ease. All of the lights that Rico installed made the room bright, the colors of paint Connie and Rose picked were just right, and Tucker's expert trim work gave the room a neat and tidy appearance. Connie even washed and waxed the linoleum tiles. Although the floor would never look good, the sheen made the room glow.

It took everyone, and everyone had a part. By the time they had finished, his crew, and his family, had returned. The house had become a home.

The two weeks also closed out fall and officially moved them into winter. Tucker had the HVAC company install the remaining radiators so that all the living spaces were now warm. As the temperature plunged, Rico, Rose, and Connie moved into their bedrooms without any of the finish work completed, but having a toasty-warm room and big beds more than compensated for the inconvenience. Beginning before Thanksgiving and lasting to the middle of December, the two bedrooms were finished and painted, new comforters bought, rugs laid down, and curtains hung. They were now continuing their progress with the last bedroom, the hallways, and the stairwell.

Tucker also added hinged doors to the cistern holes in the pantry floor. The cistern represented too much history to cover permanently. He was thinking about returning the play boats to the cistern's rim as a memorial to Sam, but it was hard to let them go.

The man peering over the rim of the cliffs was not seen again. Now that the winter snows had begun, Tucker thought, it was unlikely the man would be back. Even when the snow melted, backcountry roads turned into muddy ruts that precluded heavy vehicles. Someone might make it in an ATV, but since nothing had come of it, the guy must have just been looking the place over. Everyone still kept an eye on the rim, however, knowing that the man's visit was not accidental. Somebody was planning something.

Tucker leaned back in his chair and relaxed as he watched the snow quickly fill the dry stalks of the clump grass. It was better than television. Expecting another good dinner, he lowered his head into his hands, worked a few of the cricks out of his neck, and let his mind wander.

It was all good, he was thinking. Rico had passed his GED the previous week and was now working on the house every day, unless he was needed to help ferry Rose back and forth. She only had two more weeks before the long holiday. She and Rico would then join her parents for a long visit at her grandmother's for Christmas while Connie celebrated at her sister's house in Albuquerque. Tucker would be alone for a few days, and so, of course, he was identifying things at the house that he could do on his own.

But he wondered what Lynn would be doing and if she'd like to spend some time with him. She had not been to the ranch since her November tongue-lashing. He had thought once or twice about dropping by her office when he was in town buying supplies, but he did not do it. It was her move, if she wanted anything to do with him.

Tucker thought about his dreams of Sam, but he was no longer obsessed with them. He remembered his feeling of misery with Sam's surrender at Fort Sill being cut short by Lynn, making him wonder if he had made his misery worse than it actually was. Had he amplified his emotions associated with the other dreams as well? He was still curious, and he would have probably tried to dream again—it had been more than a month—except he didn't want to risk all that he had gained back. Besides, he had no object to access another dream.

Maybe the dreams were over, he thought. Tucker might never know what happened to Sam. He still couldn't justify why the dreams had ever happened in the first place. They had been fascinating, spooky, and considerably outside his comfort zone; but he couldn't see that they had brought any change to him. He considered his obsession temporary. Certainly, the occurrences had been dramatic, and drawn him and the others into a world tinged with the supernatural, but he couldn't see any long-term effects, unless he counted Lynn's absence. He was hoping that could be turned around. He still remembered the good times at the beginning of the summer, and how much he had enjoyed a good friend.

Tucker resumed his walks through the house in the evening, though he no longer listened for the heartbeat. He wasn't sure what he would do if the heartbeat was not there. Something had changed in the relationship between him and the house, maybe on the house's part and maybe on his. But when the flagpole didn't clang when the man appeared on the cliff, he began not to trust the house. For a year and a half he had felt a positive, continuing presence, and he had always assumed that the house was on his side. He thought that they had some sort of pact between them, an agreement of mutual respect, protection, or restoration...something. But not having been warned of an obvious danger seemed like a snub, or worse, a change in attitude; or worse still, it seemed like the house was up to something.

Fear that the house could do evil things slowly crept into his mind. He wasn't worried, he told himself, but perhaps he felt less naïve.

Tucker raised his head and looked again out the window.

There was a woman standing in the light, the snowflakes swirling around her.

He sat upright, startled, and leaned toward the window, making sure that he was not imagining it.

The woman waved.

Tucker stood, grabbed hold of the window frame next to him, and felt his hand trembling.

He waved back.

Letting go of the window frame, he noticed that it was not he who was trembling.

It was the house.

Tucker forgot his coat as he went out the front door and around to the side yard, passing a Jeep Cherokee parked in front. How had he missed hearing that? The flagpole, again, he noted, had not made a sound.

The woman walked toward him, the snow gathering in the folds of her soft hat.

"Hi," he said. The woman was elderly, maybe in her seventies. She wore jeans and cowboy boots, which even in this country were not the boot of choice when it came to walking through snow. Her coat was more appropriate—a heavy red-and-black woolen blanket-patterned Western jacket with a hood. She stood ramrod straight, a cane in her right hand.

"I wasn't sure anyone was home," she said. "I saw a light over here and decided that I should take a look before I knocked."

"We're still in the early stages of remodeling and don't have any rooms in the front of the house with lights at the moment," Tucker replied.

He looked up into her face as they talked. She must be the tallest woman he had ever met. Tucker was not short, but this woman towered over him. She had to be six-four, maybe six-five. And she was not thin. The way her coat fell, he could tell that she had broad shoulders and a trim waist.

He was more startled by her face. She looked familiar, but he was sure that he had never met her before.

"Are you Tucker Whitby?" she asked.

"I am," Tucker replied, extending his hand.

"I'm Elizabeth Aston, and I'm from way up in Montana. I've come to see the house."

"Well, you are most welcome to do so. Let's go inside and warm up, and I'll give you a grand tour."

Tucker walked with her, awkwardly holding onto her arm to steady her, though she did not seem to need it. Walking with her gave him time to think, but no thought seemed to stick. Montana? What in the world was she doing out here this late at night and in a snowstorm? Who was this woman?

"Did you have any trouble getting here?" Tucker asked. The canyons along the road were always in the shade long before sunset. In December, the sun was low in the sky, making the canyons very dark. Add a snowstorm to the situation and he was surprised she hadn't turned around. His biggest puzzle was how she got through the gate. Connie had brought Rose from school that afternoon, and so she must have left the gate open, he realized, which was not like Connie at all. Locking the gate was a rule.

It occurred to him that the house may have opened the gate, as it sometimes had. But this woman was from Montana and could hardly have had any interactions with the ranch for the house to know her.

"The snow didn't even get deep until a mile from here," she said. "And I printed a map off Google. I apologize for it being so late in the day, but I was in Denver this morning and it seemed a shame to quit when I was so close."

They reached the front steps.

"I'm afraid that only the kitchen is fully functional," Tucker said as he went up the steps. "We'll set a place for you for dinner so you can look forw…"

The woman had stopped, obviously not listening to him. Her body was moving slightly back and forth, her free hand twitching somewhat against her coat. She was muttering, lost in thought.

"Ms. Aston, are you okay?"

She slowly approached the steps. When she put her foot on the first step, the front door knob turned and the door swept open.

Tucker knew he had shut it firmly. With a breezy snowstorm, he was trained not to be gentle.

There was a string of clangs as the flagpole cable beat against the metal. It caught Tucker off guard. The flagpole hadn't made that much noise in a month. What in the world was happening?

Tucker saw Connie, Rico, and Rose in the front room, the construction lights now on, watching through the doorway. They had probably heard him rush out the door and were now as surprised as he by this visitor in the night.

Elizabeth had seen the door open by itself, but she just shook her head, looked down, then up, and continued to climb the steps. Slowly, hesitantly, she walked across the porch and through the door.

As she stepped over the threshold, the house shuddered. Squeaks were heard from the floor as it began to slightly flex up and down, and the old plaster on the walls around the entryway popped and cracked. The pots and pans in the sink made clattering noises, and the legs of the dining table scraped against the floor tiles. Rose uttered a few expletives as she grabbed the parlor doorway. Rico slid to her side and grabbed his mom, and holding both of them, he looked around with wide eyes.

Tucker's mouth fell open as he followed the woman. The house hadn't done anything like this since he and Lynn stood on the stair landing that first day.

Defiantly walking ahead, Elizabeth passed through the vestibule, then jerked to a stop as the house stopped shaking and a low moan started, not of pain but of relief, as if someone who had been lost suddenly finds himself in the place he wanted to be. A small whirlwind of snow whipped through the door and surrounded her, gently spraying snow particles against her coat.

Professor Elizabeth Aston of Montana State University weakened, stiffened herself against her cane, and collapsed on the floor.

28

Tucker closed the door and ran to get the blanket from his chair in the library while Connie rushed for a wet towel. Elizabeth was already coming around when they returned, looking up at Rose as she cradled her head. The elderly woman lay quiet for a moment, then, excusing herself several times, sat up, then stood up, and was helped into the dining room.

She barely fit into the chair at the table.

She accepted a glass of water from Rose, and as she was drinking, Tucker saw her face in the full light for the first time. He gaped at her, stunned at his recognition. He had seen her face before—in his dreams. If Elizabeth Aston let her hair down and added a deeper shade of red, he was looking at Samuel Mulvaney. She had an obvious feminine cast to her appearance, but the intensity of the eyes, the spacing of her features, the cheekbones and her chin—they were an exact match.

Tucker struggled to get a deep breath. Muttering, he walked quickly around the room, his jaw adopting an involuntary tremor. The others watched him, bewildered. Elizabeth Aston, fully recovered, also watched, curious.

Tucker finally sat at the table across from her, breathing erratically and trying to control his emotions, trying to think. Was this it? Was this the purpose of the dreams, that he would know what Sam Mulvaney looked like?

"I'm sorry," he finally blurted out. "For a minute, I thought that I recognized you."

"I'd be surprised if you would have met me and not remembered," Elizabeth replied. "As you can see, I'm not exactly average in appearance."

Tucker was still trying to calm himself. Was she related to Sam? He hadn't died in his dreams. And if he had lived after Fort Sill, he could have married and produced a bloodline. He decided to take a long shot.

"Ma'am," he said. "Are you, by chance, a descendant of Samuel Mulvaney? You look just like him."

Elizabeth Aston jerked up straight in her chair, her mouth open as her jaw dropped slightly. She struggled to say something, then cleared her voice, her face becoming stern. She looked now at Tucker with suspicion in her eyes.

"There are no existing photographs of Samuel Mulvaney as a man," she said carefully. "How can you know that I look like him?"

Tucker didn't quite know how to answer. "Uh," he began. Was he going to tell her about the dreams? He'd sound crazy. This woman has been here, what, ten, fifteen minutes? He didn't know a thing about her, but the house obviously did. The house had come unglued when she walked in. There had to be some explicit connection to the house or to the Mulvaneys or to something.

"Beginning in August," he said slowly, deciding to be honest and direct, "I've been having some remarkable dreams. Samuel Mulvaney has been at the center of those dreams, and I have seen him as a young man. If these dreams are true, then I know exactly what he looked like. And you look just like him."

Elizabeth Aston looked at him intently, then sat back and took a deep breath.

"I am not a descendant of Samuel Mulvaney," she said distinctly. "I'm a descendant of his sister. I'm Lucille Mulvaney's great granddaughter."

Tucker was flat-out dumbfounded, his expression matching the expressions of the others around the table. He had never really thought about the little sister that had been sent back to St. Louis. All he remembered was from the first dream, where the little girl chatted away during breakfast.

"Welcome home," he finally said to the lady across the table.

His words jarred Connie out of the household's collective trance. She gave a little scream and rushed to the kitchen, checking

[202]

immediately for anything burning. This broke the hypnotic spell that had been cast over everyone.

His attention returning to his visitor, Tucker told Elizabeth that she should expect to be staying for supper and for the night. There was no way she was leaving. She acknowledged it as well, and offered no resistance, as if she had hoped for such an invitation.

With that settled, Rico and Tucker set out to the dormitory to get a mattress for their new guest while Connie and Rose finished preparing the meal. After the mattress was placed in the spare bedroom upstairs and made up with sheets and blankets, and after the thermostat on the room's radiators were turned up, Rico and Tucker returned by way of the kitchen, hearing a heated exchange dominated by Rose.

"But the floor was shaking! You saw it! What the hell is going on here? I think we should get out of here. I don't need ghosts in my life! I don't care who this lady is, and I don't care about the dumb little Indian boy or his sister. I've had enough of this spooky crap!"

Tucker decided to join Elizabeth.

"I should introduce myself," she said as the others were busy in the kitchen. "I'm a history professor at Montana State University. I was given the URL to a newspaper article about the house."

"Ah," Tucker replied "You've read *The New Mexican* article. That's how you knew about the house. But it can't be a coincidence that you're also directly related to the Mulvaneys. How is it that you've never been to this house?"

Elizabeth was obviously embarrassed. She leaned forward and lowered her voice. "Well, I didn't know it existed. I'll go into more detail later, but a rather mysterious circumstance occurred to bring me here."

Tucker introduced her properly as the others returned and as supper was served. There was a little chit-chat during the meal. The people around the table were nervous and expectant, not sure what to make of the happenings in the entryway nor of this strange lady who sat before them. It was after the dishes had been gathered and put away that the new visitor finally began her tale.

"I hope that you will forgive me for such an abrupt and dramatic entrance," Professor Aston began, "but I am as surprised as you are. I never knew this house existed until a month ago. I had known the story about Lucille Mulvaney ever since I was a teenager, but I assumed that the house had been gone for decades. To be truthful, my family didn't really know where it had even been located."

Rico had brought Elizabeth's bags from the car. She reached over and retrieved her briefcase, opened it, rummaged through a few file folders, then laid one on the table.

"When I received the URL from a friend and looked at the newspaper online," she continued, "I was amazed to find that the house still existed. I loved the story, and I especially loved the pictures. I was most enthralled with the picture of the front of the house.

"As soon I saw the house, though, I knew that I had seen it before. But I couldn't have. My family certainly had no photo of the house, and our photos go back several generations. But it kept bothering me, so I went home and looked at the family photo albums.

"My parents died several years ago," Elizabeth continued, "and I was the dutiful daughter who ended up with all of the albums of family photos. I must have a thousand pictures, and most of the people in the pictures are people I don't know.

"Trying to find what had struck me so definitely about the picture in the article, I sifted through the photos until I found what I remembered."

Elizabeth opened her folder and took out a plastic sleeve. In this sleeve was a small photograph, perhaps four inches by four inches, with tiny scallops along the edges. A woman stood in the center of the photograph and behind a short stone wall. A small girl sat on the wall to her left and a larger boy sat on the wall to her right.

They were obviously on a porch. On the right side of the photo, the stone wall, covered by a capstone on top, supported two round posts that led out of the top of the picture; and to the right of the posts, the stone wall stepped down to a row of bannisters. In the background, windows were set into a curving brick wall and a door some feet to the side peeked over the shoulder of the girl.

Elizabeth passed the photograph around without commenting.

When it got to Tucker, he gingerly took it out of the sleeve and held it up.

His jaw dropped and his eyes went wide. "Wait a minute! This is the front of the house! That's the rockwork around the gazebo."

Elizabeth gave a little laugh. "I believe that it is. That wall, in fact, matched the wall in the picture from the article. The photograph is of a woman and two children on the porch of this very house."

Tucker could hardly sit still. "But is that..."

"I think it is," Elizabeth answered him before he finished his question. "I think that the woman is Violet Mulvaney. The little girl to her left is Lucille, and the boy on her right...well, that boy is her son, Samuel."

Tucker stared at the photograph. The lady looked familiar. It could have been the woman who was mixing the pancakes in his dream. He realized that he didn't have a clear image of the woman in his mind. He had seen Violet, obviously, but hadn't focused on her enough to make a strong impression.

But the boy! Now he was remembering Sam looking in the mirror in the first dream. The old photo was surprisingly sharp but the faces small. The longer he looked, however, the more the image of the boy in the picture looked the same as the image in the mirror.

It was him. It was Sam Mulvaney.

Tucker fell back against his chair, stunned.

Rico, Connie, and Rose crowded around the photo when Tucker passed it back to them. Knowing now who they were supposed to be looking at was clearly mindboggling to them. It would have been almost a hundred and fifty years ago.

"Wait a minute," Rose said. "There's a photographer's date on the back of this. It says 1921. The people in the picture couldn't possibly be the Mulvaneys. They were long dead by then."

Elizabeth nodded. "That's why we had always ignored the photograph. We couldn't connect the photo to any of our relatives in 1921. Nobody could figure out who it was, and so the photo was put in with other unknown photographs. My dad kept them in a bunch in the back of a photo album, but because it seemed so odd, I've remembered it all these years.

"The woman and the children had clearly been at this house, on its very porch, as proven by how the house appears today. But if it was of Violet and her children, it was dated fifty years after she died. How could that be? I studied the photograph and am convinced that I know what must have happened."

The others looked at her.

"The photograph seems all wrong for being taken in 1921. It is much too precise, the color is wrong, and the photo just doesn't appear like the other photos that we had of that time period. I think it must be a photographic copy of the original. In the late 1860s, a photographer would probably have produced a tintype. After the original was taken, someone, probably Violet, sent the original back to her family. Maybe to her sister, or maybe her mother and father. It would have been kept with other family photos. But keeping a tintype would have been awkward. I think that the original was taken to a studio in 1921 and a regular photograph was taken of it so that it would be easier to keep."

Tucker listened intently, his hands folded on top of his head as he stared at the ceiling. What an incredible story. A picture of Sam Mulvaney. There was no doubt it was the house. He'd had the masons add mortar between the rock and the bottom of the capstone and down the side to the railing. And now he had no doubt that it was the boy in his dreams.

"When I realized what I had, I was astounded," Elizabeth continued. "No one in my family had ever imagined a connection between this photograph and the Mulvaney story, and then, suddenly, I believed I had an actual picture of Violet and the children. Plus, the photo was taken at a house that I always thought no longer existed, but, now, did exist. I just had to come to visit. I had to have a chance to be in this house. I finished up my classes for the semester, hopped in my Jeep, and here I am.

"As for my collapse on your doorstep," Elizabeth said. "I have no idea what happened or why. I felt like I was being squeezed like a frantic mother might hug a lost child. That is, in fact, exactly how I would describe it. I was coming home, and the house knew it and so reacted as a parent might react."

"But how could the house know who you were?" Tucker said, wondering out loud, forgetting to be discrete. "It's done some pretty remarkable things before, but being able to sense a lineage of generations is hard to conceive."

"What do you mean about the house sensing stuff?" Rose said as she leaned forward in her chair.

Tucker motioned for her to sit back. "I can talk about it later, but for now just accept that the house can sometimes…uh…respond to various things," he said, not wanting to talk more about the subject. He wanted to listen to the woman across the table.

"You're talking ghosts, right? You're finally going to admit that this place is haunted, right? And the stuff that happened tonight—it's a ghost, right? I'm out of here!" Rose exclaimed, jumping up from her chair. She was caught on the arm by Rico.

"SIT DOWN!" he said. "Just, please, sit down."

Rose yanked her arm away, hesitated, then sank back in her chair.

Tucker looked at Elizabeth. "Go ahead."

She took a deep breath. "Okay, finding the picture was the primary reason I wanted to come. But there's a second reason, and it has to do with a mystery that has been in my family for generations. I was hoping that I might find something here that would help me solve it."

Connie gently put her hand on Tucker's arm and suggested that perhaps everyone needed a break. She had made a cherry cobbler for dessert, and there was always ice cream in the freezer. Tucker agreed, Rico nodded his assent vigorously, and Rose was already up and through the dining room door. Elizabeth smiled her agreement and, looking a little worn, relaxed into her chair.

After Connie and Rico had distributed bowls of cobbler with scoops of ice cream on top, the professor resumed her story.

"Much of the interest through the years has been around Cyrus and his wife because of his suicide and her insanity. I've always been more interested in their daughter, as you might imagine. No one knows what happened to Samuel, but I can tell you quite a lot about Lucille.

"Lucy Mulvaney was six years old when the Comanche Indians stole her brother. That was on the morning of Samuel's tenth birthday, August 10th, 1870. A month or so later, Cyrus Mulvaney, her father, booked stagecoach and train passage for Lucy and a housekeeper from Las Vegas to St. Louis, intending that Lucy would live with his wife's sister and brother-in-law until such time that he and Violet could join her.

"The first leg of the trip was by stagecoach from Las Vegas to Trinidad, Colorado, then on east by various trains. Lucy and the housekeeper arrived in St. Louis on the twenty-ninth of September. Unfortunately, by that time her father had murdered his old partner and hanged himself, and was already buried. And her mother had disappeared and was presumed dead. That information reached Violet's sister before Lucy ever stepped through their door.

"Violet's sister and her husband, Neville, in fact, hated Cyrus Mulvaney for who he was, what he did, and for taking Violet to an unwashed and uncouth country of heathen white men and flesh-eating Indians. That's, at least, what they believed, according to a letter that Violet's sister had written to their mother. And Cyrus's using Violet's dowry to become rich was the icing on the cake, so to speak.

"As soon as she arrived in St. Louis, Lucy was taken ferociously to their breasts, adopted as quickly as possible to erase the Mulvaney name from her memory, and subsequently never told a single true fact about what had happened to her parents. She was told they both died of cholera. The brother, Samuel, was seldom, if ever, referred to, and always in the past tense, for he was certainly dead.

"Lucy Mulvaney, now named Lucille Simpson, had a normal childhood growing up in a wealthy home and never heard an additional word of her birth family. What she knew was what little she could remember, and nothing happened that would have brought any of the real truth to light.

"Until 1879. In May of 1879, this arrived at the Simpson house."

Professor Aston opened the file folder and removed a second plastic sleeve that contained an envelope. She removed the envelope, opened it, and removed a piece of yellowed paper. She handed it to Connie, who looked at it, then passed it on. It measured about 5 inches by 7 inches and had the heading "Western Union" in faded letters across the top.

"It's a telegram," the professor said. "The lettering is quite faded, but you can still make out most of the information. The telegram was sent from Las Vegas, New Mexico Territory, on May 6th, 1879 by a Mr. Smith. It was sent to Lucy Mulvaney in care of Neville Simpson, St. Louis. The message consists of only three words:

Run, Lucy, Run.

"You might expect that a cryptic message like this would have demanded an immediate explanation. In fact, Lucy, who was now 15, was in Chicago at a finishing school and so not even at home when the telegram arrived. The Simpsons discreetly shoved it into the back of a drawer and that was the end of it. Anything connected to the name Mulvaney was not to be paid attention to. Lucy never even knew the telegram existed."

Tucker held the telegram, turning it from one side to the other, carefully examining the print, the date, the individual letters, the letterhead—every aspect of the paper. It was mysterious, he thought, and fascinating. The others sat still, their eyes focused on the tall woman at the end of the table.

"Many years later, in 1930," Professor Aston continued, "when Lucy was herself a grandmother, her foster parents finally succumbed to old age, and an envelope containing this telegram was found in their records.

"The details are few, but Lucy, surrounded by lady friends helping her sort through the many boxes of the Simpson's belongings, undid the envelope, removed the telegram, read it, then screamed and stood straight up as if hit by a lightning bolt. She continued to scream, then staggered and then fell over as dead as if the devil himself had snatched away her soul."

A chill passed through the room. The wind blew the snow in giant waves against the window, the storm picking up speed and changing the tenor of the snowstorm to a blizzard. There was no sound from the flagpole.

"An investigation followed and the real story of the Mulvaney family was revealed, the one that we're all familiar with. The telegram was passed down to my mother, who kept the mysterious telegram in a safety deposit box, as I do now. I hadn't thought about it in years, but when I read the article and then found the picture, I felt like lights were being turned on in a dark room. I could not resist the chance to look at what the lights were revealing."

Tucker continued to look at the telegram. He was completely puzzled. Who sent the telegram? Who was Mr. Smith?

And where was Sam?

29

Tucker coughed, sat up in his chair, and leaned forward on the table. "I expect that it's my turn to talk about what has happened in the last several months. But everybody here has heard my dreams and probably doesn't want to hear them again. Let's take a break, get a cup of coffee or hot tea, and then I'll tell Elizabeth what I've experienced. The rest of you can stick with us or go on to bed. I'm sure that tomorrow is a snow day at school, and so I don't imagine anyone will be going anywhere in the morning."

Rose was on her feet, tugging at Rico. Connie followed, offering to get the coffee pot going before she went upstairs. Tucker told her to go on to bed unless she wanted to sit with them.

It took a few minutes to get a pot of coffee fixed, and Tucker took the opportunity to get more cobbler. Elizabeth was satisfied with coffee, and she leaned against the kitchen island as she sipped from her cup.

"Let me show you something," Tucker said.

He led her to the pantry door and pointed at the notches on the facing. "This is where it all started."

Elizabeth ran her fingers over the notches, did her own guessing at the progression of height that they reflected, and finally put her hand up to the two notches at the top. Tucker had brought his box of Sam's belongings from the trailer and placed them on the dining table: the tiny boats, the cigar box and its contents, and the arrow. Beginning with the door facing, he described each remnant of Sam's presence in the house and where it had been found, the dream that followed, and the aftermath that Tucker endured.

Elizabeth listened intently, not asking questions. She fingered each of the items from Tucker's box as he spoke, lining them up in front of her.

"This is remarkable," she said, once he had stopped.

It was late and the wind continued to buffet the windows. Looking outside, Tucker could see the snow still swirling in the light. There was more than six inches on his pickup.

"It's late and I expect you're tired. And you didn't even get your tour of the house. But we'll have lots of time tomorrow. I'll take you around in the morning. Let me show you one more thing, and then I'll take you to your room."

He plugged in the construction lights for the upper floors and took her up the stairs. On the second floor, he pulled back a corner of the plastic that covered the next stairway, and they walked up to the third floor and into the first bedroom.

"You're convinced this is it?" Elizabeth asked.

"No question. It's the wallpaper." He pointed to the section next to the window. "My first dream started with Sam in bed and looking at the sunlight coming across the wallpaper. That's exactly what I saw when I woke up after the first dream. Lucy may have also slept in this room when she and Sam were younger. I suspect that the family lived on the whole third floor."

Elizabeth looked around, touched the walls, the sill of the window, and walked from one side of the room to the other. Then, with a wistful look, she followed Tucker down the stairs and to her bedroom. Rico had brought up her bags and left them beside the bed, and she had brought her briefcase, returning the telegram and picture to it before it was closed.

"Not the Ritz, but give us time," he said. "This will be a nice room when we get it finished and the bathroom functioning. We've also grown pretty countrified out here, and so we've given up some social graces. There's a wide-mouth jar next to your bed, your pee bottle if you need it. It's a lot better than slogging through the snow to use the toilet in the dorm."

Elizabeth laughed. "I've done my share of sleeping in barns and stables. So I've learned to pee in many situations. Thank you."

"Connie's always the first one up, and breakfast will be an informal affair. Have a good sleep."

Tucker unplugged the lights as he went down the stairs and out the back door, stepping through the snow on the deck and over to his trailer.

* * *

I am stunned. My mind is racing from what I've learned.

I thought it was SHE. When her car entered the canyon and I was aware of her, I felt sensations that I hadn't felt in more than a century. I was confused and knew that I needed her closer to learn more. I opened the gate and waited. Even when she stepped out of the car, I felt strong vibrations but still was not sure.

I was bewildered. What should I do?

When she came to my steps, though, when she walked on my porch, I *knew* it was SHE.

I didn't mean to be so strong in my reaction, but I was out of control. All these years of waiting, all these years of considering my charge to be vacant and impossible, all of these years of wanting her to return so I could encircle her and squeeze her with my welcome. I hope that I did not frighten her; that was the opposite of what I wanted.

But even as I wrapped myself around her, I realized that it was *not* SHE. I was confused. Then, when she told the others the story of SHE, all things became clear. I now knew why SHE had never come, why HE had not returned, and why I was stranded and abandoned by the ones who belonged within me.

I am humbled by being part of this story, but I am also horrified at the turn of events. Not reading a simple telegram changed the course of their lives, and of mine.

I felt weak as she told her stories. What do I do? What can I do?

I have been the constant in this long story of tragedy. I was in the beginning and I am now in the end. I have orchestrated the dreams for the man and brought him to the brink of redemption. There are more moments to play out, and I must be patient.

But this woman's arrival makes me wonder. My charge, can it be fulfilled? Can my secrets be revealed? The man is becoming HE; the woman could be SHE. Dare I plan for fulfilling the purpose for which the shaman brought me to life?

[213]

More dreams are needed.

30

Elizabeth couldn't sleep; her brain would not slow down. It had been four weeks since she'd read the article about the house, and the chain of events that followed had filled her with the anxiousness of unanswered questions. Was the picture really of Violet and her children? How could she be sure? How had the house survived for so long? Would she find new information about the telegram? How had Mr. Whitby's dreams happened? Was he really seeing Samuel Mulvaney, really watching his life evolve? And the suffering that he endured afterward, the wounds that clearly imitated those of Samuel in his dream, how was that possible?

Elizabeth turned on the light beside her bed and sat on the side of her mattress. From her briefcase, she removed a writing tablet and a pen. Leaning forward, she scribbled a timeline that ran from the moment she had driven past the gate until Tucker had brought her to the bedroom. Carefully, with as much detail as she could remember, she wrote paragraphs on separate pieces of paper and then ordered them on top of the timeline.

She sorted the papers on the floor in front of her bed, looking them over, adding more comments, adding more detail.

She had finished a rough accounting of her time at the house when she heard a child crying. It surprised her. No one had mentioned a child in the house, nor had anyone done anything to indicate that there was one.

The crying became more of a whimper, but the desperation in the voice was still clear. It was a child in distress, a child who needed help.

Elizabeth slipped on her coat but did not bother with her boots, fearing that they would make too much sound. Her socks were thick wool, and so she felt confident that her feet would stay warm. Her pajamas were thick fleece, a requirement during the harsh winters in Montana. She thought about waking Connie but decided to investigate first.

She turned on her flashlight, opened her door, and followed the sounds of the child, carefully stepping up the treads of the back stairway to the next floor. She hoped that she was not disturbing anyone.

Elizabeth crept down the third floor hallway, following the impassioned cries through the various rooms. The crying became less distinct and harder to hear, and finally faded altogether, leaving her perplexed.

She found herself in the last room, the bedroom next to the stairway that looked down on the building that Mr. Whitby had called the dormitory, the bedroom directly above her room one floor below. But it wasn't until her light flashed across the wallpaper that she realized that she was in the bedroom that Tucker believed belonged to Samuel Mulvaney.

She caught her breath, then relaxed as best she could in light of the exciting coincidence. She was standing in the very place that her great grandmother had played with her older brother so many years ago.

It was surprisingly warm, whereas she remembered the chill in the air when she previewed the room with Tucker.

Elizabeth extended the bulb on her flashlight and it became a lantern, giving a faint light to the whole room—the tilted ceilings, the dry, dull wallpaper, the worn floor—and she imagined how the room would have looked almost a century and a half before. A bed, night tables, a chest or two. Certainly an armoire to hold Sam's clothes. The fireplace and its wood box and a mantle that held…pictures? drawings that he had made? mementoes? There would have been rugs on the floor and at least one oil-filled lamp, probably more.

She remembered the boy in the photograph with his mother. Tall, thin, with hair that looked like it refused to be combed. Even though the photograph did not reveal it, she knew that both Sam and Lucy had the glowing red hair of their father. It was one attribute that had continued down through the generations. Her own hair had been a deep red as she was growing up, as was the hair of most of her siblings and cousins. The unusual size of the descendants was also common, although boys were more favored with it than girls. She had been one of the exceptions.

She walked down the hallway, looking at the various rooms, then returned to Sam's room. She agreed with Tucker's assessment and could see the whole family living on the third floor. The main bedroom that was the parents' would have been augmented with one room that served as a large closet and another as a dressing room. There would have been a sitting room and perhaps a reading nook in the round space created by the house's tower. The children probably shared a connecting room separated by a tall, sliding pocket door. Lucy would have had dolls, toys, maybe even a tiny table and chairs that belonged with every little girl's tea set. In boyish style, she could see Samuel arguing soon for a room of his own, and he would have loved this particular room because it looked at the cliffs, down into the yard, and across the river.

Tired from her long trip and absorbing evening, Elizabeth sat on the floor and leaned against the wall next to the window. She was happy, and she was thoroughly pleased that she had come.

She was weary, though, and needed to sleep. She had many questions for Mr. Whitby, and she had so much more to understand, but her questions would have to wait for the morning. And she wanted to see the house, all of the house, every square inch of the house.

The house where Lucy lived.

Her head nodded, then fell gently to her chest.

Small wisps of cloud came from around the walls, making small ocean-like waves as the room slowly filled with smoke.

31

Mother pumped water into a bucket, then poured it into the heater tank on the stove. She tried to nurse the fire back to life, but finally put new kindling and straw in the stove and restarted it. She got the flames to stay, and laid in three heavy sticks of pine. She needed enough hot water to clean the dishes, the counters, and to mop the floor. With people coming in the middle of the afternoon, she needed to start cleaning as soon as she could. The housemaids were already dusting the rooms.

"You want to go find your brother?" she asked the little girl. "He might let you ride one of the cows if you promise to give him a big slice of his birthday cake."

Lucy squealed with delight. She had been playing with her dolly at the table and now held it secure in her hand as she ran out the back door.

The barn was a short run across the yard, but hearing the clang of the cowbells ahead on the road, she ran past the big doors and took the foot path along the river. She loved running on the path because the grass was taller than she and would keep her hidden as she crept up on her brother.

But she was not hearing the cows' usual good sounds and wondered if one of them was sick. When she came out of the thick grass onto the road, all she could see were two men bending over one of the animals on the ground.

The two men were Indians, she could tell. She needed to run back to the house and go to the safe place. She was to go right now, yelling to Mother and Father as she went.

But she knew that Sam was ahead of her, that he must have seen the Indians, and that he was probably running this way. She wanted to wait until he came.

Lucy backed up, retreating onto the narrow path until she was again hidden by the tall grass. The men ahead were cutting on the cow, and Lucy started crying when the Indians yelled their awful yells and shot arrows into the poor creature that still kicked and squirmed on the road. She knew that the arrows were hurting her friend.

The Indians were yelling more and shooting arrows toward the house. They reached into the brush along the road and pulled a bag out of the bushes. Lucy saw red hair and the straps of overalls, and then she knew it was Sam. The Indians were taking Sam.

She cried more because of the surprise she was feeling and for the wrongness of what was happening. She ran, but she did not run to the house. She ran in the direction of her brother, tears burning her eyes, yelling his name so he would know she was there.

She made it up the road, stepped carefully around the now dead cow, and tried to see Sam as she looked up the canyon. All she caught was a glimpse of him riding behind one of the men on the back of a horse, and for just a second, he looked back at her.

She screamed his name and held up her hand as if her wave would be a comfort to him.

She turned and ran for the house, crying and screaming down the road and across the yard. She was caught in the arms of Father, who had heard the yells of the Indians. He quickly set her down and looked into her face with fear in his eyes. "Run, Lucy, run," he said, and pointed to the house. Mother was screaming from the back porch.

"Indians! Sound the bell," he yelled and ran for the road.

Mother stumbled down the back stairway and ran for the bell on the pole next to the front porch, used for calling the hands to dinner. It was a big bell and could be heard a long way. Mother grabbed the rope and pulled and pulled and pulled to alert the ranch to danger.

Lucy was inside the house now, but she knew that the Indians were no longer at the ranch. She stood in front of the window that looked down into the yard, crying, holding her dolly, and listening to the constant clanging of the bell. She watched and waited, and then Father came back. Mother still rang the bell, and Father had to pull her hands from the rope to get her to stop.

"I'm going to get the men," he said in a voice clouded by his heaving breaths. "You find Lucy and lock all the doors. I'll be back."

He hadn't said anything about Sam, but Lucy knew that Mother was thinking about the Indians up the road. Sam had been up the road where the Indians were. He had not come back to the house so Mother knew that Sam had been taken or was dead. She screamed and screamed and screamed.

Father caught a horse in the corral, pulling it hard to the barn so it could be saddled. He was soon galloping up the road, whipping the horse furiously with the reins. Lucy knew that Father would find the ranch hands with the herd in the upper pastures, and he would send them after the Indians. There had been raids before, but the Indians had not come this close to the house.

There were other ranches close-by, and Father would ride to them, calling out the danger, calling out for help to get his boy back.

Lucy stood and watched. She still heard Mother screaming outside. She knew what she was supposed to do, but didn't. She raised her hand, thinking of Sam, hoping that he would know she was still waving at him.

32

"We're leaving."

Rose had waited until everyone was seated at breakfast. Elizabeth had passed through on the way to the dorm's bathroom.

"As soon as the road is clear, we're moving to town. I talked with Lynn and she knows an apartment that we can move into as soon as we're ready."

Her tone was defiant but measured as she spoke, but Rico looked like he had a hangover. Connie's surprised, Tucker thought, as he looked at the faces around the table. Apparently, she hadn't been in on the conversation.

If Rose was expecting someone to protest and talk her out of it, it wasn't happening. There was only silence. Tucker hadn't any warning of the announcement, but he couldn't find it in his heart to ask her and Rico to reconsider. He was, quite frankly, tired of putting up with her, but he still felt a twinge of sorrow that he had failed. He didn't doubt that she needed more space and more control and more comfort, but she had become increasingly negative about the work and the amount of time and effort spent on making progress that, to her, seemed pitifully slow. She continued to place the blame for any bad karma on ghosts within the house. So, if she was looking for reasons to leave, then it was probably time for her to move on. Since Rico didn't have a job in town, Tucker was sure that he would be returning every day to the house to work, which was good. He was needed.

It was interesting that Rose had already called Lynn. Tucker had been in the trailer since before breakfast, and so Rose must have used the phone last night, probably while he and Elizabeth were talking in the kitchen and dining room. That was the only way it could have happened without him knowing.

He was still thinking about Lynn when Elizabeth came in and joined the others around the table. She greeted everyone with a smile.

Breakfast was subdued. Rose did not say another word, and Rico was as silent as a stone. As soon as the two were finished, they disappeared. Tucker expected they'd spend their day in the bedroom or the basement, wherever everyone else was not. Connie was silent as well. He expected that she and Rico would get together at some point and discuss the situation. Tucker sympathized with her. As much as she did or did not like living so closely with her son and his maybe-to-be wife, she would miss them. And she'd be alone.

After breakfast, Tucker and Elizabeth toured the house.

"This is one big house," Elizabeth said as they finished with the upper floors and were walking down the stairs into the basement. Even though Tucker had not yet installed radiators in the basement, if you added a blanket it was comfortable enough to watch TV. Tucker had laid down strips of carpet, and so walking on the cold floor was tolerable.

"Let's sit for a minute," Elizabeth said, lowering her large body into a corner of the sofa.

She told Tucker her dream from the night before. He listened intently, curious and amazed at the same time. That she had the dream so quickly after coming to the house puzzled him. He wasn't surprised that she had not needed an initiator, something comparable to the boats, the cigar box, or the arrow. Her bloodline would probably be enough to provide her access to all the dreams she wanted. And he didn't even feel jealous for her having a dream. It at least proved that he wasn't crazy.

He and Elizabeth returned to discussing Tucker's dreams, going through the details of Sam's life as it had been revealed. The last scene in the story was Sam surrendering at Fort Sill. What happened after that? How would they find out?

Letting go of the intensity of the family's tragedy for the moment, they talked about the Comanches on the plains, the other Indian tribes, the demise of the buffalo, the growth of the big ranches, and about Charlie Goodnight, the great plainsman of Texas. According to Elizabeth, it was probably Goodnight's herd grazing outside of Las Vegas in 1866 and on its way from Texas to Colorado that provoked Cyrus Mulvaney to try his hand at becoming a cattle baron. And it was Goodnight's choice of moving his cattle trail to the east the next year, avoiding Mulvaney's land, that had helped turn Mulvaney's planned cattle depot into a failed idea. Later on, in the last part of the century, Goodnight would go on to become the most influential cattleman in Texas, founding huge cattle ranches that would establish Texas as the world's cattle empire in the 1900s.

Tucker loved the stories of the 1800s. There was nothing that they discussed that Elizabeth didn't know in depth, and he quickly became an ardent admirer.

Along the way, he made a major decision.

"There's another side of the house that you should know," Tucker said. "It sounds like our paths are merging here, and I think you should know the whole story. I kind of hinted at it last night. What you do with the information is up to you, but I imagine you'll understand that discretion may be best."

He gazed at her for a moment, then took a deep breath.

"This house is a little more than your average house," he began.

He described the first impressions of the house, then related the specific incidents of supernatural behavior: the porch, Sam's initials in the basement, the stairwell, Sam's birthday cake, and Elizabeth's entrance into the house. He described the house's breathing, the heartbeat, and the smaller manifestations like the opening and closing of the gate and doors and the clanging of the flagpole cable. As he did, he was surprised at how many things he could cite as manifestations of an imbedded spirit.

The house itself was not content only to be described. When Tucker had finished his details, the basement had a brief moment when the air was filled with the smell of lavender, and the flagpole clanged twice.

Elizabeth leaned back into the sofa, wide-eyed and apprehensive, and gave a heavy sigh. "My goodness" was all she said.

They sat quietly for a while. Connie broke the silence when she called downstairs. There would be no lunch, but a meal was planned for four o'clock. To hold everyone's hunger at bay, she had prepared a snack—a large bowl of chili con queso, two bags of tortilla chips, plus a baking sheet full of cookies. She invited everyone to come share.

Tucker decided to give Lynn a call, and so he told Elizabeth to wander through the house and to nap if she wanted. He figured that she had heard enough bewildering news for a while.

The storm outside continued. The wind was strong, snow-filled gusts lashed the house, and the temperature hovered around twenty degrees. At least a foot of snow covered the grounds, and some drifts were far deeper. The storm was significantly more brutal than what Tucker remembered had been forecast. But the house was snug. He felt no drafts and the windows were performing well. The boiler was chugging right along, and everything seemed perfectly comfortable. He was proud. They were in a world of their own, he thought, and they'd be fine.

Tucker figured that, if the canyons had a big snow, Las Vegas would have had more, and most businesses would not have opened for the day. Lynn should be at her house.

Lynn was in fact at home and seemed surprised by his call. Eventually, she was laughing because she could not get a word in edgewise. So much had happened, Tucker told her. He described Elizabeth's coming and her fainting in the front room, and he told Lynn who she was and what she had learned. He described the photograph, the telegram, and Elizabeth's dream. He found himself unable to stop.

He was surprised when Rico pounded on the trailer door, letting him know that supper was on the table. Tucker had talked for almost two hours and he still did not want to hang up. He finally asked Lynn if she would come to the ranch whenever the roads were clear, most likely in a couple of days. He wanted her to meet Elizabeth.

The meal was full and satisfying. Not New Mexico fancy but good Hispanic fare. Connie had roasted thinly sliced strips of steak; sautéed green, yellow, and red bell peppers with onions, garlic, and squash; and all of it was layered on top of refried beans spooned onto hard corn tortillas. The combination was covered with salsa, lettuce, tomatoes, cheese, and sour cream. There were also cups of a green chile stew, and then sugared *sopapillas* covered with scoops of ice cream for dessert.

"I'm now a firm convert to green chile, and I consider myself lucky to be your guest," Elizabeth said as she leaned back in her chair.

Connie wanted to know more about Lucy: her life, her loves, her adulthood. Elizabeth was happy to oblige.

Lucy was raised a proper Victorian woman with good manners and graces, and she was well educated. Having been raised on the frontier gave her a sharp edge, and she, although accepted into the St. Louis society, was never a favorite. It only became worse when Lucy hit her growth spurt and soon towered over her friends. With flaming red hair and a massive body, she found herself treated more as a novelty than a lady—tall girls were never asked to dance. She tolerated it, however, and refused to give up her tinge of wildness.

She married a man taller than she, produced a house full of kids, and lived an ordinary life, being known for her generous nature and happy demeanor. Elizabeth offered a general overview of the family tree, tracing her ancestry to herself and her brothers and sisters.

Having warmed up her audience, Elizabeth continued with a few tales of the West, telling of the Lincoln County wars, Billy the Kid, Pat Garrett, and cattle baron John Chism. And because of their proximity to Las Vegas, she recited a string of stories about it being a rip-snorting, rip-roaring frontier town that witnessed the likes of Wyatt Earp, Billy the Kid, Doc Holiday, Kit Carson, and a string of other names her audience recognized.

"And besides the brothels and the bars," she continued, "the local *patrón* ruled the sheriff and the judge and so the liquor flowed freely and bullets flew often. Las Vegas gave Santa Fe a run for its money when it came to political intrigue…"

The storm continued through the evening. After supper, Tucker cleaned off the satellite dish on the trailer, giving Elizabeth a chance to read her email and catch up on the news from Montana. After an hour, the network went dead. The phone died soon after.

The ranch was now cut off from the world.

Without the dish, the TV downstairs played only movies, and so Connie, Rico and Rose camped out on the sofa. Tucker went to his trailer to read, and Elizabeth was in and out of her room, working on different papers and articles but mostly wandering through the house.

One by one, people adjourned to their bedrooms and the lights went off.

Just before eleven, Tucker quietly appeared at Elizabeth's door. Precisely on the hour, she opened the door, slipped out, and followed him upstairs.

He had suggested it that morning. He was a patient man until he smelled a scent on the trail. Then he wanted to go forward as quickly as possible. She was much the same, she admitted, especially when she was consumed with a sense of discovery.

They carefully and quietly climbed the stairs to Sam's room.

Tucker had brought up several blankets and pillows during the evening without being seen, and he now made a pallet on the floor. Both of them had their coats, and he reserved two blankets to pull over them, but the room, like the night before, felt unusually warm.

His description to Elizabeth of the supernatural happenings in the house made Tucker realize that the house must have been involved with his dreams from the beginning. He had always considered the dreams separate from the house, but Elizabeth's dream had proved that the house had to be the common link to everything—the smoke, the voices, the physical attributes that he had felt afterward. Whether it created the dreams or just orchestrated their happening, he wasn't sure.

But if the house had been involved from the beginning, then the house had wanted him to have his dreams and Elizabeth to have her dream, and that meant that the house was leading them somewhere. There had to be a purpose to it all. It made him feel better that perhaps the silence of the house in the last few weeks had not been the house ignoring him. Perhaps it was working toward a purpose that required silence. If the house was connected to the dreams, then the house had been active all along.

Tucker helped Elizabeth down to the floor, then slowly knelt, turned, and lay beside her. He pulled up a blanket, placed his head on a pillow, and waited.

Elizabeth removed the photograph of Violet, Lucy, and Sam from her coat pocket and laid it on the floor next to them.

Surrounded by the house and lying on the floor that had felt the feet of the children, she felt at home.

Tucker heard a slow drawing of air, as if the house was breathing deeply and then felt a long, full, satisfied stream of air across his face. It had a hint of smoke.

Elizabeth Aston, great granddaughter of Lucy Mulvaney, and Tucker Whitby, sometimes buffalo hunter of the plains, heard the wind pick up, heard some sand hit the window pane above them, and fell asleep to what seemed to be the clopping of hooves.

33

The Assistant Superintendent walked through the center of the beds arranged in two lines down the large room. He stopped at the last bunk and looked sternly at Sam. "Get up, savage. There's a man here to see you. Try anything and we'll get the whip."

Sam did not react immediately. He hated the man at the foot of his bed, and he hated the others who always came with him to make sure any command was obeyed. He sat motionless, watching and waiting for a movement that might betray the real reason he was being sought out.

The compound near Fort Sill was a school for Indian children established and controlled by the Dutch Christian Church. There was a smattering of children from tribes across the plains and the Southwest—Wichitas, Apaches, Kickapoos, Comanches, Arapahos, Kiowas, Caddoes—but the majority were from the different tribes within the Indian Territories.

The school was meant for their own good: training for living in a white world. The school also served as the gathering point for kidnapped children retrieved from the various Indian tribes, children who had been taken, adopted into Indian families, and used as slaves, wives, or warriors. Ranging in age from youngsters to almost adults, the captives were brought to the school, cleaned up, and had their pictures taken.

The photographs were circulated among towns and ranches where children had been kidnapped or had gone missing. Sometimes the children remembered their names and so their kin were easy to find, but many were confused, not only about their names but the country they had lived in. In some cases, they could not remember their birth language. Parents and relatives would come, hoping against hope, and sort through the children, trying to imagine what their lost child now looked like.

Sam finally set his feet on the floor and rose. The men at the foot of the bed flinched as he moved toward them. He moved slowly out of the building, leaned his head into the sand-laden wind gusts, crossed the yard to the offices and was herded to a room at the end of a hallway. As he approached the door and looked in, he heard the conversation.

"You don't want him, Colonel." It was the voice of the Superintendent. "He's too far gone, just a man-killing savage. We've had him for months and it hasn't made a spit's worth of difference. I would have let the army hang 'im, but he's white and the President's policy is clear about the whites. Your letter said that you knew his family and were willing to talk about taking him. No one else has come, of course."

The man across the table spit on the floor beside him, wiped his lips, and grunted.

The interview room was sparsely furnished, having only a table, a few chairs, and a corner table with a lamp. Maps of the territories were framed and hung on the walls. A picture of President Grover Cleveland was prominently displayed by the door.

Only the two men sat at the table. Sam knew the Superintendent, but not the other man, who was much smaller and had a full beard that was straggly and unkempt. His sweat-stained Stetson sat on the table next to him. His clothes were nice but worn and dusty, and a narrow string tie gave him a more formal appearance. His hands and face showed him to be a man who had lived outdoors. When he stood up, Sam could see that he was bowlegged, indicating the man had probably ridden a horse most of his life.

Sam was prodded from behind, and he bent his head to fit through the doorway. Both men in the room stood as they watched him enter.

Samuel Mulvaney was three-quarters of a foot or more over six feet, with broad shoulders covered by too small a white shirt, the sleeves coming only to his mid-forearm. He wore coveralls due to the school's inability to find large enough pants, and moccasins for the lack of available shoes that fit. The clothes could not hide that he was rawboned like a renegade prairie stallion, his body dark against the white of his shirt. He was angular and rough, his hands large and calloused. His hair had been cut with a pair of sheep shears at some point, but a thick matted layer of unkempt red hair now covered his head.

His skin was stretched like well-worn leather, deep brown and wrinkled, and splotches highlighted his cheeks and forehead, the evidence of a once light-skinned complexion. Several small scars set off one large scar that ran from his left ear to above his temple. Even though his features showed a hard life, the proportions of his face and body indicated he was not too old, perhaps not even yet an adult. An older teenager, maybe.

As Sam now sat in the chair vacated by the Superintendent, he moved his eyes around the room, across the two men, to the table, to the window, to the ceiling. Not with purpose, but with intense alertness, like an animal warily measuring his surroundings.

"Mr. Styrus, would you excuse us that we might talk privately?" the man across the table asked.

The Superintendent was openly nervous. "I can provide other men if you want."

"That will not be necessary."

The Superintendent cautiously backed out of the room and closed the door, indicating that he'd be right outside if needed.

The man across from Sam spat a stream of tobacco juice on the floor, leaned forward on the table, and spoke clearly.

"I will be plain and talk straight. I'm Goodnight. I know who you are. I know what you've done. You and I have crossed paths three times, oncet up in Kansas, oncet when you hit my outfit in Colorado, and oncet on the Canajin when you were stealin' my horses. Each time you were set on takin' what was mine and I was set on killin' you when you tried. I was obviously unsuccessful."

Goodnight paused to spit, while Sam sat silent across from him.

"What your people did all over the plains, from north to south, is open knowledge. You were called Red Hair for obvious reasons, and you led parties that killed men, women, and children with the same regard that I kill rabbits and snakes. I have killed, but I am not a savage. You are a savage, though I doubt you were born that way. You became one at the hands of your captors.

"Nothin' you did was right or can be excused, but this is tough country and people have to become tough if they are to survive. You are what you are, by choice or not, but you don't have to now do what you did then.

"You got a Comanche heart and head, and I expect that it will take quite a while for you to let go of that Injun in you. You won't get that time here. You'll be more likely to die on your own, or they'll eventually make up some excuse and hang you in spite of what the President says.

"This is my proposition. I've lived my life in rough country and in rough ways. Now I'm building a ranch in what used to be your backyard. So far, I'm the only one there and I plan to use that fact to get as much land as I can. I especially need the waterholes. I need help doing it, and nobody knows the canyons of the Llano like the Comanche.

"I'm offerin' you a deal. Work for me. Stay with me, earn your keep, do honest work, and I'll stake you to a string of workin' ponies, grub, a roof to get you out of the rain. After five years, you make the decision. You can stay on with me or I'll give you a place on the middle fork of the Red to work as your own—or you can just leave."

Sam had not met a white man who talked like this.

"If you go back to the old ways," the older man said, "I'll hunt you down and kill you."

Goodnight spat again and leaned back in his chair. He had said what he needed. More words wouldn't tame the mind.

He sat.

Sam remained silent. It was a full five minutes before he spoke. Finally, in a halting voice not yet fluid in a language mostly forgotten, he said, "I have...business. I have business in New Mexico. Then I come."

Goodnight spat again and leaned forward. "Well now, I thought so. I knew your dad and I didn't like him. He was a corrupt and dishonest man who dealt badly with poor people. He lacked integrity. I don't tolerate men who have no integrity.

"But the snake he was in cahoots with was worse, and he treated your dad badly. Most of Las Vegas was just a dad-blasted den of vipers, but Hetley was the worst of a bad lot and deserved what he got.

"I reckon by now you know all of the details. But, being as you are a little hard to miss, you show up to claim your inheritance and people are going to know who you are and what you've done. You'll find your enemies numerous and powerful. Ending up in jail is no good, nor is dangling from a rope. You're too young. You ought to live life. You have been in the wild too much to sit behind bars and die. That would be a waste.

"So, I have a second proposition. You come work for me. We'll get the range in order for winter, and in the spring, I'll go with you to Santa Fe where there's a better breed of people. I know someone who can help you straighten out your estate, legally, and keep you out of trouble. If you have business after that, I'll ride on and leave you to finish it. You can catch up with me if you're still alive." Goodnight leaned back.

Sam gave no indication of his emotions, but he knew that he could not reject the hope that the man had just given him—that he might leave this compound, regain his freedom on the Llano, and once again ride under the broad sky. It had been a long time.

He remained silent for a couple of minutes, wary of any white man's proposal, then nodded his assent.

Sam did not have many possessions. They had taken what little he had, but the Superintendent had agreed to store a quiver of arrows and a decorated bow, his buckskin clothes, and an old leather pouch. He had never had a hat.

Mounted on an extra horse Goodnight had brought, he towered over the man beside him, his feet dangling beneath the stirrups. The Superintendent held Goodnight's bridle for a moment longer.

"You won't be able to do it, Colonel. He's a savage and you won't make him better. He's too set in his ways."

Charlie Goodnight looked thoughtful for a moment, then spit. Dirt from the large wad of juice splattered up from the ground.

"Well," he said, "that's what some people say about me."

The horses turned and hit a good trot going through the gate.

34

The weather cleared by midmorning the next day, leaving the canyon sparkling with a foot-thick coat of unperturbed fluff. Even the river was shrouded in snow, leaving a narrow ribbon of water barely visible.

Tucker sat in his trailer feeling like a fortune hunter discovering a clue here, a clue there. He had most of the pieces to a puzzle but not all. No picture existed to show how the pieces looked together, making it even more difficult to see how the pieces fit. And with so many new pieces—the revelations of Lucy's life, Elizabeth's dream, and now the dream that he and Elizabeth had shared—it was almost more than he could comprehend.

The two of them talked only briefly after breakfast. It was clear that Sam had lived past the Dutch school, and according to Elizabeth's calculations, Sam could have been as young as eighteen when he rode off with Goodnight. That left a lot of life untold. And the fact that the dream told of Samuel Mulvaney becoming associated with Charlie Goodnight delighted her no end. There would have been no better mentor and protector than Charlie.

After a quick lunch of leftovers, Tucker worked on the satellite dish but could not revive the internet or the TV. Leaving Elizabeth to rest from their early morning—they had both awakened at five and snuck back to their respective beds—he went to the trailer and put on snow boots, a down jacket, hat, and gloves. Fully outfitted in his snow gear, he grabbed a snow shovel and began clearing the side porch, carefully lifting the snow over the railing so as to not scratch the twin's handiwork. The front porch followed, and then he started on the long loop of the sidewalk.

It took the first part of the afternoon. Taking a break to relax and read a book, Tucker woke up in his chair in the trailer when Rico knocked to announce supper. Stretching, a little embarrassed, he joined the others. Everyone seemed in good spirits, having had a full day of rest, and Connie, as usual, produced a good meal.

Guilty about the unfinished sidewalk, Tucker returned to the snow shovel and went back to work. It was darkening in the sky when he began, but a three-quarter moon gave the right kind of light to see his way. He quickly worked up a sweat even though the snow was light and the air cold. The idea of walking Elizabeth around the big loop and showing her the different views of the house kept him at it. Between clearing the path and his pauses to look at the vast whiteness around him, more than an hour passed before he had shoveled to the front steps of the house.

Leaning against the stone of the steps, he remembered that he hadn't checked the gate in two days. He had asked Elizabeth if she had opened it. She replied that she found it open, and she of course had not known to close it.

Tucker assumed that the gate had been opened by the house and that the house would have closed it behind her, but…well, mark it up to an obsessive/compulsive disorder, he thought. He leaned the shovel against the front steps and set off up the road to check the gate, shuffling his way through the deep snow by the light of the moon.

When he topped the hill, Tucker's throat clinched in panic. The gate was closed, but there was a pickup parked on the other side.

He carefully looked around him, then cautiously walked down the incline. He touched the gate. He took his glove off to be sure, but there was no mistaking the movement. The gate was vibrating like an alarm.

Why hadn't the flagpole sounded?

Taking a flashlight from his pocket, Tucker looked carefully as he approached the passenger side. Maybe a late-90s four wheel drive Ford F150 with deep-treaded snow tires. The cab was unlocked and a nasty smell came out as he opened the door. It was littered with beer cans and empty McDonald's sacks. On the seat lay a folded copy of *The New Mexican* with the Mulvaney house article. The names and location of the ranch were circled in red.

He checked the glove compartment. No registration, only more trash. Snow in the truck bed partially covered an old spare tire and more beer cans. The sound of the engine must have been muffled by the snow.

Boot prints led from the driver's door to the hinge side of the gate. Someone had climbed over the gate, knocking off the stack of snow balanced on top of the pipes, then left the road and went up toward the cliffs.

They were large boots, and Tucker could think of only one person who had a reason to show up here and walk in that direction. A house isolated from town, vulnerable, without help from anyone, a dead phone line, which he now thought was no accident, and an impassable road: bad things could happen and not be known for days.

The pickup was parked close against the gate so no other vehicle could squeeze by, a deliberate maneuver to block the exit.

Tucker tried to run but found it impossible in the snow, and so he slogged as fast as he could shuffle his legs. His heart racing, he couldn't help but think how the house was quiet during two obvious threats after it had been a vigilant protector for almost two years. The flagpole should be going crazy; why wasn't it?

It seemed a reasonable conclusion that the house didn't want Tucker to know that Armando had come.

A barrage of more practical questions invaded his mind. How much time had passed since the pickup had come to the gate? How long had he been shoveling the damn snow while Armando was making his move? What was Armando going to do?

Tucker, bending low, came up behind Elizabeth's Jeep, then slogged along the side of the house. Voices were coming from the dining room, and so he carefully maneuvered below the windows. The sills were too high for him to look in. As soon as he was past, he quickly shuffled to the corner. Satisfied that there was no movement around the back of the house or down the path to the dorm, he made his way to the trailer and found his closet in the dark.

He opened his gun safe, removed his pistol, holster, and belt and fastened them around his waist. He positioned the holster so it put his handgun just above his right hip, hidden in the back by his coat. Thinking better of this strategy, he removed his coat to have less material to work through if he needed to draw his gun.

He stepped through the snow, up the deck, and through the back door without a sound.

The kitchen was empty, pans from dinner sitting on the island. Only a single voice disturbed the silence. Steadying his breath, Tucker stood tall and walked through the pantry hallway into the dining room.

"Ah, this must be the fine house builder who has been gracious enough to offer my family a fine house, fine food, and fine jobs!"

Armando was bigger than Tucker had imagined. His big belly held the chair back from the edge of the table so that the man had to lean forward, his thick forearms and elbows on the table, to eat from a plate in front of him. Rico, Rose, and Connie sat across from him; Elizabeth sat on the end. Their heads were down but Tucker could see all their faces were drained of blood. Except for Elizabeth, who had a look of anger and determination.

Tucker moved to the end of the table so that no one was between him and the big man.

"You must be Armando, beater of women and unborn children," Tucker said. His anger was growing. The little family holding hands beneath the table had spent the last few months in terror, the man's absence even a threat. Now he had finally come, playing some game of fear and intimidation. He deserved to be pistol-whipped and hung from a tree. The household had lived in fear for the last six months and Tucker steeled himself to finally stop that fear. It was time.

"Oh, gringo," Armando said, his smile turning to a smirk, "I am not those things. You must have been lied to, or perhaps there has been a miscommunication."

"Leave this man out of it," Connie exploded. "He's a good man, something you know nothing about."

The big man threw his tortilla in her face. "Shut up, woman. Let men speak together. He's got money, Chiquita! Look around! You think he cares about you? No, he just needed labor. He's got enough money to steal my family and bribe them to stay with him so he has lots of meat to choose from. Has he tasted you, yet? Have you shown him a good time? Huh, Chiquita? He can buy a boy away from his father. He can buy loyalty and buy servants to do his bidding, but I'll bet that he did not have to buy you, huh? You were free, maybe? And so he has thought that he was safe to do what he pleased with another man's wife. But, oh, what has happened, Chiquita? He's not so safe anymore."

Armando grinned, a string of lettuce hanging from his lips and beans smeared across his teeth. "Is that true, gringo? You not feeling very safe now?"

"Oh, I feel very safe, Mr. Mares," Tucker replied. "It seems you are the one who should feel afraid."

As soon as he said it, Tucker realized that he hadn't thought about Armando bringing friends, people he could have let out of the truck before he reached the gate and so Tucker would have missed their tracks. They could have crossed over the fence above the gate, out of sight. Maybe, somewhere in the darkness, there had been another set of boot prints.

Damn, he thought. He should have spent more time looking and less time planning.

"Afraid? Is there something to be afraid of?" Armando asked. "Maybe you think I should be afraid of you? Let's see. No, I'm not afraid of you. In fact, I am your friend. I come to visit my family. I read about you in the newspaper, gringo, and you're a fine man, a good man, friend to all the little people. A man who hires little teenagers and teaches them how to build things and how to respect one another. A good man who gives his workers room and board and then makes them sweat like pigs while they serve him. A good man like that, he certainly welcomes the fathers of his workers to come visit their children, even when their children have white whores for girlfriends!" With this last sentence, Armando threw his plate in Rico's face.

The big man was now standing and shouting at Connie, and she was shouting at him as Rico threw the plate back across the table. Rose had stood and backed away from the table. Elizabeth moved beside her, the cane gripped in her hand.

In one graceful movement, Tucker moved from the end of the table to Armando's side, one hand sliding to his pistol and the other pulling Armando's chair, one foot swiftly moving to kick Armando in the back of the knee. The big man's body bounced off the floor as Tucker's pistol was placed in his face.

"Enough," Tucker said. "Roll over."

[241]

Armando's eyes darted across the floor of the room and he began to laugh.

Damn, Tucker thought, and he backed off the big man and was turning when the first bullet hit his left arm. The second shot missed and shattered the window glass behind him, but the situation had become academic—Armando had grabbed Tucker's pistol. Tucker sunk to the floor in pain.

"My manners! Where are my manners!" the big man said as he struggled to his feet. "I forgot to introduce my friend, Miguel."

A considerably smaller man stood in the doorway, a large pistol in his tiny hand. Tucker squinted through his pain at Miguel and assumed he was the man who had watched from the canyon rim.

Miguel was dark and thin and wore a winter work jacket. His face showed no emotion. He would have killed Tucker without blinking—Tucker knew from the lack of anything akin to compassion in his face—but Armando waved him off.

"No, no. We haven't had our fun, yet." He yanked Tucker off the floor and struck him across the face with the pistol. Tucker went down on one knee. Armando shoved the pistol into his own pocket, grabbed Tucker by the throat, and dragged him across the hall to the library. Connie was screaming until Armando slapped her on the way out of the room. She stumbled into the hallway. Rico jumped him and got twice what she had gotten. Rose and Elizabeth backed across the floor toward the kitchen.

Using ropes he had brought with him, Miguel tied everyone's hands behind their backs, then pushed each of them into a sitting position against the wall in the library. "Hey, Mando. You seen this woman? This is one big woman!" He laughed as he shoved Elizabeth to the floor. The hallway, library, and parlor lit up as Miguel went to the kitchen and plugged in the construction lights.

Tucker was dragged to the far wall, and when the others were in place so they could watch, Armando beat him without mercy.

Tucker curled up, trying to protect his stomach and chest, to roll with the kicks and punches, to survive. His face and head were bloody and the sleeve of his shirt was sodden with blood. A stream of red ran down Tucker's arm and dripped from his fingertips. He couldn't focus, and his eyelids and cheeks were already swelling. Cuts across his eyebrows fed even more blood down his face.

Armando finally tired. He grabbed Tucker by the neck and threw him across the room next to the others. Connie was screaming again, and Miguel whacked her in the back of the head with his pistol. She slumped silently to the floor. Rico had backed Rose against the wall and crowded in front of her, hoping to protect her against the coming onslaught.

Armando signaled his friend. Miguel went out the back door and returned with a gasoline can. Armando then dragged a chair in from the dining room and sat down, facing the people cowering against the wall.

"You done me wrong. I did not deserve to be humiliated in front of my friends." The big man wiped the sweat from his forehead. "I can't go home again, and I liked my home. I can't even return to my town and my friends. You would make me a prisoner, but I will not allow that to happen." He smiled and scratched his fat chin.

"You made me a fool. My fine son, an idiot, has to poke a white girl. That's no problem. I don't have a problem with white meat. Poke all the white girls you want, even give them babies. I don't care. But don't make them part of my family. Our blood is good blood and goes all the way back to Spain. My family is descended from kings. None of you understand how important that is to me. I have always been a humble man, but I have royal blood.

"I support my family. I take care of things. I make a fine home, and bring home good money. Then my good wife gives me a sop for a boy. I wanted a man! She gives me a boy that will never be a real man. My descendant, my responsibility to maintain the bloodline of kings, is a big crybaby who can't poke a white girl and walk away. Well, if I can't go home, if I can't even see my friends again, then I think it's time I start over."

Miguel made a second trip for an armload of lumber scraps. He dropped them into a pile in the parlor and poured gasoline over the top.

Connie, now awake but woozy, coughed and choked as the stinking odor of the gasoline spread into the room. Miguel took a lighter out of his pocket and held it in his hand.

"Then my woman moves in with an old gringo, and I look even worse," Armando continued. "My brothers in Mexico, they make fun of me. You have no shame, whore. None of you have any shame. How about you, crybaby? You even know what shame is?"

Armando left his chair and grabbed Rico by the throat. He gave him a vicious slap across the face and threw him against the doorway. He grabbed Rose by her shirt, lifted her with one hand, wrapped his left arm around her neck in a choke hold, and dragged her to the other side of the room.

"I'm going to burn all of you. There won't be any bones left to show anything but an accident. Some crazy accident in an old house that burned to the ground, the fire killing all those hard-working, dedicated people. This house is going to make for one big fire. And we'll all cry for the baby, right?" He twisted his arm even harder against Rose's neck. She gargled a scream, cursed his ancestry, and tried to pull his arm away.

He took Tucker's pistol out of his pocket and held it against her cheek.

"Or maybe since the girl was killed with your white guy's gun, they'll think he murdered the whole bunch. I want you to watch, gringo," he screamed across the room.

Tucker had tried to focus on what Armando had been saying, but he was feeling increasingly sick from his battering and loss of blood. He struggled to stay conscious and kept looking in the direction of Armando's voice. He managed to get a hand up to his face and wiped the blood from his eyes, making the picture in front of him clearer. He was confused.

The big man was holding a pistol to his daughter's head, and he was smiling. Tucker had told his bosses that the man was a lunatic.

"Please, don't kill my daughter. Please." His voice was weak and he spit blood onto the floor as he begged. He slipped to his knees. "Please, please. She's all I've got."

The man with the pistol grinned, then nodded to his partner.

Miguel struck his lighter and got a good flame on the second try.

He threw it on the pile of wood.

35

An explosion lit up the sky outside the house. Blinding light burst through the library windows as a fireball shot up from the yard, followed by a loud boom that reverberated through the hallways.

Miguel jumped to shield himself behind a wall. Armando whipped around, stunned, then hurried out of view, dragging Rose with him. He stole glances out the window as flames swelled into a yellow ball outside.

Beyond the windows, a monstrous bonfire now burned not twenty feet from the house, its tall flames launching upward, uncontrolled, the wood popping from the heat and a roar cutting through the air as smoke and embers spread everywhere.

"Cops?" Miguel yelled. Armando shook his head, shrugging his shoulders.

There was another burst of light through the front windows, another booming sound, and another bonfire roared and crackled in the front yard.

Miguel was frantic, slipping on the gasoline-wet floor as he ran to the front wall. His lighter lay on the floor, no flame licking at the spilled liquid. He turned and stared at Armando.

"Not haunted, amigo? You said not to worry. You see this?" He was screaming at his friend, angry and scared as he pointed at the fires blazing in the yard.

In the north yard, a third fire burst into flames, spraying the dining room windows with pellets of charred wood behind a flash of light and another deafening roar.

Armando stared across the library and out the dining room windows. He was sweating now, his eyes wide as he jerked his head back and forth looking between the different fires outside. He held Rose even tighter, her feet swinging across the floor as she struggled for traction. She was hanging from his arms, her hands trying to pry enough space to breathe.

Boom! A fourth bonfire exploded outside the back door, beyond the deck, bolts of light racing down the hallway.

Four raging fires belched smoke and flames around the house, embers shooting up as smoke billowed into the night sky.

The flagpole cable swung freely in the air, beating against the metal pole, pounding out loud clangs that echoed against the walls of the canyon. The front door slammed open. The back door slammed open. Smoke poured in.

Miguel, his eyes wide with terror, ran for the front door, which slammed before him and refused his attempts to pull it open. He broke the oval window with the butt of his gun, shot the handle, kicked it, screamed at it, and cursed it. It did not open.

He ran back through the hallway, making for the back door, his hands in front, swimming through the billows of smoke that wrapped around his legs, his arms, and his face. He could not contain his screams, the full-throated sounds of a man pulled into a situation he could not comprehend, that he had no defenses for. Something was after him, reaching for him, grabbing for him. It was as if hell itself was after him.

He dodged into the dining room, then down the short hallway. There was a muffled scream and the slamming of a trap door.

Armando stood in terror, the pistol straight out and swinging from side to side. Rose was still in the crook of his arm. He had fired at the doors as he had heard them swing open. Now he was shaking, his eyes wide as he watched ribbons of smoke curl around his legs. He too began screaming uncontrollably.

Tucker rolled up to his hands and knees.

"Please, don't kill my girl! Please! Sara!"

Armando, his eyes full of fear and confusion, put the pistol back against Rose's cheek, not knowing anything else to do.

"Please!" Tucker screamed, focused enough to be angry now, and filling with hate, deep-down killing-type hate. "Don't!"

The smoke was getting thicker. Tucker tried to stand. Pain shot through his arm and he stumbled, then picked himself up again. He finally managed to get upright, his hands on his knees, taking a deep breath as he prepared to lunge forward. He had to try. There was no option; he had to try.

His breathing became easier as he inhaled the smoke, and he stopped feeling the pain of his wounds and strangely relaxed his withering arm. Am I dying, he wondered? He flexed his body. His arm did not hurt. His face did not hurt. His legs did not hurt.

This is what death is like, he decided. You stop feeling pain as your brain shuts down your body, preparing to let go of its functions, of its connection to life. He squeezed a cry out of his mouth and tears rolled down his face. He would be dead before he could do anything. And Sara would die.

Tucker began to sob, viciously gritting his teeth and screaming against them as he shook in anger.

But his sobs caught in his throat and he felt something else, a pull, a gnawing in his muscles and a swelling of his torso as he stood taller. He stretched his neck, rolling his arms, which were huge now and made of hardened muscles. He felt his legs as equally large as he stood up. He felt massive and strong, his hands and feet growing bigger. He inhaled the smoke deeply, longingly, as if it were food; he sucked it in as if it were water.

Tucker felt himself towering above the floor, an unrestrained power coursing through his body. He smelled the campfires, the incense that he had added, and he heard the chants and the songs and the prayers that he had offered. He felt the cut on his hand and the blood that he had dripped on the threshold of the door.

Tucker roared, straining as his hands and arms slowly raised above him, his fingers outstretched, his hands and arms shaking with rage. He filled the air with a powerful noise that shook the room.

He had returned.

Elizabeth lay on the floor, hoping that the smoke would rise above her. She could hardly see through the darkness as she tore at her rope, trying to get free.

But what she did see left her breathless.

A man was standing beside her, a huge man barely visible because of the smoke, a man so big that even she felt small. She watched as the man strained against his muscles, raised his huge arms above him, and screamed a long, throaty yell. Then he was gone, leaping across the room in one bound, his arms raised high in the air like an animal descending on prey.

Armando's eyes were wide open, staring in shock at the beast bounding toward him, stunned at the huge creature that had risen up out of the smoke. The pistol was still pressed against Rose's cheek, but a huge hand suddenly encircled the weapon and yanked it to the side. Thick, calloused fingers slid around Armando's throat and the huge body slammed into him, bowling him over as the gun clattered to the floor.

Rose slid to the floor, coughing, choking, rolling away to escape, to protect her unborn child.

There was no fight, Elizabeth said later. Armando crumpled under the big man, screaming in terror—horrible screams. She also heard growls and snarls. Then Armando had bellowed like a child, scrambling across the floor, trying to stand, falling down, then stumbling to his feet and running awkwardly across the room toward the stairs. Armando's flailing limbs had kicked the pistol across the floor and he grabbed it as he disappeared into the smoke.

The giant man straightened up, stretched his arms out from his chest, tipped his head back and his yell consumed the room. The sound from his throat faded as Elizabeth watched him evaporate into the swirling clouds.

She must have fainted or blacked out, she said. When she came to, the smoke had condensed into undulating waves that glided across the floor, draining from the room, currents of cold wind pushing the clouds out the now open doors. There were no leaping flames, no bonfires to be seen through the windows, no light from any source outside. The construction lights were still on, swinging from the ceiling. Tucker was on the floor where Armando had been, his arms clasped around Rose as she sobbed into his chest, shaking so much that Tucker's blood was slung across her face. Rico was struggling to stand up, and Connie lay on the floor to Elizabeth's left. Her eyes were open but she was not moving.

When the smoke finally bled away, the doors closed. The ropes that had bound their hands lay in a pile by the fireplace.

Elizabeth was on her knees, crawling first to Connie and violently shaking her. Connie shuddered, blinked several times, then slowly propped herself up with her arms. Elizabeth was already crawling to Tucker, her knees and hands smearing the pools of blood on top of the linoleum tiles. Tucker was unconscious, his arms now fallen away from Rose.

Elizabeth pulled off Tucker's shirt and ripped it into wide strips that she used to bind the gunshot wound in his arm. Rico had found Rose and was dragging her to a protective corner while Connie struggled across the floor to help.

Elizabeth yelled at the others to wake up and to get Tucker out of the house and into the Jeep. Knowing that her bandage would only temporarily stop the blood flow, she wrapped Tucker in a blanket and used the ropes to secure it around his shoulders and arms to slow his bleeding as much as possible. Then she and Rico dragged him through the front door as Rose helped Connie across the porch and down the stairs. The cold air slapped them awake and Elizabeth started the Jeep as Rico lowered the back seats. Tucker was shoved in behind her.

They flew through the open gate, Armando's truck on its side in the ditch as if it had been scraped from the road.

36

When they got within cell phone range, Rose called 911, then Lynn. They saw flashing lights as they reached the I-25 interchange and pulled over as the ambulance reacted to the on-off-on-off of their headlights. Tucker was switched to a gurney and hooked to various tubes and bags as the EMTs wheeled him to the ambulance and slid him into the back. Connie and Rico refused to wait for another vehicle and rode to the hospital with Elizabeth and Rose. Lynn met them in the emergency room as three different bays swelled with doctors and nurses and rolling carts.

Lynn asked that Rose be examined and an obstetrician was called. He did a sonogram and a general check and said everything seemed fine. Thankfully, the nurses also helped Rose clean the blood from her hair, face and arms, and gave her a gown to put over her blood-stained T-shirt.

Elizabeth cleaned as much of herself as she could in the bathroom, then borrowed a gown as well.

Rico emerged first. He was limping and had bruises on his face, and he was missing a tooth. He had a large mark on his thigh from Armando's steel-toed boots, but his ribs had not been reinjured. Connie followed an hour after that. She had a split lip, a large bump on the back of her head, and a minor concussion. She'd been given something for her headache but still kept her eyes closed after she sat down.

It was a row of gaunt faces immobilized by exhaustion, fear, and worry that finally looked up as an emergency room doctor came into the room. Interpreting his stern face as a sign of bad news, Lynn buried her face in her hands.

"The wound in his arm is severe," the doctor said. "The bullet missed the bone but severed an artery and shredded some of the nerves. We brought in Dr. Selven, an excellent vascular surgeon, and Mr. Whitby is now in surgery. It is a severe trauma, and so he may have a little loss of mobility and maybe some discomfort, even after it heals. He lost a lot of blood. We checked his ribs and didn't find anything broken, but he'll feel like they are. He'll have a good number of bruises too. He probably has a concussion, but we couldn't get him alert enough to check for one and we needed to get him into surgery as soon as we could.

"We'll get him up tomorrow or the next day and have a neurologist give him an evaluation. He'll be in the recovery room sometime tonight, and we'll get him into a regular room tomorrow."

They all thanked him, then sat awkwardly, too nervous and frightened to let go of their energy. Elizabeth volunteered to find a Starbucks and was warmly sent on her way. Within an hour, each was hunched over in a chair sipping a drink.

A bell went off as the automatic door of the emergency room opened and a Deputy Sheriff came into the waiting room. He looked them over before speaking. "I need to talk to the Mares family privately."

Elizabeth and Lynn volunteered to step down the hall. A few minutes later, Rose came to get them and they returned. Connie was crying; Rico had his head down. The Deputy stood in the corner.

Rose spoke in a low voice. "Armando's dead. They found him hanging from the third floor bedroom balcony. They figure he must have been running down the hallway and went into the bedroom to hide. The outside door to the porch was open and snow had blown in. He got tangled up someway in the cord of the construction lights, slipped on some ice, and went through the door and over the railing. The cord got wound around his neck, and when he went over, the cord pulled the door closed behind him, clamping it so it became tight. He either choked to death or broke his neck. They'll know after the autopsy."

Rose took a deep breath and sat down. The Deputy spoke.

"We're still looking for the other man. There are tracks in the snow going back and forth to the house, but nothing leading away from the house."

Elizabeth looked up. "There's a pantry room off the kitchen. It has a lift-up door in the floor that leads to a room below that holds the cistern. Look in there."

"Why would you think he might be there?" the Deputy asked.

"Just a guess. I heard some noises when he was running away."

The Deputy stood to the side and made a call on his radio. A minute later, he sat down next to her.

"You called it. The guy must have fallen right through the opening of the cistern. He either broke his neck or suffocated. It'll take a while to pull the body out, but we'll let you know when it's done."

The Sheriff's Department hadn't yet accounted for the guns—Tucker's 9 millimeter and the .45 that Miguel had used. They were assuming that Armando had Tucker's pistol in his hand as he went over the railing and so it must have been flung into the snow of the front yard. It would take daylight to search for it. Miguel's pistol may have been missed in the darkness of the cistern, the Deputy said.

"It's going to take all night to wrap up the investigation, ma'am," the Deputy told Connie. "Is it alright if we use the kitchen to set up a command center and coordinate everything?"

Connie nodded, then told them to use the bathrooms in the dorm if they needed.

"Uh, Deputy," Rose said. "When you're in the house, you probably shouldn't use bad language, drink, or play loud music. And don't leave trash around."

"Ma'am?" he responded, raising his eyebrows.

"Yeah. You don't want to piss off the house, that's for sure," Rose replied.

The Deputy, his eyebrows still raised, rolled his eyes, and shrugged. "Okay. Whatever you say."

After speaking into his radio, the Deputy took each in turn to the hallway for preliminary statements. After recording all of the interviews and confirming the situation with his chief, what happened seemed pretty straight forward, albeit odd, and so far, all the evidence they had found supported their initial conclusions. Satisfied, the Deputy left.

Elizabeth had told the others as they rode to the hospital that their answers during any police interviews shouldn't contain references to opening and closing doors, bonfires outside in the snow, billowing smoke, or a giant man who materialized out of nowhere. Nothing would be gained by complicating the situation with the truth.

About two in the morning, Tucker came out of the operating room. They kept him in post-op for several hours, then moved him into a private room when the day nurses came on their shift. Lynn had taken Rose and Connie to her house for the night, then returned to wait with Elizabeth, napping as they could. Rico told Lynn that he needed to stay at the hospital to make his wife and his child proud of him.

Everyone was back by nine in the morning, gathered around Tucker's bedside, their eyes moving from an unconscious Tucker to the green screens of the monitors above him.

The sheriff stopped by about ten o'clock to let them know that the road to the ranch had been plowed and Armando's truck was on its way to the county impound. Tucker's pistol had been found in the snow on the sleeping porch, where it was apparently dropped before Armando went over the rail. Retrieving Miguel's body required ventilation equipment from the utilities department and a portable wench, but his corpse had finally been pulled from the cistern. His pistol was found beneath him.

During the night, an officer had taped cardboard over the broken window of the front door and stapled a kitchen towel over the window in the dining room so the house was relatively secured against the weather. The sheriff left a card from a company in town that offered crime scene clean-up, implying that the family might not want to return to the house until the floors had been mopped and the walls wiped down. He indicated that the blood spills were extensive.

Tucker's surgery had been delicate—an artery close to the armpit was a difficult place to work. The surgeon wanted him to remain immobile as long as possible. When the nurse pushed more sedative into his IV, Lynn decided that it was a good time to return to the ranch. She would take Connie and Rose and they would

[254]

return in Tucker's pickup. They could change clothes while they were there. Lynn would bring back Elizabeth's bag and she could change at the hospital. They were on their way in a matter of minutes, anxious for relief from the intensity of waiting.

Lynn had heard the others' descriptions of the previous night, but when she opened the front door and saw the parlor and library, she almost vomited. Pools of blood had solidified on the library floor; splotches and splatters of blood were all over the rooms and hallway; and blood trails led to the dining room, where Tucker's blood dripped down the wall below the broken window. Complicating the mess were a thousand boot prints with mud tracked in by investigators.

Connie wretched when the reek of gasoline hit her.

It took a few minutes for all of them to put off the horror and move through the rooms. Connie and Rose immediately went up the stairway to change. Lynn cowered in the kitchen and tried to stop her body from shaking.

When Connie returned, she refused to leave without cleaning. Lynn argued that it would be done quicker and without the trauma if they called the cleaning business the Sheriff had identified, but Connie would not hear of it. And so Lynn and Rose joined her with pots of hot water laced with a strong antiseptic and a whole bag of paper towels.

It was hard work and Rose was overwhelmed with the smell after half an hour, puking a spot of her own to clean up. She was sent to sit in the Yukon while Lynn set the limit of one more hour before she and Connie would quit and they would all return to the hospital.

Lynn started with the bedroom and balcony upstairs. There was not much mess beyond the water that now stood where the snow had blown in, but she decided that it was a job that Connie should not do. It was bad enough to stand where Armando had plunged over the railing, but handling the extension cord that the investigators had taken from around his neck and left in a pile in the center of the room was not a memory that Connie should have.

When she had finished upstairs, Lynn took the mop from Connie and held her breath as much as possible as she repeatedly wiped the parlor and library with disinfectant. It took three rounds of emptying the pail and a full bottle of Lysol, but the pools, splatters, and boot prints were erased. Calling it good enough, Lynn took several large trash bags full of dirty paper towels outside to the deck.

Connie worked on the dining room, pantry, and kitchen. The mess was not so much blood as caked mud and melted snow. She cried as she wiped Tucker's blood from the wall and window sill.

Rose did not stay in the SUV. After her stomach had settled, she put her coat back on and walked around the sidewalk. She knew that Tucker had shoveled it the night before. With the strong sunlight of the new day, except for some patches of ice in the shade of the cliffs, it was clear around the whole path. She cried through most of her walk, the stress now rising to the surface as she was alone for the first time. She specifically looked for any evidence of the bonfires from the night before. There was nothing. The snow around the house was pristine except for tracks of those coming and going.

Not wanting to go back into the house, she settled for sitting on the toilet in the ladies' bathroom in the dorm, huddled close to the electric heater.

Lynn had moved to cleaning the fireplace and the gasoline-soaked wood, hauling the pieces out the front door and dumping them in the yard. They could be disposed of later. It took a whole roll of towels to soak up the gasoline, adding another bag to the pile on the porch. But once it was done, she was surprised at how quickly the toxic fumes disappeared.

It was when the reek of the gasoline was replaced with the rich aroma of lavender that she allowed herself to wonder about what had happened. While on the way to town after Tucker was in the ambulance, Elizabeth had told her passengers the bare bones of what she had seen as she lay on the floor. But it wasn't until the quiet hours of the night in the waiting room that she carefully led Lynn through the full details of her visit. Even under considerable stress, Elizabeth had a way with words and of analyzing the world around her. She drew pictures with her voice, Lynn thought, and she was as taken with her as Tucker was.

Rico had listened but made no comment.

Elizabeth began her story in her office in Montana and ended with a detailed description of getting the wounded Tucker into the Jeep. She described her finding *The New Mexican* article and the photograph of Violet and the children. She went over the history of the telegram. From her arrival at the house for supper the first night through lunch two days later, Elizabeth drew careful pictures of the various "pieces of the puzzle," as she termed it. Some of it, Tucker had told Lynn over the phone, but it was a world of difference to hear it from Elizabeth. Tucker had hurried through it, as anxious to explain as to describe, but Elizabeth allowed Lynn to savor the information, to ask questions and to understand for herself the significance of how each new episode blended with the others.

As Elizabeth recited the last dream, the dream that was shared with Tucker, Lynn was taken with how the dreams had intimately bound Tucker to Sam. Lynn had never doubted that the house was responsible for the dreams, regardless of what Tucker told her, but the fact that Tucker had become Sam and was able to rescue Rose in a way that Tucker had not been able to rescue Sara had to have been a carefully orchestrated plot. If that were true, then the house had chosen to act on Tucker's behalf. It had, in fact, created a path for Tucker to find redemption.

Lynn had never considered a situation where a haunted house might be tinged with nobility.

Elizabeth confessed that she did not know how the story was going to end, but Lynn believed her when she said that it was not over.

Returning the mop and bucket to the dormitory, Lynn found Rose on a toilet seat in the bathroom, the electric heater glowing close by to give the frigid room a hint of warmth.

Rose was shaking. "Is he going to die?"

Lynn turned the mop bucket upside down and scooted it in front of the helpless girl. She took Rose's hands in her hands. "Are you afraid?"

Rose's eyes filled and the tears flowed. "I've been afraid of everything. I was afraid they'd take the baby from me, that Rico would go away, that Connie would hate me, that the baby would be born dead, that I'd be left alone...I was afraid of everything, and I took it out on everybody. I am so sorry," she said as she buried her face in her hands.

"Sweetie, listen to me," Lynn said. "Every mother is afraid. I was strong with my first one, but I was sure that my second one had a bad heart and would not survive. I shook for the last three months that I carried him, I was so afraid. And you having this house stuff and Rico's dad—it's a wonder that you're still standing."

Rose sniffled and took a deep breath. "I am so sorry about Mr. Whitby. I should have done more. I don't remember a lot, but he got beat so bad!"

"Did he ever tell you that you reminded him of his own daughter?"

Rose was surprised. "The daughter that was murdered? I don't remember him saying anything."

"Well, he wouldn't, you know, but he loved his daughter. And from the very first time he met you, he thought that you had the same eyes, the same look as she did. He told me several times how much you reminded him of her."

"Is that why he was pleading with Armando about Sara? He thought I was Sara?"

"I imagine he was pretty whacked at the time, but I expect so. His own daughter was killed by a man with a gun, just like Armando was going to kill you. All Tucker could see, I expect, was that he was back in the moment that his daughter was murdered."

Rose wiped her eyes. "What happens now?"

Lynn stood up and moved, and Rose got up and followed her.

"I don't know, Rose," Lynn said. "We'll just have to wait and see. Don't think for a minute that any of us understands what happened last night—the house, the fires, the fight. We're out of our league on this one, but all we can do is work with what's in front of us. Tucker is not going to die but he may not be the same. None of us may be the same after this, but we have to keep going.

"It seems like forgiveness is in short supply around here, and I think that we need to understand how important it is now, and how much more important it will be in the future. Tucker needs to forgive himself for being human, and you need to forgive yourself for being where you are.

"And God only knows what the house is going to do next."

Inside the house, Connie had finished with the kitchen. The leftover food was sacked as garbage, and the dishes, pots, and pans were in the dishwasher, and the counters washed. The dining room table was clean, as was the floor, the wall, and hallway. She was waiting, anxious to get back, as Lynn and Rose came in the back door.

Even though the ranch road had been plowed, the yards of the house had turned to slush and mud from the Sheriff's Department vehicles. Connie struggled to get Tucker's big pickup out to the gate while Lynn sat in her Yukon watching them pull away.

At the last second, Lynn put the SUV back into park, jumped out, and ran back onto the porch. Standing before the door, Lynn hesitated, then placed her hand against the wood of the door as she remembered Tucker doing so long ago. She closed her eyes.

As she rushed back to her vehicle, the cable of the flagpole clanged against the pole, and it continued to clang until Lynn had driven through the gate, which closed and locked behind her.

* * *

My work is almost complete. It was hard watching the pain and the suffering, and it was difficult to cause fear and horror without regretting the confusion and distrust that accompanied it. But physical pains heal, while mental pains bring change. It is change that brings the salvation of people's souls. As resolute as the man has been for years, it was basic to his soul that freedom would be a gift were it ever to be granted to him. It has now been granted and I will see if he regains his life.

I have reconsidered about this woman. I like her. She sees the absolution that must occur for the man, and she perceives the changes needed to release him from the weights that burden him. She desires him to love again, freely.

And for me? My charge is fulfilled. I lack only one more action.

It is time to reveal my secrets.

37

Tucker returned to the ranch after three days in the hospital, his arm in a tight sling cinched to his body. The nurses instructed him to spend at least a week in bed, moving as little as possible. He did his best to follow their instructions, but his desire to reconnect to the house and the ranch was too persuasive for total obedience. It was difficult to lie in his bed and not imagine himself walking around, having done it for so many months.

He did not move much, though. Any movement was difficult. Dark red bruises were scattered around his torso and thighs. The cuts to his face were patched with either stitches or butterfly Band-Aids. A whole day of wet cloths over his swollen eyes had returned his eyesight, but his lower lip still looked as if he had a marble between his teeth and gum. Two of his fingers, although not broken, were taped together where the doctor suspected Armando had stomped on his hand.

Tucker could not lie down for long, and neither could he sit up for long. And his head hurt. But he was home, and for that he was thankful.

Following the first supper after his return, Tucker asked everyone to tell their story, leaving out no detail or feeling. He faintly remembered the fires exploding outside, but events afterward for him were confused or missing entirely. Pleased to be asked for total truthfulness, each person carefully recited what they had seen, smelled, or heard, and more was said than any sheriff could have ever written into a report.

Eventually, Tucker was satisfied; even some of his aches and pains had subsided with the mental closure that the conversation had brought. It was over. The dread hanging over the family was gone. Armando was still to be buried, and Connie was making the arrangements, but his death erased any of the legal problems a divorce would have introduced. Rose was safe, the baby was safe, and Rico could now measure his life from his own perspective and not from his father's.

How the house made everything happen was a mystery. Tucker was sure that the four fires were significant, as was the resulting smoke. He reminded the others that there was smoke before each of his dream episodes, and he told them he was convinced that the smoke had a specific meaning but wasn't sure what it was. He could not remember anything about becoming the giant man that Elizabeth saw.

Tucker also recognized the similarity between Rose's situation and that of his daughter, Sara. He did not remember calling Rose by his daughter's name or of wrestling the pistol away from Armando, but deep down he felt a sense of relief that he had not failed. He had redeemed himself, even it had been by proxy.

He wished he had been more aware. He would have liked to have the memory of putting monster hands around Armando's neck. Holding Sara in his arms, even if it was actually Rose, would have also been sweet. And to have this tale end with Armando hanging in the same way that Cyrus Mulvaney had hung was interesting, to say the least; the house was obviously capable of poetic justice.

Tucker knew the upstairs bedroom door had not been open, and that getting a light cord accidentally wrapped around one's neck was not easy. The house had played the final hand and he was glad of it. Any inherent guilt from Armando's death resided in no one.

Elizabeth took the opportunity to express her appreciation for everyone's hospitality and to say that it had been quite an experience. All of the new information on her ancestors was fascinating, and the fact that her heritage was tinged with the supernatural she couldn't even begin to appreciate. In her schooling in history, she could remember professors teaching their students to never accept a supernatural being as a prime cause of anything. History was made by people, not ghosts.

[262]

Well, she said, she might just have a different viewpoint after meeting up with the Mulvaney Mansion.

She said she hoped that everyone would heal quickly and asked to stay a little longer, which was readily accepted. Tucker even offered to finish the bathroom upstairs if she would move to New Mexico.

"And I'm looking forward to having my own little fire in my own little room," Elizabeth said. "My thanks to whoever brought in the firewood. My old bones will appreciate it."

The people around the table looked at her with blank faces.

"You mean, real firewood?" Tucker asked.

"Sure. It smells wonderful. If my nose is not fooling me, it's *piñon* stacked neatly in the box next to the fireplace."

This was a puzzle. There had never been any real firewood at the ranch. Tucker routinely cut up scrap lumber into fireplace-sized pieces, leaving a huge pile next to the dorm to burn through the winter after they had gotten all the different flues cleaned. Tucker knew that this wouldn't be true for at least another year.

Tucker sat silent for a moment, thinking, while Elizabeth's expression went from thankfulness to suspicion.

She finally smiled. "I knew we weren't finished."

As opposed to what used to be a grim challenge in the face unknown forces, and possibly the haunted, Tucker watched as the people around the table were almost giddy at the idea that a new piece of the puzzle might be at hand. They filed up the stairway, Tucker slowly bringing up the rear. He'd had more than his share of ghostly happenings, and it was now their turn, he thought.

In Elizabeth's room, Tucker struggled into a kneeling position in front of the wood box next to the fireplace while the others formed a semi-circle around him. The wood box, a plank-lined cavity built into the wall next to the fireplace, was about four feet tall and perhaps two feet wide. It was deep enough to hold good-sized logs of around sixteen inches in length. When full, the wood was probably enough for a week's worth of nightly fires in the fireplace.

Elizabeth's wood box was, indeed, filled with small, split logs. The smell branded them as freshly cut, and so Tucker knew that they had not come from the ranch property. If anyone had cut a tree in the valley, he would have known it.

Leaning slightly to the left to protect his slinged arm, he used his right hand to pull out a log and lay it on the floor next to him. He waited to see if anything happened.

Nothing.

He grabbed another log and removed it the same way. Nothing.

He pondered for a moment, shrugged, and then put the logs back. The last one was a tight fit and he gave it a good push to get it to the back of the box. The box moved. Everyone saw it move and pointed to where the box now formed an open crack along the side. He pushed the log harder, and the box moved more.

Rico helped Tucker push steadily and the box moved straight back a foot or so, then pivoted away from the fireplace to reveal an opening behind it. In the light of the room, he could see a narrow landing. Borrowing Elizabeth's flashlight, he pointed the beam into the darkness.

"Well, I'll be damned," he said. "There are stairs inside the chimney."

Tucker and Lynn didn't have flashlights, and Tucker wasn't about to struggle downstairs to find one. He asked Rico to pull down the string of construction lights in the hallway. Rico returned with a long length of cord that held several wire-caged bulbs, the end still plugged into an outlet downstairs.

"I'm going in and check it out," Tucker said as he started to scoot into the opening.

"Oh, no, you're not," Lynn said emphatically, the others shaking their heads in agreement. "We're in better shape than you are, and I'm not going to let you go anywhere by yourself."

Tucker looked back at her, then reluctantly agreed. But he wouldn't go last, muttering something about being the owner of the house. It was soon settled—Elizabeth would go first, Lynn second, and Tucker, helped by Connie, would follow. Rose would be behind her, then Rico.

A large loop of light cord was handed to each person, a cage and bulb on each loop.

"It looks pretty tight in there, so be careful," Tucker said.

Elizabeth had to get down on her hands and knees to crawl through the opening. Once inside, she slowly stood up, tested the strength of the wooden landing, and moved onto a small spiral staircase in the center of the chimney space. Lynn soon followed, and Tucker limped as he maneuvered himself through the opening. Asking Lynn to hold her light up, Tucker examined the inside of the chimney.

It was crowded even without people. The fireplace next to the wood box jutted out into the space, its bricks fully supported by wooden girders under the bottom. From the top of the fireplace, the brick flue, attached to the inner wall of the chimney, snaked its way upward. Adding to the profusion of brickwork, flues from the fireplaces below came up beside it and joined in a regimented march upward.

In the center of the space was an iron staircase that spiraled tightly around a center pole, narrowly missing the landings and fireplaces as it went both up and down the chimney shaft. It had no railing.

Looking below and above, Tucker could see that each fireplace in the different rooms projected into the chimney space in the same way. Each fireplace had a narrow landing next to it, which told him that each of the wood boxes probably opened like the one they had come through. That's why there are wood boxes next to every fireplace, Tucker realized, and why a wood box was built into the base of the chimney in the basement. The staircase went through all four floors, allowing anyone in the house who was threatened to slip through a hidden entrance on any floor and escape down to the basement. From there, the windows provided a way outside.

Tucker smelled a wet dirt odor inside the chimney. Perhaps the snow had revealed a leak.

Holding her light in front of her, Elizabeth crept up the narrow iron steps, carefully threading her body around the pole. Slowly, cautiously, she was followed by a caterpillar of legs and lights.

The space within the shaft narrowed at the next landing where the four flues of the four fireplaces below were joined by the two fireplaces and flues of the third floor. The third floor had the last of the fireplaces, and with no more fireplaces and no more wood boxes, the treads of the stairway should have stopped at the last landing. But they did not. They continued to spiral upward for a few feet more.

To a door.

A tiny door—much shorter and narrower than other doors in the house and looking singularly innocent with a porcelain doorknob in a simple faceplate—was above the last tread of the staircase by about a foot and sandwiched between the encircling brickwork of the fireplace flues.

Encouraged by Tucker, Elizabeth gathered her light cord into her right hand and carefully negotiated the last steps, barely squeezing into the crowded space. Her hand slightly shaking, she grabbed the knob and gave it a turn. It took jiggling just a little, but the door unlatched and swung open.

Tucker strained to see past Lynn for a better view of what was on the other side of the door.

Elizabeth held the light in front of her and stepped up into the opening.

38

Even after the small door creaked open as far as it could, the passageway behind it was still a tight fit for Elizabeth. It was a dust-laden space with a narrow wood floor and plastered walls, the ceiling maybe only four feet high. She could see the other end of the passageway, perhaps five or six feet in front of her. It did not have a door but was only a rectangular hole, complete darkness on the other side. She asked Lynn to hold her light while she knelt and crawled along the floor, retrieving her light before she ventured out the other side.

Lynn followed on her hands and knees as well, steadying herself with her shoulder against the wall. Tucker tried to crawl, but his damaged arm and bruised muscles refused to hold him. He finally sat and scooted backward using his elbow, Lynn pulling as Connie pushed. The others followed.

Once through the passageway, each stepped out and down to a floor. The lights revealed that they had entered the end of a long ill-fitted room. It was stuffy and dry and very cold, and a thick layer of dust lay over everything in sight, washing all color from what they saw. There were no windows. The ceiling sloped steeply from above their heads down to the floor on each side, leaving the room with no walls other than the ends. The wood slats of the floor were mildly warped and separated, but a number of rugs hid most of the damage.

The room had a rocking chair, a desk chair pulled up to a writing table, and an oil lamp. A short stack of books leaned against a table leg. A porcelain washbasin and pitcher sat on a short bureau with several drawers. Next to the pitcher, a hurricane lamp still held liquid in its glass base.

To the right of where they stood was a small pot-belly stove, a box of kindling, and a metal bucket with several pieces of coal. At the near end of the room was a tall gun cabinet with a glass front panel that revealed a number of rifles and pistols inside. A set of small drawers sat underneath. To the right of the cabinet, a set of hooks on the wall held two or three coats and sweaters, barely visible through the dust and spider webs.

Against the far end of the room, a bed frame held a mattress and covers. The frame was made of copper rods connected to larger copper pipes that constituted the footboard and headboard. Unburnished for more than a century, the copper was a dull black. What was left of the mattress was a thin layer of cotton bunting covered by quilts; wire springs connected to a heavy perimeter wire showed through the footboard.

All eyes were drawn to what lay on top of the mattress.

Perhaps pure white when new, the dress was now yellowed and the sheen of the satin was dull in the uneven glare of the construction lights. Fine layers of lace bordered the collar, the bodice, and the sleeves, and trailed down the long folds of the skirt to the ankles. The small lace swirls were filled with brownish drifts of soft dust.

That it was a wedding dress in decay, there was no doubt, but the body that it adorned still wore it with a simple elegance. A shear veil lay over the face, but the pale skull shown through, light tan around a perfect set of white teeth. What remained of any skin was shriveled and curled, mummified from years in the dry air of the Southwest.

Still flowing from around her head, long strands of blond hair swept from the pillow down onto her shoulders. She lay with her hands clasped above her midsection, the skeleton bones of her hands still grasping several dry stalks of flowers.

At the top of the bodice, as if placed over the heart, were two folded pieces of paper.

"L U C Y" was crudely written across the top of the first, which appeared to be a piece of stationery. The second was more formal, with thicker paper, folded and tied with a ribbon.

Tucker reached carefully and slowly picked up the stationery, tapping it against the bedframe to shake off the dust. He handed it to Elizabeth.

She opened it, gently bending the brittle paper just enough to read what was written inside.

L U C Y
W I R E   G O O D N I G H T   A T   F O R T   S I L L
I   C O M E
S A M

Taking a deep breath, Elizabeth whispered in a somber tone, "I finally made it, Sam."

After a moment of silence, Elizabeth's voice adopted a professorial tone and she instructed the others to not touch anything.

"You've got a spectacular find," she said, a slight breathlessness coming into her voice. "A room that has existed for over a hundred and forty years without being touched, without any disturbance whatsoever. Historians live for such a find." She did, however, take a peek at the other paper that lay on Violet's chest.

Not touching anything didn't mean not taking pictures. Rose sent Rico for their phones while Connie wanted her camera. Elizabeth got hers, and Tucker asked Rico to get his from the trailer; Lynn said she'd steal pictures from everybody.

More than an hour later, Tucker printed nine or ten pictures onto paper, and the family sat around the dining table looking closely at the objects in the photographs, pointing out details, and making a mental list of questions about who, what, and how. They all had a guess regarding what the drawers of the bureau might hold.

"It wasn't an instruction, after all," Elizabeth said, out of the blue. "It was a code for danger, just like in my dream."

The others looked at her.

"Run, Lucy, run," she said. "If I had small children in the middle of Indian country, I would have trained them to run to safety without having to think about it. I would have had a hiding place ready, and I would have taught them a word or a phrase that could be called out at any moment. Don't think, just go to the hiding place if you hear that word or phrase. That's why the telegram is so short. Sam had to have written it. He knew that Lucy was the only person in the world who would understand the message: he wanted her to return to the house and go to the hidden room.

"When she came to the room, she would find the two papers. One was a formal document identifying the bank that held the titles to, and remaining money of, the Mulvaney estate, and a copy of Cyrus Mulvaney's will that transferred all the property to Sam and Lucy. The document had been drawn up by a lawyer in Santa Fe, signed by Sam, and witnessed by the lawyer's secretary and Charles Goodnight.

"The second paper was the note from Sam that told Lucy to send a telegram to Fort Sill. They would get it to Goodnight's ranch over in Texas, which was about a hundred and fifty miles away along the rim of Palo Duro Canyon. Goodnight would get it and give it to Sam, who would then return to the house to get her. I'm sure that he expected Lucy to join him in Texas until his work agreement with Goodnight was completed. After that, I don't have a guess as to what he thought they would do.

"But she didn't get the telegram for almost fifty years, and when she did get it and realized that her brother had lived after his kidnapping, that he had waited for her and she had never known, it was too much for her. She died of a broken heart.

"You know what else I think?" Elizabeth said, glancing around the table. "Sam didn't know Lucy had never gotten the telegram. He assumed that she had gotten it, but had decided not to return to the house, and not to return to him. He probably thought that she had found out who he was, what he had become, and what he had done, and decided that she never wanted to see him again.

"If Sam had any heart left, it broke as well."

39

It was the first Sunday of June, and Tucker thought it was a perfect day. The winds were just enough to bring the smells of the cottonwoods down from up-canyon and mix them with the cool freshness of the grass and water vapors coming off the river. Spring had brought more rains than usual, and the clump grass around the house had suddenly become a carpet of six inch blades that added to the feeling of lushness in the valley.

He wondered what it was like the first time Cyrus Mulvaney brought his wife to the canyon. If the guy had been smart, he would have done it in either spring or fall, when the small valley was bursting with color, moisture, and rich smells. He would have sent people ahead to erect a tent, put out chairs, set up a table, and prepare food for the famished family. Then he would have let the canyon work its magic.

Sam and Lucy would have run themselves ragged—exploring, playing in the water, running through the grass. And Violet, tired from the long buggy ride, would have been restored by the beauty of the cliffs, the river, the trees, and nature's other displays that declared the valley a special place, a consecrated place where she could live in the wondrous house that Cyrus had described. Other families in Las Vegas society might have houses and yards, but she would have her own valley.

Tucker rocked at a leisurely pace in a rocking chair on the front porch beneath a slowly-turning ceiling fan. The shade and the breeze softened the June heat, and he relaxed against the back of the chair, a cold drink in his hand. On the riverbank below, a group of teenagers was making more noise than Tucker thought possible.

"Those kids had better get all that foolish behavior out of their systems today because we're starting serious work tomorrow."

Lynn laughed from the rocker next to him. "Oh, you are such a tough boss."

The twins were back, happy to have a full summer of work to look forward to. After the introductory tour of the house, even though most of them had seen it, and a welcome by Tucker, Tony and Tommy led the five new crew members to the shallow pools of the river. They had started the fun by throwing the girls into the river, which then escalated to everybody throwing everybody else into the river. The river was past its spring raging stage and now flowed softly and evenly, clear as glass, and was a temptation beyond resisting for fun and frolic under a hot sun.

"Hey, I'm not kidding, sweetie. No fooling around on the job at this house. There are rules, you know, and we follow the rules."

Lynn just smiled.

There was yet more yelling from the river and someone started a game of Frisbee.

Tucker's arm had not healed as they had hoped. Nerves were damaged and it appeared that they would not ever mend. Though he had been out of the sling for some months, he still did not have his former strength, and he was missing some dexterity in his left hand. He could hold a hammer but could not pick up a pencil. He exercised every day with the hope that his fingers would somehow remember what they were supposed to do. Until then, he relied on Larry to help out with the two-handed work.

Larry and Charlene had moved to the ranch after New Year's. Between Tucker, Larry, and Rico, the front bedroom on the second floor had been remodeled into a well-appointed suite with its own bathroom. Living at the ranch gave the Jacksons a chance to save money for their own home as well as help keep the rebuilding of the Mulvaney Mansion going forward. Charlene also provided financial expertise to Rose's passion for home decorating, and the two were thinking about a partnership to provide interior design consulting to builders and remodelers in town.

Rico was at a trade school in Colorado Springs, earning his electrical license, and he had a spot reserved with a contractor in town. When he returned, he and Rose would move into Connie's house. They would gradually remodel the house, starting with the creation of a nursery. The baby, only a few months old, was healthy and happy and doted on by Connie, and carefully monitored by Rose, who was as loving a mother as a baby might wish for.

Connie had considered moving back to town until Tucker hired her to be the ranch manager as well as the cook. He thought that, when Rico and Rose left, he might offer to house some of Elizabeth's research assistants when they needed a local place to stay. With the possibility of more people coming and going and a steady stream of summer kids from the high school, someone was needed to manage it all.

The hidden stairway and the secret room had made the primetime shows and all the news channels, and there was even a short tour on YouTube. Formal access to the room was managed solely by Elizabeth, of course, as it was her great, great grandmother they found on the bed. Tucker also believed that everything in it belonged to her as rightful heir. The room and its contents were providing a flourish to the end of Elizabeth's career, and the articles, papers, lectures, and resulting book were keeping her and her research assistants busier than they wanted to be.

Tucker was most pleased when a closer examination of the secret room revealed a small sink and a covered opening to a sewer pipe. The pipe probably led to the basement where it joined the drain system, and it was most likely used for emptying the room's chamber pot. The single spigot of the sink provided water to the people inside the room.

Looking carefully at the spigot and investigating how water was pumped to that level, Tucker discovered a small tank made of zinc that hung inside the uppermost part of the chimney. A pipe from the tank led to the spigot, providing water to the room, and another pipe ran from the tank through an eave overhang to one of the copper ornaments. It connected to a clever funnel system built to collect rainwater and snow. A hundred and forty years later, the tank was still being randomly filled with water.

The outlet pipe at the bottom of the tank had corroded to make a small leak, and, every second or so, a drop of water fell all the way to the bottom of the chimney. The result was a firm and rhythmic *thump* against the wooden landing connected to the very bottom wood box.

Tucker had found the heartbeat of the house.

Violet, still in her wedding dress, was buried next to her husband. Tucker was baffled about how to find Cyrus's grave, but a mass of wildflowers suddenly sprung up in back of the house and north of the dorm. The flowers grew in a perfect rectangle about the size of a very large body. Pretty remarkable, he thought, considering that it was January at the time.

Elizabeth and Tucker had agreed to spend time together at the end of the summer. They would map out the events of the year, look at the timeline, research the history, and write down all they knew about the house, including their dreams—everything. They were sure it would never be made public, but the story—the whole story—was so fascinating that they both wanted to record every detail.

But first, Elizabeth wanted to find out what happened to Sam.

She was already in Texas for the summer to visit the museums and university libraries. While her research assistants looked for a fuller history of Red Hair, the giant warrior of the Comanche, she would look for clues to Sam's life after he sent the telegram to Lucy. What happened when she didn't come? Did he leave Goodnight? Where did he go? Had he married? Fathered children?

She needed more closure for her book, she said. Or maybe she just didn't want the story to be over, Tucker thought.

Waking from his state of contentment, Tucker looked at Lynn. "I want to show you something that Elizabeth sent me." He went inside the house and returned with a large picture book.

"Elizabeth found a book of photographs taken around the cattle ranches in the Palo Duro Canyon area. Charlie Goodnight started his first Texas ranch in 1877, then started the most famous of his ranches, the JA, in 1878. They both included large portions of the Palo Duro Canyon area in the panhandle of Texas.

"Look at this one."

Tucker handed her the book opened to a full-page photograph. The picture was of a chuck wagon. A number of men were sitting in a row on the ground in front of the wagon, a few on the wagon tongue, and several were on horseback lined up behind the wagon. Written across the bottom in a white pen was "JA Roundup, 1881."

Each man wore a long-sleeve shirt buttoned all the way to the neck and either suspenders or a vest. All had large handkerchiefs wound and knotted around their necks. Most had hats—some tall, some short, most with flat brims, some slightly crushed, all looking well-dusted, and all with considerable sweat stains. Their pants were dark, some with stripes, some plain, and all were tucked into the tops of tall boots. A couple of the men wore chaps.

The chuck wagon was stacked high with a jumble of tied bedrolls, and several pieces of rigging hung from the sideboards.

"Here," Tucker pointed.

Along the line of men mounted on horses behind the wagon was a man considerably taller than the rest. His face was angular and gaunt, and the left side of his face seemed to be scarred. A woven pigtail of hair peeked from under his hat. The hands, folded over the saddle horn, were large, and he was broad-shouldered and thickly muscled. His horse was also larger than the others in the line, but it could not hide the fact that the man was a giant compared to those next to him.

From beneath the brim of his hat, the eyes that looked at the camera were clear and singular, as if the man was seeing beyond the camera, beyond the camp, maybe to someplace far away.

The eyes appeared unusually intense, like a wild animal's.

A few hours later, before the sun had set, Tucker, Lynn, and all the teenagers were gathered in the front yard. Rose sat in a rocking chair on the porch with the baby, watching the group and laughing.

Tucker had cleared a large circle of dirt between the flagpole and the riverbank. He had lined it with flat stones from the old quarry to make a fire pit. Finally using some of his wood pile, small pieces of lumber were stacked nearby. Tucker refused to use gasoline to start the fire. Instead, he built a small structure out of kindling and dry grass, as he had learned from his father, and brought the fire to life using only a single match.

He nursed the flame until it burned brightly, then carefully placed several pieces of wood around it. The wood pieces, some of which were more than a hundred and forty years old, caught and burned like torches. Soon, a tall column of snapping flames whooshed up into the air, letting loose embers that burned brightly, embers that drifted up into the sunset.

"Are you ready?" Tucker asked.

Lynn, whom he had asked to be his wife, gave him a smile, then nodded.

With a signal, Tony hit the play button on a CD player whose speakers had been spread across the porch. The music that came out was a waltz. A beautiful, dreamy, full-orchestra waltz.

Tucker and Lynn led the others among hoots and laughter as they all danced around the fire. They danced and danced, swinging around and around, then across the grass, along the sidewalk, and all around the house.

No one noticed that the flagpole cable clanged in time with the music.

Epilogue

The tiny door opened into a narrow passageway of no more than a couple of feet in width, the ceiling low, the air hot and stuffy and laden with the dry smell of dust. Sam bent over and turned sideways, angled himself through the door, and setting the lantern before him, used his hands to pull himself along the floor. The passage opened into an angular room tucked under the roof. Carefully unbending himself, he extended a leg out of the opening and down onto a wood floor covered with rugs. He unwound the rest of his body until he stood in the room.

The room, smaller than the other rooms in the house, was narrow and long, the ceiling half the height of the other rooms and steeply slanted from above his head to the floor on both sides. Holding his light in front of him, Sam's moccasins barely made a sound on the rugs, his feet as sure of their path as if he walked in daylight. He had been in the room many times. He and Lucy loved playing hide-and-seek inside the chimney, moving swiftly between the bedrooms, parlors, and cellar.

He looked the room over, one side to the other. It was exactly as it was the last time he was here, except that the body of his mother now lay in a heap on the floor.

He had heard the stories told by the Comancheros who traded with the Comanches. His Chief, the father he loved, had learned who Sam had been and sought details from the traders when they were encountered. He told Sam what was known, unafraid that the boy would be lured back to the house, back to being white.

Sam knew that his mother had not thrown herself into the river as the stories said. He knew she was here, escaping to the secret room when the maids turned away. The dancing woman in white was no ghost. Sam imagined that, after everyone had left, she set the piano to play a waltz, then gleefully danced on the porch, in the yards, and along the bank of the river. She would have laughed as she swung in the arms of her beloved husband.

Setting the lantern on the desk, Sam carefully picked her body up off the floor and laid it softly on the bed, her head on the pillow, arms crossed, the dress smoothed over her and down the bed, her hair straightened and her face covered with the veil.

He did not feel anything; he shed no tears. He had run out of tears years before, and death was so common in his life that even his mother's body elicited no emotional response. Whether she had died from a sleeping potion, had starved to death, or her body had merely given out did not matter.

He had gathered flowers from beside the riverbank before entering the house, and he slid them now beneath the withered skin of her hands. He placed two papers on her chest.

The telegram he had sent that morning was brief, and he knew no reason Lucy should not receive it within the week. He knew she would come when she read it. He considered staying in town, waiting for a response, waiting for her, but Goodnight had told him it was best if he spent as little time as possible in town. Wait in Texas, wait for her to come to the house, wait for her to send for him, and then go get her, Goodnight had said. Sam had years of his obligation to Goodnight remaining, and then he would make the decision for them to homestead in Texas or to return here.

Sam, in an unusual show of tenderness, laid his hand on top of his mother's forehead and slowly stroked her long hair. Then he moved to the doorway and looked again across the room, his gaze moving from the bed to the books to the guns to the stove. At the last minute, he knelt before the gun cabinet and opened the middle of the three bottom drawers. Pulling it out and setting it on the floor, he squeezed his hand inside the opening, pushed a lever, and removed a smaller drawer from the back.

His father had hidden a bag of coins to be used for emergencies. Pulling it from its tight confines, Sam untied the leather thong, widened the bag's opening, and removed eight Spanish gold pieces. He returned the bag to its hiding place, replaced the small drawer and then the larger. The coins would be enough to pay Goodnight for the clothes, boots, and hat, and to serve as travel money when Lucy sent for him. It had been years since he had ridden in a carriage, but he assumed that Lucy had become a lady and would require one on the return trip.

He grabbed the lantern and contorted himself back through the passageway, closed the tiny door behind him, then crawled out the wood box opening into the third floor bedroom, listening for the click of the latch as he pulled the box closed.

This had been his room.

He had not looked through the house when he first came in. He had come to do something that needed done and had done it. Now he looked carefully, warily, over his bed, his shelves, the curtains that had let in the light that morning, and the wallpaper he continued to see in his dreams.

He never had his party.

He touched the dust-covered blankets, sheets, and pillow. He ran his rough hands through the dust of the window sill, touched the iron of the radiator, and looked into the yard below, noticing the tumbleweeds against the back fence. It had been his job to gather them into a pile on the riverbank, waiting until night to set them on fire so everyone could see the embers shooting into the stars.

Ducking as he went through the doorway, Sam went down the back stairs, turned and went into the kitchen. He went quickly to the storage pantry. Running his hand up and down the notches along both sides of the door facing, he turned, backed up against the wood, and held his knife on top of his head. He nicked the wood, then turned to see the mark.

He was taller than his father.

He had wanted to know, and he now wished that his father could have witnessed the event, to have laughed at seeing his son so much like himself.

Sam cut the notch deeper into the wood.

He and Goodnight had gone straight south from the school outside of Fort Sill, making it to Wichita Falls, in Texas, a day later.

Goodnight knew a tailor there, and Sam had stood for a fitting, the tailor needing to stand on a chair to reach the expansiveness of the huge man before him. Goodnight then paid the man for several shirts, several pairs of pants, a coat, belts, suspenders, socks, and several pair of cotton underwear—a novelty for Sam. "If you want a suit," Goodnight stated, "that will be up to you."

They crossed the street to a boot maker, the man claiming that it might take a whole hide to get what they were asking for. Sam wasn't sure he would wear them, but Goodnight assured him that kicking cows on a regular basis made them a necessity.

Then there was the problem of a hat. Sam claimed he didn't need one of those either, but Goodnight was unmoved. Every cowboy needs a good hat, he said, just as he needs a good horse. Eventually, they found a hat maker with a mold big enough for not only the head but the thick mat of red hair that sprouted from it. Sam had already decided to return to the large braids that once fell down his back.

They waited on the clothes, the hat, and the boots, then journeyed north a few miles, back to the Red River. Turning west, they followed the river for several days, then turned northward. It was another two days before they came to Goodnight's homestead on the rim of the Palo Duro Canyon.

Sam did not remember time in the beginning. The sun and moon gave the Comanche an orientation to what was today and what was yesterday, and they didn't really perceive thinking beyond tomorrow except with regard to the change in seasons. Goodnight finally gave him a watch and a piece of paper with the times written down, if any were important, and indicated days, if any of those were important. Other than that, Sam understood when work started, when it finished, and when other work was to begin.

Sam did not remember money in the beginning either. It was a strange concept to an Indian. He felt no sense of earning it, since his equipment, horse, food, and place were given to him, and his work was just what he did. He regarded Goodnight as a Chief and he a member of a tribe. Regardless, the Chief continued to pay him wages. There was no place to spend it, and even if there had been, there was nothing that he needed. So he left his wages with Goodnight, who kept it in the bank at Clarendon.

Sam did, however, develop an uncanny ability to tell when it was mealtime. Goodnight took camp cooking seriously and prepared meals that far expanded Sam's meager dietary habits. Sam found the stews, the spices, the beans, the potatoes, the breads, and the desserts to be wonders; and still holding to the Comanche way of regarding meals as survival and unexpected lean times as a given—gorge now for you may not eat tomorrow— he ate without restraint. He developed regulation, but only after Goodnight turned the air blue with a cuss-word laden lecture on eating protocol. Even then, Sam still ate twice what the others ate and waited to lick the pots and pans without shame.

And he ate pancakes at every opportunity.

Still a teenager, Sam continued to grow, and it was anybody's guess when he would stop. After his Plains Indian diet dominated by meat, his body now celebrated at every meal at the Goodnight ranch. The raw-boned frame of the tough-life Indian filled out, and by spring, he seemed twice the size of any other man around him. Goodnight was always wiring the tailor for bigger clothes to be sent, and he was always looking for bigger horses.

Leaving the pantry doorframe behind him, Sam walked throughout the house, opening every window and door on every floor. Then he went to the stacked firewood in back of the house and gathered armloads of *piñon* and juniper. He set about building four fires, one on each side of the house, far enough away to avoid the piles of tumbleweeds. Within an hour, four healthy blazes were roaring into the sky. He threw on more wood, then covered each with green juniper branches he had stripped from trees at the foot of the cliffs. The fires coughed, smoldered, then billowed thick smoke into the air.

Sam retrieved the leather pouch from his saddlebags.

The Dutch Church administrators had opened the pouch and examined it. To their eyes, it was only smaller bags of differently colored dirt, ground up flowers, and seeds, probably meant for seasoning meat, they assumed. They threw the pouch in with Sam's other belongings.

The pouch's contents had nothing to do with cooking. Each innocent-looking powder had been carefully found, prepared, and stored by Sam's medicine man father. Knowing how to use the ingredients had taken Sam a year to learn.

He spread a number of the smaller bags on the ground, and using pieces of bark to hold various powders from the bags, he added water from the river. He mixed four colors of paste and applied them to his body—stripes of different shades and lengths across his chest and cheeks.

Satisfied with his markings, Sam centered himself in the middle of the porch in front of the entry door and slowly moved his feet in a shuffle. Adding more energy, he turned his torso back and forth to some internal cadence that needed no drum, then began sweeping his arms around him. Soon, the movements were stronger and more repetitive, and he traced a routine line around the porch and down into the yard.

Sam danced. Sam sang.

The cadence increased, his feet moving up and down in rhythm, his body turning in circles while his hands cut through the smoke that poured from the bonfires. He moved faster and faster, then broke into a run, still in rhythm, as he circled each fire, running in large curves around the house, sometimes leaping with a frenzied concentration. Sounds came from his throat, from deep in his chest, from his nose. He yelled, yodeled, hummed, and chanted.

Sweaty and stinking of smoke, he swooped by his pouch and grabbed a small bag. He danced around each bonfire sprinkling the bag's contents into the flames, causing an eruption of blue smoke. The colored vapors rose and circled the house, then darted in through the open windows and doors. The smoke invaded the reaches of the house, immersing it in holy incense, baptizing it with a swirling blend of embers and magic.

Samuel Mulvaney, called Red Hair, the mighty Comanche warrior and shaman to his tribe, called the house out of darkness and into life. He called on the house to awaken, to feel the earth beneath it, to find the vibrations of the spirits that lived in that earth, and to come alive.

He chanted, he danced, he yelled as he swirled.

Finally, tired and covered with sweat, Sam stopped his dance at the front steps. He came to the front door, which opened before him. He took more powder and threw it against the doorframe, removed his knife and made a deep slit across his palm. He closed his hand, opened it, then placed bloody handprints around the door facing, finally smearing both hands with blood and pushing them down onto the threshold.

The house shuddered, soaking from the blood all that it would tell.

"This is what I want," Sam whispered. "This is why I brought you to life."

He spoke to the house of protection, of patience, of preservation, of keeping secrets, of guarding the body of his mother. Then he gave it a charge, a command as he would give a junior warrior.

"Keep all things in order. She will come. I will return."

The smoke finally thinned and flattened, and glowing coals replaced the leaping flames.

Sam closed the windows and doors, mounted his horse, and guided him down the bank of the river. He knew a path that would take him out of the canyon country and into the plains. He would follow the Canadian River halfway across Texas, then veer south for the canyons of the Palo Duro. He knew the trails, the camps, and the sources of water. He expected to catch up to Goodnight along the way.

As his horse splashed in the shallow water along the front of the house, a very small memory came to his mind: his sister standing on the ranch road, her hand raised, waving to him as he was being spirited away up the canyon.

Sam stopped, turned in his saddle, and raised his hand, wondering if she knew he had wanted to wave back.

www.ingramcontent.com/pod-product-compliance
Lightning Source LLC
Chambersburg PA
CBHW030034180626
46810CB00001B/358